ALL RISE
FOR THE
HONORABLE
PERRY T. COOK

ALSO BY LESLIE CONNOR

FOR MIDDLE GRADE READERS
Waiting for Normal
Crunch

FOR YOUNGER READERS
Miss Bridie Chose a Shovel

FOR TEENS
Dead on Town Line
The Things You Kiss Goodbye

LESLIE CONNOR

ALL RISE
FOR THE
HONORABLE
PERRY T. COOK

KATHERINE TEGEN BOOKS
An Imprint of HarperCollins Publishers

Katherine Tegen Books is an imprint of HarperCollins Publishers.

All Rise for the Honorable Perry T. Cook
Copyright © 2016 by Leslie Connor
All rights reserved. Printed in the United States of America.
No part of this book may be used or reproduced in any manner
whatsoever without written permission except in the case of brief quotations
embodied in critical articles and reviews. For information address HarperCollins
Children's Books, a division of HarperCollins Publishers, 195 Broadway,
New York, NY 10007.
www.harpercollinschildrens.com

Library of Congress Control Number: 2015940765
ISBN 978-0-06-233346-9

16 17 18 19 20   CG/RRDH   10 9 8 7 6 5 4 3 2 1
❖
First Edition

For my Toddy family

Even people with dark pasts
can show a softer side of their soul
in the presence of innocence.

—*Kate West*

ALL RISE
FOR THE
HONORABLE
PERRY T. COOK

chapter one

TEENY-TINY SURPRISE, NEBRASKA

Big Ed is about to tell it again. He greets all the new ones. He sits them down, tells them about the place, and gets to know them as quick as he can. Being a welcomer is part of his work at Blue River, which is the biggest thing you'll find in the teeny-tiny town of Surprise, Nebraska.

Big Ed asks, "Are you from around here?"

The new resident shakes his head no. He sets his dinner tray down across from us. The answer is almost always no because Surprise is a long way from most places.

"You know why they call it Surprise?" Big Ed asks. "It's because this little nowhere-Nebraska town gets an impressive amount of snow. But the snow is not the surprise. What you find after it melts—now that's the surprise. Uh-huh. Things you never knew you lost. Of course, I'm talking

1

mostly about folks on the outside. Here on the inside, well, most of us have nothing left to lose. Or it can feel that way."

Big Ed laughs. He sounds like a harmonica. Then comes his coughing. He has to pull himself together before he can go on. "But spring comes and on the outside they find all sorts of things. Baseballs and dog bones. That favorite pair of garden gloves all flattened down into the mud and grass. Maybe even a set of keys. And don't we all wish we had the keys around here. Huh, Perry?" Big Ed gives me such a nudge I almost spill my milk.

The new rez—that's short for resident—listens nicely enough. I wonder how long he's going to be here. Maybe not so long. Depends on what he did. Depends on what's been decided. Sometimes I hear. Sometimes they tell me. I never ask.

Big Ed tells the new guy, "You'll see so much snow outside these windows it'll make you forget that grass is green." He always pauses for several seconds right here. Then he says, "Unless, of course, you're doing a catnap." A *catnap* means a short stay.

Big Ed leaves a little airtime, waits to see if the new rez feels like talking. He might tell him about his sentencing. Sometimes they do. Sometimes they don't.

This guy dips his head like he's talking to that bowl of turkey chili on his dinner tray. "I got eight months," he says. He doesn't say what he's in for. Meanwhile, he keeps eyeing me. Big Ed claps a hand on my shoulder and tells the guy,

"This here is Perry. Perry T. Cook."

I put my hand out. The guy waits. He looks to the right and left where the supervisors are standing. He's knows he's being watched, and he's trying to figure out what is allowed. There are rules about contact.

"Handshaking is okay," I tell him. "As long as it's brief."

Big Ed says, "You can listen to Perry. He knows it all."

I push my hand closer to the new rez. Last try. Finally, we shake.

"Name's Wendell," he says, and I don't know if he means that's his first name, last name, or only name. Mom's rule is, I can call the adults whatever they tell me to call them, but she wants me to add Mr., Mrs., or Miss to the front end. For Big Ed, well, I just added "Big," and I guess nobody ever corrected me. It was such a long time ago. He's the only rez at Blue River who's been here longer than Mom and me.

"What's a kid doing here outside of visiting hours?" The new guy wants to know.

"I call him my Morning Son," says Big Ed. (It's an old story.) "Perry makes sure we all wake up on time."

"The kid will be here in the morning?" Mr. Wendell looks confused. New ones always do until it dawns on them that I live at the Blue River Co-ed Correctional Facility here in teeny-tiny Surprise, Nebraska.

From behind the serving counter in the kitchen, we hear Eggy-Mon dishing up the last trays of supper for the evening. He thinks all food deserves poetry. Tonight he calls,

"Get your gobbling-good order from south of the border, with a hunk of corn bread, or white rice instead."

Mom comes by with her tray in her hands. "Perry, down the hatch with that milk, pal." She sounds impatient, and she has left more than half her supper. It's strange because she doesn't waste food, and the turkey chili is not that bad. I take my milk carton in both hands and gulp it back so fast my throat aches. Bad manners. But Mom needs me to move along tonight. Something's up with her, and I don't want to add to her trouble. Neither does Big Ed. He gives me a pat on the back and says, "Good man, Perry."

Earlier today, Warden Daugherty called Mom into her office for a conversation. Whatever that was about, it put Mom on a tilt. Now it's one of those weird days when everybody knows something's going on. Everybody but me.

"I want to have one more look at that map of the middle school with you before lockdown," Mom says. She glances at the gray clock on the wall, and so do I. We have to pay attention to the time at Blue River. At nine p.m. I have to be in my bedroom next to the warden's office off the Upper East Lounge.

Mom has to be in her room down at the end of the hall on Cell Block C.

chapter two

ALL RISE

It's 6:23 a.m. I scoot forward and put my lips close to the microphone of the prison PA system. I always begin quietly. Warden Daugherty comes to wake me every day, and she is gentle about it. So I do the same for all the residents at Blue River.

"Good morning," I say in my slow, low voice. "This is Perry at sunrise. It is Tuesday, the sixth of September. If you need a reason to bother getting up today, well, it's probably not the weather. 'Tut-tut, it looks like rain.' That's the quote of the day—comes from Christopher Robin, by the way, and if you don't know who he is then maybe it's time for you to get some literature in your life. Mrs. Buckmueller and the Bucking Blue Bookmobile will be here to restock the Leisure Library from four o'clock to five o'clock, and don't forget, she takes requests."

I glance at Warden Daugherty. She smiles as she leafs

through a stack of papers. She likes it when I give literacy a plug. The clock on the wall above her desk reads 6:26. I lean toward the mic again.

"The news on the outside is, it's the first day of school in Butler County. That means I'll be gone all day. Don't miss me too much. The good news for all of you is, waffles are popping out of the toasters down in the caf. Scrams are in the pan. They're even letting some fruit cocktail out of the jar. Choice of beverage, as usual. Remember, there are no knives in the flatware trays at Blue River, so get used to that spork for however long you'll be with us."

I lean away from the mic and whisper to Warden Daugherty, "That last part is for the new intake, Mr. Wendell."

She whispers back to me, "I'm sure he will feel most welcome now." She points to the clock without looking at it. She doesn't need to. The warden is so precise you can almost hear her ticking.

Six twenty-nine and a half a.m. Time for me to get louder. I grip the mic in my hand like I'm about to fly a plane.

"Ooo . . . kay, residents of Blue River! If you're not up by now, time to get up!" The finish has to be big. It's the same every day. I take a deep breath and bellow. "Al-l-l-l-l rise!"

I turn off the mic and hustle toward the door. I stick my head into the hallway and listen for morning release. Six thirty a.m. Locks disengage. Doors click and creak. Toilets flush, and the residents yawn themselves awake.

Foreman Joe is coming up the hall from Block A, which

is one of the men's wings. "Good morning, Fo-Joe." I started calling him that when I was little. (*R*s tripped me up when I was first learning to talk. I used to call myself *Peh-wee*.) "How's things?" I ask. But I don't really want to know, not right now, and Fo-Joe knows it.

"Things?" he says slowly. "Well, let me see . . ."

I chew the inside of my lip and wait. He's being slow on purpose.

"Things are fine. But I'm wondering what they fed you all for dinner last night. Was it burritos? Because . . ." He stops, pinches his nose. Fans the air. "That morning release had some fire on it."

"Turkey chili," I tell him. "With beans." Then before he can go on and on about that, I remind him, "Hey, Fo-Joe, it's the first day of school."

"Oh yeah!" he says. "Thus the new sneakers, hey?"

I look at my feet. "Can I go?" I ask.

"To school?"

"Fo-Joe!" He knows what I want. I am already facing Block C. I'm crouched into a runner's stance. But I have to wait for permission. It's one of the rules. "Fo-Joe. Puh-leese!"

"Perry?" he says.

"Yeah?"

"Are you still here?"

I am not. I am off like a flash, sprinting toward Mom's room at the end of the hallway on Block C.

chapter three

JESSICA

Jessica Cook liked to be out of her room before Perry reached her in the morning. Maybe it was silly. Her boy knew that his mom was locked in at night. He knew that she had to wait in her room for morning release just like any other resident at Blue River.

Release. The word ricocheted between her ears. Not morning release. Get-out-of-prison-for-good release. Jessica shook her head. She tried to will herself not to think about it until there was something definite. Trouble was, she couldn't think of anything else. She'd been awake most of the night, and the thought stuck while she did her morning push-ups, crunches, and hamstring stretches on the person-size patch of floor beside her bed. Jessica had coached at least a hundred residents through the release process at Blue River. That was her work here, and it was a little bit twisted considering she had not had the pleasure herself. But that day should be coming.

She had served nearly twelve years of a fifteen-year sentence. She could apply for parole in just a few more weeks. *Finally.* There would be a process. But up until yesterday, she'd had every reason to think—every reason to hope— that come the frosts of late October she'd be a free woman. She'd had been coaching Perry for the day they'd leave the only home he'd known.

But now, this glitch. The warden had received word that there was a wrench in the works. No details, just yet.

Do not lose hope, she thought.

She propped her door open while she brushed her teeth. Foreman Joe usually let Perry head down immediately after the all-rise. Her boy would be sprinting, and he was fast— and getting faster.

Minimum security meant that she stayed in a narrow, dorm-like room, not a cell behind bars. This was not a crusted prison from a late-night movie. In fact, Blue River was a campus with natural light in some of the common areas, and not-so-horrible colors on the walls. Those were the good things she told herself about this place. She was locked up. Hard fact. But being assigned to the facility in Surprise had been a little spot of good inside a blurry nightmare of bad.

The years had been bearable because her boy had lived with her for eleven of them. Such arrangements were unheard of. So lucky. Still, she longed to get him out of here and begin that new life on the outside, when her time, and Perry's time, would be their own.

Jessica spat toothpaste into the saucepan-size sink at the back of her toilet. She ran the faucet to wash her hands then quickly pulled her hair into a high ponytail. She checked her bed again, though she'd already tucked it tight as a spring-board. A surprise room inspection could come at any time, and if there was one thing she hated, it was being repri-manded in front of Perry. Jessica toed the line.

She heard her son's sneakers slapping along the low-pile carpeting, pounding his way toward her. She broke into a grin as she jumped out into the hallway.

Perry was arriving, nostrils flaring like a racer and blue eyes wide beneath the cap of dark hair. (More and more he looked like another boy she'd once known.) He was beautiful, she thought. He was hope in a new pair of cross-trainers. Jessica opened her arms, her boy leapt, and she caught him for the swing-around, which she was pleased she could still manage. So far. Then with Perry back on his feet again, the two exchanged good mornings and started down to breakfast.

"How are you feeling about school?" she asked.

"Nervous. Excited." Perry rocked his head side to side as he spoke. Jessica tucked her fingers into his hair for just a moment.

"I'm feeling the same way for you," she said. "But some

things won't change. Miss Maya will still pick you up here. Now that you are in the middle school you'll see her during the day."

"Yup," he said, and Jessica felt her son give a little shrug beside her. They'd already gone over it. Perry was his quieter self this morning. She should let him be.

"I'm glad Zoey's on Team Three with me," Perry offered. "Same homeroom."

"I'm glad too," Jessica said, and she was. This was where Perry's not-so-ordinary upbringing had worried her. There was the stigma of the prison. But also, for a kid, he had a strangely adult social circle—the nearly impossible mix of ragtag and colorful, half-lost and fate-tossed nonviolent residents at Blue River. Meanwhile, she, his mother, had never been able to meet the one young girl he called his "best friend on the outside."

When Perry had first mentioned Zoey Samuels, Jessica had pulled Maya Rubin aside and said, "Please tell me she's not imaginary." Maya, Warden Daugherty's niece and Perry's main escort on the outside, had promised that yes, Zoey was real. She'd also remarked that Perry was as good a friend to the girl as she was to him.

Jessica felt relieved to know he had a friend. That part hadn't been easy. A lot of questions might be asked. Rumors might be whispered behind the slender back of a boy who called a correctional facility home.

Well, the day was coming—or was supposed to be coming—that she and Perry would both leave Blue River.

"Mom?"

"What?"

"Is something wrong? Something you can tell me?"

"No, no. I am just never going to be a 'Yay, September!' mother," Jessica said as they passed the warden's office. "I'm only lending you to that school because I'm nice. I'm really going to miss you today."

"I've got the camera. I'll bring you pictures."

"Boy, that was the best gift ever," she said, and not for the first time. The camera was a hand-me-down; the benefactress was Zoey Samuels, who had somehow ended up with two. The camera had been a boon for a locked-in mother who ached not to be locked out of those hours her son spent on the outside.

Jessica and Perry accidentally brushed hands as they walked. He looked up and gave her a comforting half smile.

Her boy had not seen her in her tiny locking room this morning. She noted it as a win. It was one of the ways Jessica preserved hope. You do a lot of that when you have fifteen years to serve—parole after twelve. *If* everything goes right.

chapter four

WELCOME

The middle school is three times the size of the elementary Zoey and I went to. Miss Maya brought me to the open house last week. The hallways were jammed with kids and their parents. But Mom pointed out that the school building is much smaller than the Blue River campus. I started finding my way around that place as soon as I could walk. I figure I won't get too lost in a school. It's a good thought to be having as Miss Maya turns into the parking lot. The schoolyard is already busy even though she has brought me here teacher-early. I see a lot of new faces.

We stand under the clock in the foyer. Miss Maya shifts her tote on her shoulder. I tuck my thumbs under the straps of my pack. "Okay, Perry. I'm off to my classroom," she says. "You have plenty of time before you have to be in yours. You remember where you're going, right?"

"Room 208. Second floor."

"Okay. I'll see you for Language Arts in my room this afternoon and here in the lobby at the end of the day. Actually, I bet we'll cross paths a few times. I'll wave to you," she says. She turns, and all her ropy rows of hair swing and follow her like a curtain.

"I'll wave back," I say.

I turn around and there is Zoey Samuels. Her hair is pale and her skin is tanned. She was away all summer.

"Perry!" she says. "Hey, Perry! Come on. I want to show you something."

I follow Zoey up the wide stairs to the second floor. "Hello. Hope you had a nice summer . . ." I use an under-mumble like Bid Ed's. It's for when you don't expect an answer. When we reach the landing, Zoey stops and turns. She points to a set of high windows where a whole lot of morning light is streaming in.

"Sun," I say. "Huh. It was supposed to rain all day." I am thinking about the report I gave during the all-rise.

"That's why I rushed you up here. Check it out." Zoey is pointing upward. Someone has stuck colored cellophane letters to all the windows. WELCOME. Zoey shuffles backward and presents the floor to me with both hands. "Look!"

The colors from the windows are being sun-cast on the floor at our feet. *Welcome* is spelled upside down and backward. Zoey sticks her leg out, and a purple *M* curves over her shin. "Is that cool or what?"

"It's cool," I say. I start to haul my pack off my shoulder.

"I should get a picture of the welcome message for my mom . . ."

The landing darkens. *Welcome* disappears. Zoey and I look up at the window. Large spatters hit the panes. "Aw, rats!" she says. "Well, maybe the weather will clear later this week. You can get the shot then." She tags my shoulder. "So listen, I found out that we don't get seated alphabetically." She says this like it's the best news in the world. "Even though you are *C* for Cook and I'm *S* for Samuels, we can sit together. But we better get in there before it fills up. Come on!"

Zoey is quick, weaving around kids in the hall. She is through the door to the classroom. I'm caught in a bottleneck, but I can see between shoulders. She lands her backpack onto the top of one desk and sits down at another right beside it. Claims two with one blow. When I finally get to her, she pulls out the chair with her foot and waves me into it.

Zoey Samuels is always on a mission.

chapter five

A TALE OF SURPRISE

Zoey Samuels was mad when she moved here. Mad about her parents' divorce, and mad that her stepdad was trying too hard with her and coming off like a big fake. She was mad about the house she had to leave, and mad about having to start at a new school in the middle of the year. She was mad that it was snowing. I never would have found out all of that if it hadn't been for Big Ed.

Zoey sat by herself at lunch. That's pretty much what I did too. Not because I don't like people—I do. But a lot of things changed right around fourth grade. Kids started to talk about karate and music lessons, soccer teams, and playing for the ice hockey club in David City. Those were all things I couldn't do. Fourth grade is also when the trouble with Brian Morris began, and it was all because of the one-mile run. That's the first year they timed us in gym class. Brian didn't like the way that turned out.

He's one of those kids who other kids magically follow, so if you get in trouble with him, it sticks on you. Brian is also the boy who started calling Zoey Samuels Mad-Zoe. That stuck to her.

I watched Zoey sitting alone for a few days. Then I went over and stood beside her with my lunch tray in my hands and said, "Welcome to Butler County. I'm Perry Cook. I live in Surprise. It's a tiny place."

"Isn't everything tiny?" she said.

"Well, it's a tiny place *and* it has a funny name. I'm guessing you're not from around here."

"Not at all," she said. She rocked her head and rolled her eyes. She probably wanted me to go away.

"Do you want to know why they call it Surprise?" I asked.

Zoey Samuels looked right at me. Her mouth twisted to the side. She pointed to the seat across the table, so I sat down. "Okay, tell me. Why is it called Surprise?"

I could have told her the real story. I had written a report about it in third grade. But I liked Big Ed's story better. "It's because of the snow," I said. We both looked out the cafeteria windows at the January whiteness. "But the snow is not the surprise. It's what you find when the snow is gone. All the stuff you never even knew you lost. Like a mitten that you dropped. Or a dollar bill. Or a letter that you meant to mail. You look down on the ground and things are—"

"Flattened," Zoey said. She smacked her palms together. "Stuck to the driveway. Or frozen to a rock under a bush," she said. "And so . . . you should give yourself the dollar bill because you're the one who found it. And you should just open the letter and pretend it's from you to you. Because it's been there so long that you will have forgotten what you wrote, and when you read it . . ."

"Surprise!" I said.

Zoey Samuels cracked up.

She's been my best friend ever since. I've never been to her house, and she can't come home with me after school. But Zoey knows exactly where I live. She knows why too.

She's never said a bad thing about it.

chapter six

SWIPE

It is lunchtime in the new school. My meal card won't swipe. The cashier tries again and again. Her name pin says "Miss Jenrik." She's not very old. In fact she looks like she should be down the block at the high school. She has pink spiky hair and long earrings with feathers at the ends. She is wearing rings on every finger. Each time my card fails she shakes her head and something on her jingles.

"Did you activate this?" she asks. She gives my card a hard look.

"Yes," I say.

"Did it go through the washing machine?"

"Not yet," I tell her.

Zoey is right behind me. She laughs. Miss Jenrik laughs too as she squints at the display on the machine and wiggles all her rings at it.

"I don't know why this thing is asking me for a code,"

she mumbles. "I'm new on the job. But I haven't seen this all day . . ." She punches a few buttons. She tries the card again. The line is backing up behind us.

I tell Zoey, "You should have gone first. You could be eating by now."

Zoey leans around me to speak to the cashier. "Hey, what if we swipe my card twice? Just for today."

"It's not going to let us do that." Jingle-jingle. "Hmm . . ."

The line is pressing on Zoey now. I'm pretty sure the edge of someone's lunch tray is in her back. She plants her feet like she's holding our ground.

"What gives?" someone asks from the back of the line. I look and see a tall boy with his empty tray clamped in one hand. He points to himself with the other. "Starving here!"

"Well, look who's holding things up." I know that voice. It's Brian Morris, and he's leaning out of the line to sneer at me. "Not so fast today, *are you?*" he says. As if I ever sprint through a lunch line.

Miss Jenrik asks me, "Did you pick up this card here in the school office?"

I lean forward and tell her, "It was mailed to me. From the state."

"The state? Oh! This is an assistance card!" She seems to get louder with each word. "You're on assistance! That's why it wants a code."

Zoey lets a puff through her lips and shakes her head.

Brian Morris makes a duck-call with his hand from

behind us. "It's Perry *Crook!*" he squawks. "Escaped from Surprise!"

Miss Jenrik's head snaps up when she hears that. Her face turns five shades of red beneath her pink hair.

"I'm s-sorry," she says. She's very quiet now. "My fault. Totally my fault." She puts in a code. My card goes through.

Zoey and I sit across from each other at the very end of a long table. We both lean into the cranny where the table folds out from the wall. Zoey is giving her hot macaroni a cold stare. She's mad about the card. I'm thinking that the harder won a lunch is, the more I want to eat it. I'm also thinking that soon I won't have a card from the state. When Mom is paroled, my card will be like everyone else's.

"She didn't mean it," I tell Zoey. I pick up a forkful of noodles.

"She was loud, Perry. Megaphone loud."

"But she was just glad she figured it out. Tomorrow will be a breeze."

"She could have done better," Zoey says. "Way better."

"Hey, Zoey," I say, "where did you get that ring?"

"Trying to change the subject?" She twirls the ring as she speaks.

"Yeah," I say. I can't hide much from Zoey.

"Stepdad Tom gave it to me," she says. "He bought it in the gift shop at the bed-and-breakfast we stayed in this summer."

"Cool," I say.

"I suppose," she says. "But it's like I've told you before, he gets me things that I don't really want or need—like the camera," she says, leaning up a little.

"I'm glad he got you the camera." I say it with a shrug and a grin.

"It's not just the gifts with Tom. It's that he has to talk about why he gave them. 'This ring is to celebrate the vacation we took as a *fam-i-ly* . . .'" Zoey grumbles. She starts to imitate Tom. "'Isn't it so great how far we've come, Zoey? You and your mom and I, we have made ourselves into a *fam-i-ly* . . .' And then there he is this morning asking, 'Are you going to wear your new ring to school today, Zoey? Huh? Huh?' I felt bad because I didn't even think about putting on the ring this morning, Perry. But I pretended that I did. Mostly to make my mom happy."

I've met Zoey's mom a couple of times, just to say hello at the window of her car in the school parking lot. But I've never met Stepdad Tom. I don't always understand exactly how Zoey feels about him. But I know that he is her biggest thing to need to talk about.

"It's been two years, Perry," Zoey goes on. "He still does it. He still talks about how great we're doing. You want to know what?" (She is going to tell me.) "The best times are when he says normal things like, 'Please pass the rice.' That's when I feel like we are a family."

I nod my head. I think I get the part about Tom trying too hard.

22

Zoey says, "It *is* a very cool ring though." She props her elbow on the table and tilts her fist toward me. "Put your face up to the stone, Perry. Don't put your chest into your macaroni," she warns. "Get real close. See your reflection? It's like a mirror in a fun house. Your nose gets really big. See?"

"Oh yeah!" I say. She is right. I am one giant nose-face with tiny eyes way up high. I crack a smile and see giant horse teeth in Zoey's ring. It's too funny. I drop my ridiculous face into my hands.

"Made you laugh!" Zoey is triumphant.

Zoey says that I never laugh. I say I'm just quiet about it.

Four boys come to sit at our table, including the loud, tall, hungry one. I shift over and slide my tray back in front of me like I'm making more room. But I am stuffed into the wall already. They are talking about what team everyone is on and about which school they came from. There's some whispering, and they keep looking at me. Then up comes Brian Morris to sit with them. He knows where I live. He probably told.

"Hey," says the tall boy, "how about tomorrow you take your assistance card to the back of the line, *Blue River Boy*."

Yep. Brian told.

I wonder what else he said, because he makes stuff up. He told the whole fourth grade that I sleep in a cell with no mattress, that I only get white bread and water for supper.

The boys are staring. Zoey's jaw is set off center. She

23

doesn't like it when people are into my business.

She looks at me. She jabs her straw onto the table and pushes the wrapper down into a tight accordion. She slides the paper across the table right in front of Brian Morris. She uses her straw to wet it with a dot of milk. It grows.

She looks up at Brian and says, "Worm?"

chapter seven

THE FIRST
TIMED MILE

When we ran our first timed mile in fourth grade, the gym teacher told us it was a fitness test required by the State of Nebraska. "Don't worry. But do your best." That's all he said. Right away I got it into my head that I wanted to finish first. So did Brian Morris.

It wasn't that close; I think I bested him by ten yards. I'd done a lot of running at Blue River. Mr. Halsey had taught me to breathe, *hoo-hah*, *hoo-hah*, and to exhale every time my left foot landed. It worked. I was already walking off that run when Brian barrel-brushed me and almost took me down. Instead, he stumbled, and he's the one who ate dirt.

"Are you all right?" I asked.

Brian got to his feet, still fighting for breath. He rubbed the long muddy smudges on his arms and legs. Then he let me have it—bad language. He even spit on the ground near my feet.

"You're fast because you run from prisoners all day," he said.

I got one of those ice-cold rushes inside—the kind that keep spilling through you. No one had ever said anything like that to me.

"I don't run from them. I run with them."

Brian twisted up his face. "What?"

"With the residents. There is a track at Blue River. I run—"

"I'd rather be *dead* than live at a prison!" Brian swept past me, knocked me in the shoulder. I had to step backward to keep my feet underneath me.

Dead? Really?

That night at the Blue River supper table I told everyone within earshot that I had the fastest timed mile in the fourth grade.

"Yeah, Perry! Victory feels good!" Mr. Halsey put his long arms up in a big *V.*

"It felt good. But only for a few seconds," I said. "This kid, Brian Morris, was *mad.* Like he wanted to punch me in the gut. I think I should let him win next time."

Every single rez shouted, "No, no, no!" Mom was firmly with them.

"But if it will make him feel better?"

"No! No! No!" It was practically an uprising.

26

Even the warden stopped by the table to see what was up. "What has you all so excited and united?" she asked.

Eggy-Mon, who loves a rhyme, clicked his fingers from behind the serving counter, and repeated, "Excited! United!"

Mom said, "You should always do your best, Perry. Stay proud of yourself!" She gave me a nudge. "Besides, if you let Brian win, he might sense that's what you're doing. That won't make him feel better."

"Hmm. You know what else Brian said? He said he'd rather be dead than live at a prison." Everyone fell silent. Mom hummed a sigh and clicked her tongue.

"You know, Perry, before I came here, if I thought about being incarcerated—if I tried to imagine it—my mind would shut down on me after just a few seconds. I couldn't bear the thought. It seemed *deadly*. Maybe that's what Brian really means."

Last year, in fifth grade, we ran the mile again. At the starting line, Brian Morris told me he'd bury my sorry butt, and he did—by three seconds—fair and square. I'm curious as to how this year will go. I want to win.

I also want to keep Brian Morris off my back.

chapter eight

JUMPERS

I'm sitting outside my bedroom door in the Upper East Lounge right outside Warden Daugherty's office. This is the smallest lounge at Blue River. That's because Big Ed and his Special Projects crew from the woodshop walled off part of it to make my bedroom. I know the story because Big Ed likes to tell it.

"The residents were so sore about it!" He laughs. "They grumbled about losing the morning sun." (It sure does flood in on a clear day.) "Everybody said, oh, what's Blue River need with another broom closet? Or, is that warden going to hog the light to expand her own office? What's going in there?"

The story goes, the partition went up and Mom's belly grew out. Then a crib arrived. "I set that up myself," Big Ed likes to say. "Soon everyone knew that a baby was coming to Blue River. We had ourselves a little-bitty prison nursery for one."

Mom left Blue River to have me in a hospital. (She only leaves on medical passes.) She says that when she walked back through the entrance with me asleep in her arms in a blue blanket, Big Ed was beaming. He called out loud in the Blue River Common, "Oh boy, it's a boy!" He raised both his arms into the air. "Hey everybody, you can quit moaning about your morning sun." He pointed to the Upper East Lounge. "We've got us a new Morning Son!"

This lounge shrank because of me. Mom says it's the best place to hold small meetings. Fo-Joe calls Mom the Blue River U-Hauler because she likes to circle up the chairs. He can be a little bit of a jerk about it. He makes her put everything back, and he'll make her late to supper if the job isn't done.

Today, I am here on my own. No homework on the first day of school. I'm sitting on the floor, dangling my legs over the common. I have permission. The railings, which happen to be candy-apple red, protect me. Mom says it was all anyone could do to keep me from licking them when I was little. These days, I just rest my chin on the low rail and watch everything that goes on below.

The rezzes are coming in from the woodshop and the greenhouse. Some have been to meetings or classes. The dinner bell will ding in ninety minutes. This is free time for the rezzes. Sort of free. Some will go take showers. There is a schedule for that. Some will go to the gym or to another meeting. The men and women can socialize before dinner.

But only in the common. Mom says it's hard for anyone to have a private conversation that way. But it's the rule. There's no dating and no getting married at Blue River. You can't kiss anyone. Well, Mom can kiss me, and I can kiss her back. But anyone else will get an infraction ticket. Their pay will be docked, and they will have less to spend at the commissary. Some rezzes sneak hugs and quick kisses anyway. I see it happen. I don't tell.

At this hour there is lots of handshaking and high-fiving down in the common. That's how the workday ends for everyone at Blue River. The warden says it's how you show your gladness. Some rezzes like it. Some, not so much. There are some that stand with their backs against the wall. They cross their arms over their chests and stay stone-faced. They are the Cold Ones—I think it to myself. I see ice in their eyes, and that tells me they have the kind of hearts that don't want to care. Mom tells me, "Steer clear, Perry." And I do. But sometimes I see that even the Cold Ones go a little softer when they see me—a kid—around the halls of Blue River.

Mr. Halsey and Mr. Rojas are like family. They look for me to be up here. They know I am usually in this spot at four p.m. Sometimes I call down to catch someone's attention. But I stay quiet if I see people who look like they might be having a heavy time of it. Almost every rez at Blue River has troubles that come upon them pretty hard from time to time. I don't go jiggling people out of their deepest thoughts.

30

"Perry, my man!" Mr. Halsey is looking up. He's been to the commissary. He's got a plastic grocery bag tied closed at the top. He hands the bag to Mrs. DiCoco. "Protect this for me, will you, Callie?"

She will. Just about everyone likes Mr. Halsey.

Mr. Rojas plays lookout for him. He checks the common to see if Fo-Joe or any other supervisors are watching. "You're clear, man. All clear."

Mr. Halsey takes a few running steps and jumps up. He reaches high with one arm, like he's dunking a basketball. Only there is no ball and no hoop in the common. He's reaching for me. Easy-peasy. He tags my sneaker. "Check it out!" he says as he lands. "Perry's got fresh kicks! Woo-hoot!" He takes a look around to see if he is caught. He's not. He gives Mr. Rojas some skin. "Your go," he says, and then Mr. Halsey is the lookout. Mr. Rojas is lots shorter. He jumps, stretches, and just misses my foot.

"Give that man a booster seat!" Mr. Halsey teases. Mr. Rojas shakes a finger at him for the diss. Some of the younger rezzes join them taking jumps.

It's a pretty good game. They are getting away with it. Everybody at Blue River likes to see a little bit of that. Meanwhile, I like the thumps on my feet. I like it when Mr. Halsey asks about getting me and my new sneakers out onto the track for a run. I love to run with him. But we only have Saturdays now that school started.

Mom comes up behind me. "What's going on down

there, Perry? Are those fools jumping again?" She looks into the common just as Mr. Halsey leaps and smacks the bottom of my foot. He lands, spins, and looks up at Mom.

"Hey, hey, Jessica!" he says. He's smiling but he sounds a little serious when he asks, "How's it going? You doin' okay?"

I see Mom nod. But she's got that worried, not-enough-sleep look. She rests her elbow on the railing and plants her chin in her hand. She gives Mr. Halsey a thin smile. "Hey, Halsey," she says. "When are you going to play a real game in the yard?"

"I don't know," he says. "I've still got some work to do." He points to his own chest and says, "Gotta know that I can keep a cool groove."

"Play your first game with me," I say. "One on one. Whenever you're ready. We can keep it cool."

"That's a plan, Perry."

I look at Mom, but she has gone sort of blank. Maybe it's because crabby Mr. Krensky is skulking by at the top of the stairs on his way to the law library. He's a Cold One. We steer clear. But there is something else about Mom. She's not carrying the New Start file folder. This is the time of day that she usually sits in the lounge shuffling through it. She keeps lists of jobs she wants to apply for once we are out. She crosses them off if the positions get filled. "It's still early for me to be looking," she will say. "But this way I know what's out there."

The New Start file is also full of apartment listings. We'll need to rent. Someday. Those come and go too. I know her favorite: it's the whole second floor of a blue house on Button Lane in Rising City. That's the next little town, seven miles north of Surprise, where Zoey Samuels lives. The photos show a place with little rooms and long windows, wood floors, old radiators, and round knobs on all the doors. But the best thing about that one is that we could make it back on Saturdays to see Big Ed and the others. Week after week Mom checks on that blue house. "The ad is still there," she'll say. "Maybe it'll wait for us." She could be right about that. I get the feeling nobody else wants it. Mom's parole hearing is coming up. We'll be leaving soon.

Below us, Mr. Halsey takes his grocery bag back from Mrs. DiCoco. "Jess-i-ca!" he calls up to Mom. (He loves to say her name in three broken syllables.) "Think fast!" He comes rising up, the grocery bag sitting easily in his palm. He gives it a push to send it up over the railing. Mom comes to life. She reaches to catch it. She gives the bag a gentle, guessing-game squeeze. Her eyes brighten.

"Broccoli?" she says. "Did you buy me fresh broccoli?"

Mr. Halsey taps his long index finger to his lips. "Shh-shh-shh!" He looks over his shoulder then whispers up to her. "Don't get me in trouble!"

Mom covers her mouth. There's not supposed to be

giving or trading of goods from the commissary. But that's a rule that gets broken all the time.

"Thanks, Halsey," says Mom. "Lookie here, Perry." She says it with a smile. "Green gold!"

chapter nine

JESSICA

Jessica Cook had two weighty pieces of news on her mind all afternoon, and she carried them both to the dinner table. The first was the incident at Perry's school—the business of the assistance card for his lunches. The school had called to apologize for what had happened. They said she should please know that the privacy of every student was of utmost importance to them and that Perry should feel no stigma or discomfort using the card.

Jessica thought she should say, *Oh it's fine! Don't you know I'm in jail? Being outed for an assistance card is nothing to my kid.* Instead she'd squelched her sarcasm and thanked them for the call.

Perry hadn't said anything about the card. He'd been fairly quiet all evening, watching the jump game in the common and then sharing the snack of steamed broccoli with her in the Block C kitchenette. They had joked about how they were spoiling their supper on the healthiest thing they'd eaten all day. Sad truth.

But her boy was onto her. He sat close to her at dinner, his huge blue eyes searching her face for the big tell. Perry always knew when there was a stink in the clink. He just didn't always know the details, and he knew not to ask. He'd been raised to respect everyone's privacy at Blue River, including his mother's.

The second piece of burdensome news had come from Warden Daugherty, in another private meeting in her office just hours ago—and it was far more haunting. "I'm afraid," the warden had said, "that we have finally come upon that one person who knows about my unusual arrangement as Perry's foster care giver and is unwilling to look the other way."

Jessica's breath had collapsed into her chest.

But who? After all this time? Why now? How bad is this? She was certain she had pondered the words, not spoken them. Yet it seemed the warden had heard.

"We have to stay calm. I'm on this, and I'll keep you informed. I promise you."

Sitting at dinner now with Perry and a cluster of female residents, Jessica struggled to be present. Sweeps of cold fear overtook her. She closed her eyes and let a deep breath slide over her lips.

Shake. It. Off.

Eat supper with your beautiful kid. Jessica ran her hand

along Perry's back where he sat beside her. He was wearing one of the new back-to-school shirts she'd sent Maya Rubin to buy. It'd taken the better part of two prison paychecks, but oh, nice knit, nice fit.

At least something was in place.

chapter ten

SITTING NEXT TO SCISSORS

"I can't believe we can't go," Miss Sashonna is complaining at the dinner table. "It's not fair. Not fair. We made all the decorations. That's all us." She pats her chest with the flat of her hand. Miss Sashonna has long, skinny arms and sharp elbows and she never stops moving. We leave a lot of space around her at the table. Sitting with her can be like sitting next to a pair of scissors.

Mom says Miss Sashonna is one of her biggest challenges here at Blue River. Sashonna thinks everything is "not fair." Nothing bugs Mom more. When Sashonna first got here she mouthed off about everything from the shower schedule to the sporks in the cafeteria. "You see this, you all?" She held her spork up high. "Know what this is? I'll tell you what. This is unnn-necessary, that's what. They can give me real flatware. I'm no stabber."

Mom told her, "We're all nonviolent, Sashonna. Sporks are practical. One utensil. Easy to wash." Then she added, "And isn't it your job in the kitchen to wrap napkins around sporks?"

"Two hundred of 'em a day," she answered with a waggle.

"That's a lot of sporks," said Mom. "You better find some love for those until you get promoted."

"Yeah, I find some love for my big eight dollars a week," Sashonna said. "I can't even get a little jar of that chocolate spread at the commissary. It's not fair."

One day Miss Sashonna brought up the fact that Mom got to have me with her at Blue River. "What's up with that?"

But Warden Daugherty was quick, saying, "Sashonna, if you know of a facility where you think things would be *more fair*, you let me know. I'll get you transferred." That shut her down in a blink. She's no dope. Anybody would choose Blue River in a heartbeat—anybody who has to be in a prison.

Tonight, Sashonna's whine-o-meter is all cranked up because of the Dads and Daughters Dance. It's the first one ever. Warden Daugherty has decided to try it for the men at Blue River—the ones who are dads. Everyone is going to knock off work early on Friday afternoon to get ready.

"We should all get to go. They got a suit for every guy. Did you hear that? All donated. Shoot, we never get to see them looking fine like that. I'm so sick of blue shirts," she says.

39

"I don't care so much about them," says Mrs. DiCoco, flapping her hand. "It's the little girls I want to see. Little ones like my grandbabies. They are going to come in wearing their dresses and looking adorable. Like tiny princesses."

"Well . . . ," Miss Gina says. She has dark crusty eyelashes that look like they will break when she blinks. "I wish it could be a dance for all of us too."

"Yeah! Yeah!" Sashonna whirls her knobby fist in the air.

"That could happen someday," Mom says. "You never know. The warden is always working on new—"

"Jessica! You're just on the other side about everything around here," Sashonna says.

"Hey. No, I'm not," Mom says, shaking her head. "It's hard as heck, but I try not to think about sides in here."

"Well, that's because you're due to get out." Sashonna curls a lip at Mom. She sits back hard in her chair. Folds her arms. "It's two years since I've seen a guy all dressed up nice."

Mom makes a tiny sound in her throat like she's kind of agreeing with Sashonna on that point. "Well, I'd love to have eyes on that event too," Mom says. "But the dance is for the guys. To remind them what's waiting on the outside." She sounds drifty. "Remind them to keep on doing the right thing, keep on rising up—even on the bleak days."

"I'm glad one of you gets that." Warden Daugherty has done that thing where she rolls up out of nowhere like some life-size wind-up toy. She stands at the end of the table with her clipboard tucked in her elbow and her pen in her hand.

Miss Sashonna straightens her spine and puts both hands up. "I get it! I get it too," she says.

Miss Gina rolls her eyes. Mrs. DiCoco lets out a laugh and pushes at her silver hair.

"That dance is going to be emotional," Warden Daugherty says. "And emotions are fine. We are human. But for this, the fathers deserve some privacy." She looks over the tops of her eyeglasses and pokes her pen at the group like she's popping a balloon. "End of discussion," she says. Then she looks at me. "So, Perry. Good day at the new school?"

"Yes," I say.

"I'm glad to hear it," she says. "If you need anything, you come see me. Any problems, just tell me." I'm guessing someone told her about my unswipeable lunch card. When something like that goes wrong for me on the outside, the warden gets it fixed in no time. But the only thing I want to know tonight is what's up with Mom. I can't ask that question right here and right now. Besides, the warden is already motoring through a turn. Then she is gone.

Miss Sashonna plunks her elbows on the table. "Okay, so we can't go to that dance." A grin creeps across her face. "But Perry can." She jabs a finger at me.

Mom says, "First of all, don't point at my kid. Second of all, he's not a dad or a daughter."

"But he's a photographer! He's got that camera." Miss Sashonna is pointing at me again. Mom gives her a wicked look, like she'd like to grab that finger.

"Pictures would be nice," Miss Gina says, and Mrs. DiCoco likes that idea too.

"So do it, Perry!" Miss Sashonna pumps her skinny arms and dances in her seat. She sings, "Have a party! Be a dancer!"

"Perry does have a nice camera," says Mom. She makes a rectangle with her fingers and thumbs. "It's tiny, and I love how you can view the shots right on the screen. It's the most brilliant thi—"

"That's called digital," says Sashonna. She puts a long bony finger in Mom's face. "Don't you know? Digital."

Mom looks up. "Right. Cameras are one of those things that have changed a lot in twelve years," Mom reminds her.

"What do you say, Perry?" Miss Gina pretends to hold a camera to her eye. She clicks down with one finger and shuts one furry eyelash.

"Can I, Mom?"

"If the warden says you may—and if you want to do it." She always lets me decide. I am the guy with the most freedom at Blue River.

I try to deliver.

chapter eleven

DADS AND DAUGHTERS

On Friday afternoon I come in from school and find the Blue River Common transformed. Twists of pink and white crepe paper float from the railings. Paper birds made from magazine pages hang from strings. "Wow!" I wave my arms to move the air. Everything sways. The common is breathing.

I have permission to hang out in the Upper East Lounge and take pictures of the Dads and Daughters Dance. But only for the first half hour. Fo-Joe likes the idea. He thinks we should print pictures for the dads. Some of the girls who are coming are the ones that can't always make the trip to Surprise.

When the fruit punch and trays of cookies are ready, Fo-Joe and the other supervisors clear the common. Mom and the other women will have tea and free time in their block kitchenettes this afternoon. Dinner will be an hour later than normal. This is a rare day at Blue River.

The men come in, and I have to look twice to tell who is who. They are wearing the donated suits—some baggy, some tight, but all of them sharp. When I watch them through the viewfinder of my camera, I see the men standing tall. They are well dressed and smiling. All of Blue River is outside the frame. They are *free* this afternoon. For the first time I wonder, what about Mom? Will she look different when she's released? Will she be different when we're on the outside?

Below me Mr. Rojas laughs. He helps Mr. Palmero pin his boutonniere to his jacket. There are some upside-down carnations in the common. But everyone is having a laugh about it.

Then the daughters arrive. Just like Mrs. DiCoco said, the little ones look like princesses—or cupcakes with little heads, legs, and arms. Most tiptoe right up to their dads, glad to see them. There are a couple of criers, some sad, some not so sure about being here. Their fathers wait, talk to them sweetly. Then bend low to lift them up.

Cici and Mira Rojas know me from visiting days. They wave to me, and Mr. Rojas holds a girl on each arm. He says, "Look up! Smile for Perry!"

I frame the shot and squeeze the shutter. More dads and daughters look up to be photographed.

There is a holdout. She's a bigger girl, about my age. I don't know her dad, except that he's called Talon. (He has bird claw tattoos that come up his neck and behind his ears.)

He's a bit of a Cold One. Tonight he seems softer. But his girl looks mad as heck. She stands against the wall, one foot up behind her and arms tight across her chest. Her chin juts forward. She won't look at her father—won't look at much of anything, except to give me the stink-eye.

"There's some dumb boy up there!" She points at me. Mr. Talon goes to stand beside her. "What's that boy doing?" I turn away. I don't know what else to do.

The music is playing. The dancing begins.

Some dads and daughters kick out, jump, and shimmy. But most dads hold their daughters close, rock them, and twirl in one place. There are still some tears. The warden said emotional.

I see Talon and his girl step away from the wall. She won't take his hands, but they dance a little. I don't get their picture. Maybe they don't really want one.

I watch the clock. I don't stay long.

Later, Fo-Joe comes to my door with a cup of punch and a napkin full of shortbread cookies. "Brought you a snack, since dinner is late. The party's breaking up down below. Give it five and you're free to roam," he says. I don't usually have to stay stashed away, especially not on a Friday afternoon.

When the music dies I step out and look down. The common is empty. The paper birds hang still. I see Mr. Rojas coming up the hall from Block A on his own. He has changed out of his donated suit, back into his light-blue shirt. He carries an apron. He's a server in the kitchen tonight. He doesn't see me. When he gets to the common he stops and looks at the decorations still hanging there. He sits back against the wall. He pulls a handful of tissues from his pocket and blows his nose three times in a row. I remember what Warden Daugherty said about privacy. I back away from the rail. I hear sobs and then a few deep breaths that let me know he is trying to stop.

I know what he did. Mr. Rojas ran a gambling ring. He said it was good quick money. He thought he could sack away everything he'd need to send his little girls to college then walk away from the illegal stuff. I heard him tell it. "I got greedy," he said. "Just a little more, just a little more . . . ," he mocked himself. "Now I'm just a dumbass in the slammer who messed up on his family."

But actually, Mr. Rojas is smart. He helps the rezzes up in the law library. You have to understand your own case when you are in prison. Mr. Krensky is a good jailhouse lawyer too—maybe even better than Mr. Rojas. But Krensky isn't nice. He makes people pay for every little thing. Mr. Rojas helps for free. He's been a good friend to Mom and me. When Mrs. Rojas brings their girls to visit, I feel like more family has arrived. It's one of the hard things about Blue River. I'm glad that he has been here for us. But I know how much Mr. Rojas misses home.

I inch up to look down. I see him tying on his apron. I

hear Eggy-Mon call from the kitchen, "How do you do, my man in blue?"

"Blue is the color," Mr. Rojas replies. "I'm getting it together. But man, we have guys weeping rivers down on Block B tonight."

chapter twelve

MEETING WITH
THE WARDEN

Warden Daugherty offers me her rolling chair. I get the feeling I will not be spinning in it today. No taking a short run to land on my knees on it and surf across the floor. I might be getting too big for that anyway. The warden pushes me forward to sit in front of Mom. She closes the office door and drops the blinds over the glass that looks into the hall, and I wonder why we need privacy. The warden stands beside her desk. Mom does the talking. Her voice is unsteady.

"Perry," she says, "Warden Daugherty and I need to tell you something. There's a new bump in our plan." Mom presses her hands together. She lowers her head for a second, and when she raises it I see that her eyes are watery.

Must be a big bump. "Which plan?" I ask.

"The leaving Blue River plan." She sighs. "Things are going to go differently than expected. It's not my choice. But it may not be all bad either."

"So, what part of it is bad?" I ask. "If there is some delay, we'll just wait . . ." I feel bad for saying it. Mom deserves to be out. She shouldn't have to wait another second. It's time.

She clears her throat. Fixes serious green eyes on me. "You know that it's always been a little unusual that you live at Blue River." Mom glances at the warden before she goes on. "We've been so lucky for that, Perry. But now . . . there's someone making trouble over it."

"Why? Who would care?"

"Well . . . one can only wonder about that." Mom huffs, as if there might be more to that story. But I won't be hearing it right now.

"Um-hmm," the warden says. "The scrutiny is really on me, Perry. My practices and procedures here at Blue River— the way I do things."

"Are you saying you are in trouble?" I look up at the warden. The tiny nod of her head tells me I'm right.

"Wow," I say. I feel like I'm being slowly hit by a bolt of lightning. "And trouble for you means trouble for me?"

"It means change," says Mom. "For you and me." She grabs both my hands in hers. I can feel her shaking right up into the rolled cuffs of her Blue River chambray shirt.

"Mom?"

"Perry, I always planned for the two of us to leave here

together. And I'm staying on track. I will apply and reapply for parole. Oh boy, will I ever . . ." She gets a little quieter. "But you, Perry, you're going to live on the outside."

I jump to my feet. The chair rolls backward and hits something behind me with a thud. "What? When?"

"I'm sorry," Mom whispers. "You have to go now."

chapter thirteen

LEAVING BLUE RIVER

L ate in the afternoon on Sunday I watch the gray clock in the common. It's ticking away the minutes. Last minutes. Mom wants me to be strong. She said, "We aren't going to like this. But we will be fine. We are a family. We are a team. We are together even when we cannot see each other." I'm hanging onto her words. I want her to believe that I am okay. I've been to the bathroom two times in seven minutes.

None of this seems real. Something will happen. A call will come. An order will arrive. An indestructible dome will drop over the Blue River campus to keep me in and keep the thing that is coming to get me out.

The dark-gray SUV pulls up in the front circle drive. My insides lurch.

I stand with Mom, Warden Daugherty, Foreman Joe, and Big Ed. Someone could think that we are setting up to have our photo taken, all of us looking out the large front window together like this. But none of us are smiling. At my feet is a rolling suitcase that belongs to the warden. It is filled with almost everything I own. My school stuff is in my backpack. So is my camera. We have filled it with pictures of pictures—all the shots Warden Daugherty and the other residents have taken of me over the years. Mom keeps the prints on her wall. I photographed them all so I'll have the same set to flick through when I need them.

When Mom told me that I'd be living on the outside without her, I saw myself wandering around inside the rooms of the house she wants to rent on Button Lane. Alone. That was ridiculous. Now I can't picture anything. I can't see myself living outside of Blue River at all.

My pits are sweating. My head feels airy and floaty and cold on top. I take a few breaths to try to send some oxygen up there.

A man gets out of the SUV and takes quick, lively steps to the back of the car. He opens the gate. I suppose he'll put my bags back there. I see him brush the arm of his coat with the back of his hand. He pats back his brown hair with his palms.

"So that's him?" I ask. I cannot feel my lips.

"Must be," says Mom.

"It is," says Warden Daugherty. I guess she has met him before.

The man's name is Thomas VanLeer. I know that he has a wife and a daughter. I also know that he is the whole reason that I am leaving Blue River. I know that I'm going to live at his home. Big Ed calls that "pouring salt in the wound."

Mom is twisting beside me. Big Ed's lower jaw is pushed forward. Fo-Joe is drawing his teeth over his lip. Everyone keeps eyes on Thomas VanLeer.

Nobody likes this, I think to myself, nobody except smiling, waving Mr. Thomas VanLeer, who is striding toward the door of the Blue River Co-ed Correctional Facility. He's a big deal in Butler County. He has some important job.

Thomas VanLeer reaches for the door handle and goes to give it a good yank. Blue River is locked up tight. He nearly bangs his own head into the glass.

"Yeah, heh . . . there's a beautiful thing . . . ," Big Ed says in his under-mumble.

Slowly, the warden points to the left to indicate that there's a security call button at the side of the door. VanLeer needs to punch it. He looks around, confused. When he catches on he nods in a goofy sort of way. He gives the button a press. Then he waits. We all wait. Things are awfully silent. I begin to wonder which guard is monitoring the front cam.

"Warden Daugherty? Do you need me to run up to security and tell them to unlock?" I ask.

The warden speaks slowly, as if her batteries are dying. "That's all right, Perry. I'm sure the guard will open the door. Eventually."

I look back over my shoulder at the golden walls, the

wide halls, the stairs and red railings. No more running the Block C corridor. No more hugging the railing above the common. No all-rise announcements in the mornings. A weight falls through my stomach. I lean into Mom. She pulls me close.

VanLeer is still waiting, shuffling his feet. What if we just never let him in? I think this to myself, and I feel brilliant. I hear the lock bolt disengage. It seems louder than it ever has before. Mr. VanLeer is inside. My ribs make a tight cage around my chest.

"Hello, all. Phew! September cold snap out there." He claps his gloves together. He directs his attention to me. "You must be Perry."

"Genius," says Big Ed in that low rumble.

"Yes. I'm Perry." I say it slowly. I know that I have never sounded more miserable in all my life. I don't offer to shake hands with him.

Big Ed speaks close to the back of my head. "No reason to be friendly if it's not what you're feeling." I'm not.

VanLeer looks at Mom. "And are you Jessica?" he asks.

"Yes. Perry's mother," she tells him.

"Well, I'm Thomas VanLeer," he says. He introduces himself all around. He gets gloomy responses, but he smiles the whole time. "Pleasure to meet you all."

"Hardly," says Big Ed.

"You may know, I'm the Butler County district attorney," Mr. VanLeer says.

54

"Funny thing about that," Big Ed says. "I always thought the DA was supposed to work for the people. And here it seems to me that you're working against these people." He fans his hand toward Mom and me.

"Well, I believe I'm righting a wrong in this case," Mr. VanLeer says. He is still smiling and nodding. "Which brings me to my business. We all know why I'm here."

"Here to take away our Morning Son," Big Ed says.

The warden says, "Mr. VanLeer. You have papers for me." She holds out her hand. VanLeer pulls an envelope from the inside pocket of his coat. The warden takes her time unfolding the papers and even more time looking them over.

Mom is so silent, she is hardly breathing. Warden Daugherty keeps reading. VanLeer leans toward her impatiently. "Look, it's all in order, Gayle," he says.

"Unfortunate," says Big Ed.

"I'm meticulous with paperwork." VanLeer reaches for the rolling suitcase with my things in it. "I think it best we not prolong."

"Hmm. Sounds like you want to get away from us," Big Ed says.

The warden fastens the papers to her clipboard. She looks at Mom and nods. "It's time," she says, and I feel doomed.

Mom speaks. "Mr. VanLeer." She waits until he is looking right at her. "I hope you'll be as good at providing this interim home for my son as you seem to think."

VanLeer smiles broadly. "He's in terrific hands."

"He has always been in terrific hands," the warden says.

Thomas VanLeer tells Mom, "Perhaps it's best for you to keep an open mind." He claps a hand on my shoulder, and I feel my eyes bug out. "Perry deserves better than he has had."

"Says you." Big Ed coughs.

"This will be good for him."

I can't stand it anymore. I slip out from under VanLeer's clamp to give Mom an enormous hug. Then I reach for Big Ed and the warden, who takes her time and hums while she holds me. I give Fo-Joe a high five. He pulls me in for a short, rough hug. Then I hug Mom again. Longer. She is shaking, but she won't cry. This is my team, I think to myself.

"I'll see you all on Saturday," I say. "Six days away." I force my shoulders to shrug. "We can handle that."

Mom lets out a tiny laugh and that stops her shaking at least for a second or two. Big Ed puts his arm around her. She rests her ear against him. Fo-Joe and the warden ignore the extended contact. This is a special circumstance.

VanLeer pulls up the handle of the rolling suitcase. I pick up my loaded backpack.

Mom says, "I love you."

"Love you too," I say. "Six days. Don't miss me too much." I push my mouth into a wide smile. I hope that every tooth is gleaming.

Then I go.

chapter fourteen

A NEW STINK

When I step out of the Blue River Co-ed Correctional Facility, all I feel is wrong and dizzier than before.

I make my way onto the backseat of Thomas VanLeer's SUV, which has a new-car smell that crawls straight up my nostrils. "Got your seat belt on, Perry? Need any help with that?"

"No. Thank you." I could remind him that I am eleven, and that I ride in a car to school every day, that I know how to buckle up. But I do not feel talkative. I see him looking at me in his rearview mirror.

"So, Perry, this is a new chapter for you." He cranks the steering wheel as we begin to roll. I look back and see Mom and Big Ed and Fo-Joe and the warden all standing at the glass, each with one arm raised. I'm not sure they'll see me, but I press my palm against the glass inside the SUV.

"You'll love the house," VanLeer is saying. "You'll feel

right at home. You'll have a nice bedroom. A real bedroom. And you can make it your own. We can paint. Put up posters. Whatever you want."

I know he's still checking the mirror. I won't look up there. I'm watching Blue River.

"I understand that you'll miss your mom—and that's normal. I don't want you to worry. You'll still see her. We'll follow the schedule. Meanwhile, you'll get to know our routines . . ."

He is talking too much. That new smell of the SUV is too much. My head feels some kind of horrible.

"You'll have a first family supper with us this evening," he says. He laughs and adds, "They know you're coming! They're setting a place for you at the table. Are you hungry now, Perry? Home is not far away, but we could stop. Ever been to the drive-through? Do you like milk shakes? French fries?" His tone changes. "Normally I wouldn't suggest snack food before supper. But this is no ordinary day . . ."

My horrible floating head bobs. Once. Twice. I'm in a predicament. There is a floor mat at my feet. I lean up. The seat belt stops me. I'm trapped. I turn my face to the side and lose my lunch all down the inside of Mr. VanLeer's car door.

chapter fifteen

NOT RIGHT AT HOME

Mr. VanLeer pushes the door to his home open for me. I step inside. The walls feel close. The ceilings are low. The air is warm and smells sweet and spicy. Better than new-car smell. And throw-up.

"Ah! I think that's Thai food," says VanLeer. "Don't I smell coconut?" He cocks his head at me. He should know to stop talking about food by now. Maybe he thinks I am empty. "My wife took a wonderful series of cooking lessons in foreign cuisine," he tells me. Then he calls out, "Hello! Robyn? We're here!"

I wait for Mr. VanLeer's family, even though I'm dreading it. I'm sure my face is gray. They are going to find out that I threw up in their car. A woman comes around the corner from what must be the kitchen. Her face is turned downward for a moment. Her head is all long light curls just

59

like Zoey Samuels's mom. Another look and I realize she *is* Mrs. Samuels.

"Wha—" I don't get any words out. Something else catches my eye, and that something is Zoey. She leans around the corner.

"Z-Zoey?"

"Yeah." She gives a little shrug. "Hi, Perry." She winds her finger into her hair then makes a fist. I know Zoey. She does that when she's nervous.

"Tom!" I say it louder than I mean to. Everything is silent for a few seconds. I look at Zoey and say, "Thomas VanLeer is Tom."

I watch her eyebrows arch up. "Yeah," she says. "My stepdad. Tom."

Mr. Thomas-Tom VanLeer has been very busy this whole time with his head inside the closet, pushing his coat onto a hanger. I'm not sure he has heard me. But Zoey's mom has. I'm not sure whether to call her Mrs. VanLeer or Mrs. Samuels, but she is giving me a kind smile. I think my mouth is hanging open.

"We're glad to have you here, Perry," she says. Her head tilts in that friendly way. "Can I get you anythi—"

"Water," Mr. VanLeer says, springing back out of the coat closet. "He needs a drink of water."

He herds me into the kitchen, almost stepping on the backs of my sneakers as we go. He drags the warden's suitcase in behind us and sets it down. He pulls a glass from the kitchen cupboard and accidentally clanks it against the faucet as he fills it. Everything about him has sped up since my great moment inside the SUV. Throw-up has a way of making people hurry. He hands me the glass, and I take a tiny sip.

"And let's run a load of wash," he says, nodding at Zoey's mother. "Perry's jacket is a bit . . . soiled." He tries to talk plainly, like nothing is wrong with puking in a car or down your own sleeve.

"So, would you mind, Robyn?"

"Not at all."

"Good. Now, I've got to go back down to the car—just for a minute." He quickly grabs paper towels and spray cleaner from under the VanLeer kitchen sink. I should offer to clean that car door. But Thomas VanLeer is halfway down the hall. He calls over his shoulder. "And hey, Zoey, sweetheart, you can go ahead and show Perry to his room. And the bathroom, so he can wash up. Show him the whole house." He disappears with his cleaning supplies.

The room takes a breath. In the silence, I'm still holding the glass of water, which I do not want. I'm thinking about rules and wondering if it is okay to just set this glass down on the counter. Or do I put it in the sink, or inside the dishwasher? Mrs. Samuels or VanLeer reaches to take it from my hand.

"Looks like you are done with this," she says softly. Then she helps me out of the jacket so easily that I feel bad about what's all over it.

Zoey watches. I still cannot believe that I'm in her house on this horrible day.

"Hey, Mom," she says, "my jacket could go in too."

"Good idea," says her mom.

Maybe not, I think. But I can't seem to say the words.

Zoey's mom carries my jacket. Zoey grabs my backpack. I pull up the handle on Warden Daugherty's rolling suitcase and follow them down the hall.

chapter sixteen

THE ROOM I WILL (BARELY) SLEEP IN

Zoey and I stand in the bedroom in the VanLeer house. I am supposed to sleep here. I'm in a fight with myself; I don't want to look around the space, but I have to. It is very square and the walls are the color of Mom's morning coffee. That's with two big splashes of milk. The bed is a mound of brown and white pillows and covers and it looks like a giant dessert. All the furniture is dark wood. Lamps with big flared heads stand all around the room. Then there is Zoey, who is shifting in place.

"There isn't that much to show you," she says. She points around the room saying, "Bed. Nightstand. Dresser. Window. Curtain. And the closet is here." She pushes on a narrow door. I see a tiny empty room. "We can move your furniture around if you want."

63

"I don't have any furniture," I say.

"Well. The stuff in this room," she says. "You know what I mean."

A few seconds grind by. I think of the gray clocks at home. I scan the coffee-colored walls and don't find a clock here. I have to have a clock . . .

"Perry," Zoey whispers. "Are you all right?"

"When did you know?" I ask. I'm giving her a stone face. I can't help it.

Her shoulders slump. "They told me on Friday at supper. Perry, I'm sorry. There was no way for me to tell you. I know this is your worst-case scenario. I knew it the minute I heard. But I was hoping—"

"What? Hoping that I'd like being yanked out of Blue River as long as it was to come live with you?" My face turns hot. Zoey looks stunned.

"No. But Tom might have been thinking that. Maybe it's better than . . . well, I don't know . . . At least I'm not Brian Morris, or . . ." She sighs and does not finish that sentence. Zoey Samuels is having trouble talking to me. That never happens. After a few seconds she asks, "Do you want to put your stuff in the dresser?"

"No."

Later, I stare at the swirls of plaster on the ceiling. I am used to seeing square tiles. But it is just one of the hundred or so things that are not right. This bed does not feel like mine. I am lying down but off-balance, too high from the floor. There is something wrong with the little bit of supper in my belly. I'm not sick from it. It actually tasted good. But I ate it with the wrong people. Right about now, I'd be happy to hear Miss Sashonna say, "It's not fair!"

Lights from somewhere outside cast weird shadows on the walls, and I have a strange sense of how far down the hall the bathroom is. I didn't think to ask if I could just go ahead and use it in the night. The shower in there is messed up. The water comes out of the little spout at the bottom—like for filling the tub—but nothing comes out of the showerhead at the top. I crouched under the low spout and splashed water onto me to clean up. Maybe only the bathtub part works. I'm not used to that. There are no tubs at Blue River, except for the little plastic one that I outgrew a long, long time ago.

I hope I won't need to get up in the night. I'm afraid I'll knock over one of the lamps in this room where I am *not* sleeping. Meanwhile, I forgot to ask what I'm supposed to do in the morning, which is slowly, slowly getting closer.

I will have to wait for six days just to tell Mom how I got sick, how VanLeer has turned out to be Zoey's stepdad, how the shower doesn't work right, and how every single thing is different here. I lie in the strange bed, aching to talk to Mom. Suddenly I know that this is what new residents feel like on their first night at Blue River.

I am a new intake at the VanLeer house.

chapter seventeen

MORNING IN
A NEW PLACE

It turns out that the way you wake up here is: Mr. Thomas VanLeer stands in the doorway and hollers you right out of bed. I am feet on the floor before I have a single thought. It's not mad hollering. He's clapping too. Maybe he thinks he is cheering me out of bed.

"How did you sleep, pal?" *Clap!* Mr. VanLeer bangs his hands together again. "That's a heck of a soft bed, isn't it?"

I look at the bed and blink a few times. I don't know how I got down from there so fast. Did I really sleep? How many minutes? I saw the sunrise . . .

"Mrs. Samuels finds the nicest things for our home—"

Oh, it is Samuels! I think. She probably kept that name so people wouldn't be confused about her being Zoey's mom.

"That bed came from an old farmstead up near Lincoln . . ."

Mrs. Samuels arrives at the door. She touches her husband's arm and looks in at me. "Good morning, Perry," she says. She is sweet and quiet. "Breakfast will be ready in just a little bit. We'll let you get dressed now. Come to the kitchen when you're ready." She loops her hand into the crook of Mr. VanLeer's elbow. She smiles and closes the door.

I look for a clock again, then remember that there isn't one. Before I dress, I stand by the window and look out across the flat yard where the tall trees stand. By the look of the sun outside, I can guess that it's time for morning release at Blue River. I curl my hand around nothing but air and lean toward my thumb. Low and slow, I whisper.

"Good morning. This is Perry at sunrise. It is Monday, September twelfth. If you want to know how I slept, well, I didn't." I stop to breathe and a huge sigh comes out of me. "I don't know what you're having for breakfast. I'm not sure what I'm having for breakfast." I stop and imagine the click of the locks, and that one enormous yawn that all of Blue River makes every day. I wonder how Mom is waking. My eyes begin to burn. The sand in them loosens. I wonder if she and Big Ed sat in the common long after I left. It might have been allowed. Special circumstances. I wonder if she ate dinner and if she tossed and turned all night. It catches me—a cold stone in my throat. I want Mom so much. I want to go home.

I should be crouching into runner's stance facing Block C right about now. But this morning there's nothing to run toward.

chapter eighteen

SLEEPWALKING

Zoey's mom is driving us to school. I sit in the VanLeer SUV with my nose tucked inside my fleece. It wears a whole new smell: VanLeer laundry soap. Zoey keeps looking at me. I stay tucked.

Inside the school, I stand beside Zoey but I am searching the lobby for Miss Maya Rubin. When I see her, I know that she has been watching for me too. We put our hands up to wave at the same time. I go right to her. "Miss Maya, have you heard from the warden this morning? I'm just wondering if my mom is all right."

"I'm sure Jessica is fine," Miss Maya tells me. But Miss Maya is not a resident of Blue River, so she doesn't know for sure. "She'll be wondering the same about you, Perry. This whole thing is . . . well . . ." She shakes her head.

I think she's hesitating because Zoey has followed me.

"It's unexpected," Miss Maya says. She leans around me just a little to say a cheerful good morning to Zoey. Zoey nods. The hallway is beginning to buzz like a hive. I step closer to Miss Maya.

"Can you call Blue River today?" I ask. I'm low-talking. I'm not so sure I want Zoey to hear me. She knows it. She looks off to one side and pretends not to listen.

"I know of no rule that says I may not," says Miss Maya. Her eyes open wide and she flashes a grin.

"I just want to know how everything is."

"Sure. I'll try to call during my lunch break," she promises. "I should at least be able to reach my aunt. I'll give them the message that I've seen you today. That will comfort everyone." She smiles and turns to go.

In the middle school we change rooms for different subjects. I'm dragging myself from class to class. Twice, I walk right up the back of somebody in the hall and have to say I'm sorry. One of those times it is Zoey, and I accidentally pull her shoe off her heel. She hops out of line and backs against the rain forest bulletin board. I step out with her.

"You gave me a flat, Perry."

"Sorry," I say.

Zoey sighs and hooks her finger into her shoe to fix it. We go on in to science class, where I get a jaw-killing case of the yawns. I'm wishing for lunchtime to come. I'm not hungry. All I want to do is check back in with Miss Maya.

Standing in the lunch line, Zoey says, "Okay, so just tell me. Are you going to stop talking to me permanently because of all this?"

"No," I say. "I'm just tired." It's the truth. I'm sleepwalking. I mean to tell Zoey this, but then someone tall elbows past us. I mistake him for a teacher and step out of his way. Then I realize that he's one of the kids who was with Brian Morris that first day of school. He's the one who complained when my unswipeable card held up the lunch line.

"Hey!" Zoey says to him. "Check it out." She points to herself and to me. "Other hungry people. In line."

"I'm not waiting while someone takes forever to get his special card swiped," the boy says, and he looks straight down from the top of his tall self, right at me.

"Shut your trapola about that," says Zoey. "It's been fixed."

Another boy slides in front of us. Then another. Then Brian Morris, who also mumbles, "Move over, Mad-Zoe."

"Hey! Neanderthals! What gives?" She's getting loud.

"Shh . . . Zoey . . . ," I say. But that's all I've got. I'm too tired.

Miss Jenrik's jewelry jingles when she swipes my card. She punches the right code in on the first try. While she is swiping Zoey's card she asks, "Did somebody cut that line today?"

"Yes!" Zoey tells her.

"Thought so." Miss Jenrik tucks a tail of her flamingo-pink hair back. She glances past us to the table where the boys have gone to sit.

"It doesn't matter," I say.

"It does matter," she corrects. "People have to wait their turn. So, listen . . . I have another code for you," she says. "It's baloney."

"Baloney?" Zoey is very interested.

"Yep. You know why? Because we never serve baloney here. So if I hear someone say the word *baloney*, these multiple-pierced ears of mine will perk right up." Miss Jenrik flicks at her hoops and feathers. "I'll deal with that baloney because there is no place for it in this cafeteria. Promise you."

"All right," says Zoey Samuels, and she stands tall.

I give Miss Jenrik a weak smile and move on.

We have to squeeze by those boys to make it to the place we like to sit. Today, I would've settled for any other spot in the cafeteria, but Zoey is leading. The boys grumble. They make room for us as if we were a pair of cactus plants.

We sit. I lean on my elbows, cheeks in my hands, and look down at the food in the compartments of my lunch tray. The largest one holds three breaded chicken fingers. Another is filled with a scoop of hash browns, another with three baby carrots, two cherry tomatoes, and a piece of broccoli all tucked together. There is an oatmeal cookie in the last small square.

"Perry? Are you going to eat?" Zoey asks.

It could be that a little while has gone by.

"Yeah," I say. But then I just sit there some more. I'm thinking about the vegetables. There are never enough vegetables for the residents at Blue River. Not the fresh kind. Same for fruit. If I get an apple on my lunch tray I sneak it back to Blue River and split it with Mom.

I think of home and how much I want to go to sleep in my own bed again. I'd like to do that right now. I can see Mr. Halsey jumping in the common with the bag of broccoli. Wait. Impossible. My face is still in my hands. The skin on my cheeks is stretched. My elbows slide. My tray moves forward toward Zoey's tray then stops. My head is nodding. Something isn't right. Halsey is jumping with bags and bags of broccoli . . . throwing them over the red railing . . . again and again. But there was only one head of broccoli . . . broccoli . . . My head is broccoli . . . and it's going to fall off my shoulders. Then . . . it does. BAM!

"Perry!" Zoey is suddenly on her feet. "Oh my gosh! Oh my gosh! Perry!"

There is food all over the table. Zoey is screeching.

"Perry, you're bleeding!"

My nose feels runny. I blink and put the back of my hand up there and it comes away bloody. Brian Morris and his new friends are sliding away, leaving the table, and taking their lunch trays with them. I hear gasps and groans.

"Blech! Sick!" and "Nasty!"

It takes a few seconds for me to realize that my nose is killing me. Zoey is leaning toward me, offering her napkin. But it's as if she can't reach me across that mess of tumbled lunch.

I feel far away from everything today.

chapter nineteen

ZOEY EXPLAINS

Zoey and a school custodian walk me to the nurse's office. All the way there, the custodian holds her big ring of keys against the back of my neck just under my shirt collar. "Magic trick," she says. "It helps stop a nosebleed. I don't know why it works, but it works."

I pinch my nostrils near the top. Zoey hops along beside us saying, "It's okay, Perry. It's already stopping. You're going to be all right."

I squeeze my eyes shut several times as we walk. Something huge is rising up inside of me. I want my mom. So much. I want her to know what has happened. I can't believe that I am not living at Blue River. I can't get to her. It chokes me.

In her office, the nurse checks me over. She holds my head with her strong fingers and thumbs, she tips it and tilts it. She looks up my nose then feels my nose bones.

"Perry, that must have hurt!" she says. "But it's not

broken." She positions my fingers back on my nose. "Pinch. Perfect. Now, you might have guessed it, but I can't tape a bloody nose shut with Band-Aids. But if you pinch a little while longer, we'll have a full recovery. A wet cloth will take care of the evidence. It's a miracle you missed the shirt," she adds.

The shirt! It is new, and new shirts are expensive. Mom works hard at Blue River to earn a small pay. I always try to tell her that Goodwill shirts are fine. But she likes me to have a couple of new ones each season. Thinking about it makes me feel like crying. I gulp. I have to get myself together.

The nurse sits me in a little room inside her office. She lets Zoey come in with me. She puts a baggie of ice on my neck in place of the custodian's keys. I lean forward and continue to pinch. My hand is sticky with my own blood.

"How do you feel?" Zoey wants to know.

"Gross," I manage to say. I sound like a duck. My eyes burn, and I blink.

"Perry, did you fall asleep sitting up?"

"I think so," I say. I remember the broccoli dream. But I don't tell it.

"Didn't you sleep last night?"

I shake my head no, which is tricky when you are keeping your nose pinched.

"You hate it at my house, don't you?"

I don't answer.

"You know, Perry . . . if you are mad, I get it," Zoey says.

75

She looks at me and bites her bottom lip. Her knees begin to bounce up and down. "I feel terrible. Like, really, really terrible." Her voice turns raspy. "This whole thing happened because of me."

She sits forward, and I know that she's going to tell me why.

"A couple of weeks ago we were all sitting at the dinner table. Tom was looking over some papers. He works basically all the time. Mom and I were talking about school starting again. I asked her if we could invite you to come for supper this fall, now that we'd be in middle school. I said it was about time. We thought maybe your mom and Blue River would agree to let you come." Zoey takes a breath.

"Tom was being quiet, working and eating, and listening to Mom and me with one ear. Then I see him set down his fork. He leans up and interrupts our conversation." Zoey puts on her Stepdad Tom voice.

"'Wait, wait. Are you telling me that your school friend—this boy Perry—lives at Blue River? There is a child? Living at the prison?' His eyes were popping straight out of his head, Perry. Mom was trying to explain that you grew up there. Then he's all, 'Grew up there? How did I not know this?' Perry, I swear, I clammed up. I told Tom I wasn't going to tell him anything. I said I wasn't even talking to him in the first place. That got me sent to my room for the evening. Happens every time I speak rudely to Tom." Zoey shakes her head.

"Anyway, it seemed like he just dropped it. Nothing happened. School started, and I thought it had all blown over." She waves a hand in the air. "Then last Friday night comes, and—"

"Perry!" Maya Rubin pops into the little room inside the nurse's office. "I just heard what happened." She stoops down in front of me, lifts my bangs, and takes a look—more into my eyes than at my nose, it seems. "Are you all right?"

I nod. "Hey . . . um . . . Miss Maya," I say. I quack at her because I'm still pinching my nose. "Did you get a chance to make that call?"

"I did." She smiles. "Everything and everyone is fine at Blue River. But you are sorely missed."

"Thanks," I say.

Somehow, I feel glad about that.

chapter twenty

CLOSET LANDING

The plan for after school has changed on account of my slamming my nose on the lunch table. Zoey and I were supposed to walk to the library together, do our homework, and try to choose an after-school program to join. Instead, Zoey's mom cuts her workday short and comes to get us.

At the VanLeer house I stand in the room where I got no sleep. I let my backpack slide to the floor. Someone has moved the warden's suitcase with all my things in it into the closet. I roll it back out.

I stare at the high bed with its chocolate-colored covers. I remember that Zoey said I could move things in this room. I grab up the comforter and a pillow, or maybe it's more than one. I hug the bundle, walk it into the closet, and drop myself on top of it on the closet floor. I don't do much arranging. I've landed in my favorite sleep position—the running start—half on my belly with one leg tucked up.

My head is on a pillow. I close my eyes and cup my hand to my sore nose and breathe. The warm air returns with each breath. Before long, I am drifting.

Big Ed sits in the armchair by the window at the front of the Blue River Common. A new intake sits across from him. I keep walking around them. The sun is coming in. But it's that dusty sort of light. Like fog. I squint. Weird. I can't see the new guy's face. He might be the new guy named Wendell. But I feel like I know him better than that.

Big Ed is talking about his Mottos for Successful Residents.

"Seek to succeed," Big Ed says.

I know what he will say next; I know it by heart.

"Whatever it was that got you put in here, it's not the only thing that you are about. You're here to rise up. Go to work. Go to your meetings. Clean up your soul and feel honorable again. Believe it or not, you can be successful here."

I keep circling.

Big Ed moves on to the next motto. "Eye on the end," he says. "Keep a clear vision of how you want to emerge. If you're smart, you'll make a . . ."

"Timeline," I finish the sentence for him. My voice sounds far away and filled with bubbles.

"Give purpose to each day. Make goals. Whether you've got ten months or ten years . . . plan for that day you walk out."

"Here's the one for right now," Big Ed says. "Seek to

understand before you seek to be understood. Keep your head down. Get to know others before you reveal yourself." Big Ed sits back like he is done.

"There's one more motto," I say, but now, I can barely hear my own voice. "Big Ed," I try to call out. "You forgot to tell him about Win-Win. You forgot . . ."

"Perry? Hey, Perry? It's just me."

What is Zoey Samuels doing in the Blue River Common? Wait . . . We're not in the common . . .

I open my eyes and lift my head. Zoey is kneeling at the closet door. She holds two mugs by the handles and a stack of cookies in her other hand. I see tall boots just behind her. I look up.

"Love what you've done with the place," Zoey's mom says.

I sit up and look at the scramble of bedding all around me. "Oh. Sorry." I try to unpaste my sleepy lips. "I—I know the bed is really nice and came from an old farmhouse and . . ."

"No matter." Zoey's mom shakes her head and flaps her hand. "Do you mind if I try to improve on your new setup? Just a hair?"

"She's good at this stuff," Zoey assures me.

"Aw! Thanks, honey! But it's really more like I can't stop myself." Mrs. Samuels laughs. She reaches behind her and shows me a thin, rolled mattress. "This is for camping, really, but it'll put a little padding between you and the floor. Give it a try. I'll leave you to it. I'm going to start dinner."

When she turns to go I see her stop and glance at Warden Daugherty's suitcase. I think she's going to ask me to move my clothes into the dresser, but she doesn't.

Zoey sets the mugs down carefully and slides one toward me. She offers me a cookie, and I take it. Silently, she settles herself in the doorjamb with her cocoa cup on her knees. I sit cross-legged and promise myself I won't spill on the bed cover, even though it might not show if I do. Warm cocoa is the perfect thing to wake me up. Once I have a few sips in me, I can talk to Zoey.

"You're right," I say.

"About . . ."

"I am mad. But I'm not mad at you. I'm glad you wanted me to come for dinner. I don't think you could've known that your stepdad would decide to get me pulled out of Blue River. And anyway, it wasn't a secret that I was living there. Everybody knows. Even though nobody talks about it."

"I guess . . ."

"I'm sorry if it seemed like I was being mean. I'm not happy . . . about . . . all this . . . stuff." I swallow hard. I figure I don't have to explain that to Zoey. "And I really was super-tired," I say.

"Sorry you didn't sleep well," says Zoey.

I shrug and lean down to take another sip of the cocoa.

"And sorry you smashed your nose," she adds.

Now I'm sipping cocoa and cracking a smile at the same time.

"And flipped your lunch. Everywhere." Then she blurts, "Made you laugh!" Then I do laugh, right onto my mug. I nearly spray cocoa across the closet. That makes Zoey laugh. We both have to steady our mugs.

"Well at least I get to," I say.

"Get to what?"

"I get to eat dinner at your house."

chapter twenty-one

JESSICA

Halsey Barrows put both his arms full around her right there in the common where everyone was coming in from the workday. The crowd concealed them. It was the first time Jessica had seen Halsey since Perry had been taken away the evening before.

"Come on," he said. "Be strong. You're going to be all right," he told her. "Perry too. Because you raised a great boy."

Halsey smelled sweet from his day in the woodshop, a scent that reminded Jessica of the tree she'd played under in the yard of her parents' home outside of Lincoln. That was the only home she'd ever had besides this one. There'd been nothing ideal about either place. But at least Perry had been here. She wanted him back so much her throat ached. A few curled wood shavings clung to Halsey's Blue River chambray. She caught them between her finger and thumb.

Halsey was apparently willing to risk an infraction ticket for extended contact. Foreman Joe was around. Somewhere. But with Perry gone, Jessica felt weary of all the rules. Unfocused. There seemed less reason to toe every line now that Perry wasn't right beside her where he could see her receive a reprimand. Why not just accept this one comforting hug? Maybe Halsey's big heart beating in her ear would reset her somehow, and get her through the evening. But what about him? He had a date for his parole hearing. He didn't need trouble.

It might have been a kiss, that gentle pressure she felt on the top of her head just before she backed away from him. Or maybe it was just a brief chin-plant caused by their height difference. Whichever, it meant he understood how she was feeling.

Jessica stood in front of him, arms dangling at her sides. She sighed and said, "Thanks, Halsey."

chapter twenty-two

WIN-WIN

As the new intake at the VanLeer house, I do what new ones at Blue River do. I find someone who has been here a while, and I follow her. When Zoey's mom asks her to set the VanLeer table, I'm on her heels.

"Napkins on the left, fork on top," she says.

Easy enough.

While we work, I remember my sunny, dusty dream. *Win-Win.* That's Big Ed's other motto for being a successful resident. The first "win" means you count all small good things that happen to you every day. It takes me a second. Then I think of Miss Maya making the phone call home for me, and Miss Jenrik with her "baloney code." There was Zoey with the cocoa, and Mrs. Samuels showing up at the closet door with that camp mat. So, a call, a code, a cocoa, and a camp mat. Four pretty good things.

The second "win" means you do things that bring

victories to others. I've heard Big Ed say it at least a hundred times. "No matter where you live, you have a community of some kind. And you can be a contributor."

New intakes sometimes roll their eyes at all of this. But the ones that try to follow his advice, well, it just goes better for them. I've seen it a hundred times.

I decide that setting the VanLeer table with Zoey is a start at contributing. There is a fork, a knife, and a spoon at every place on this table. Zoey shows me how each piece goes. Tomorrow night, I still won't be home where I want to be; I'll be here. But at least I will already know that the blade of the knife is supposed to face the plate.

At dinner I keep practicing the mottos. I listen. I try to understand what the VanLeers like to talk about at suppertime. I listen to how they spend their days. There is steamy golden stew in the bowls that sit on top of our plates. Fat pieces of chicken, carrots, and potatoes float there. I wonder why I have the plate, and I wonder why I have the knife and fork. I look around the table. All anyone is using is the spoon.

I listen. I learn that Mr. VanLeer goes to the courthouse in David City every day, and he has an office across the street from it. Neither is far from the new middle school, and the library is in between. I learn that he had a pastrami and provolone sandwich on an Italian roll at lunch.

That sounds fancy. Eggy-Mon wouldn't be able to get that. He calls our sandwiches "meat and cheese on white—all right." Or "PB and jelly—sticking to your belly." He does the best he can with the Blue River kitchen budget. People miss the meals they used to eat on the outside. So he runs contests. Residents can make up food poetry. If Eggy-Mon likes your poem, and if he can get the ingredients, he'll put it on the menu. Some rezzes try for something too fancy. Like Mr. Krensky, who always seems like he's trying to stick it to people anyway. Once he asked for "tilapia fill-aze in honey-mustard glaze."

Eggy-Mon flapped a spatula at him and said, "Nice poem. Big ask. Too big."

Then Mr. Krensky crabbed at him in that voice that nobody really likes to hear. "Question is . . . are you up to making it happen?" He stuck his pointed chin at Eggy-Mon.

Eggy-Mon drew his bread knife through a bun. He held the bun up in both hands and made it talk like a puppet. "How about a day-old roll for the Blue River troll," the bun said. Eggy-Mon thumped it onto Mr. Krensky's tray.

Eggy-Mon probably can't get tilapia—whatever that is. But when Mom came up with "Curds on wheat, with a fresh-fried tweet," we got the best toasted egg and cheese sandwiches ever.

Oops. I'm not listening to the conversation at the Van-Leer table. Following Big Ed's advice is going to be hard when my mind keeps wandering back home.

I tune back in just in time to hear Mrs. Samuels talking about taking a trip to Lincoln tomorrow where she's going to pick up a dresser for the Lund family and cart it back to town. Mrs. Samuels helps people and businesses with their places and spaces. Her job is about paint colors, fabrics, furniture, and flower beds. I've already heard her say that she doesn't have enough work in these little towns.

"Wasn't the dresser pickup scheduled for this afternoon?" Mr. VanLeer asks.

"Well, it was going to be, but then when the school called, well . . ."

I realize that she's gotten to the part about changing her schedule because of my bloody nose.

". . . with the sun shining, it turned out to be a great day to stay in town and clean out flower boxes and do fall plantings. I did the Higgins and Hansen porches in gold and white mums," she says. "And then it was kind of nice to come home and start dinner early."

"Thank you," I say—or, more like, I blurt it.

All the VanLeer and Samuels heads turn to look at me.

"This dinner is good," I say. Then I think it to myself: this dinner is a win.

chapter twenty-three

IN THE HISTORY ROOM

When Friday gets here, I am psyched. I'm one day away from Saturday. That's all I've been thinking about. Mr. Thomas VanLeer will drive me back to Blue River for the entire afternoon. *Tomorrow.*

Mom and I have so much catching up to do. Little things, big things, new things. I need to tell her about the VanLeer house, the meals, the busted shower, and the bed inside the closet. I want her to know I made a timeline and taped it to the closet wall. I'm marking my *X*s through days that are done. I'm trying to keep my eye on the end. Trouble is, I'm not sure exactly when that will be. I am all about the day when Mom will be paroled and I will get out of the VanLeer house.

There is a whole week's worth of assignments from the

new school to tell her about. Mom always keeps up on what I'm doing in my classes. Just today, Miss Maya Rubin told us about a whopping long-term assignment—the kind that causes me trouble. I really need to talk to Mom about that. I want to leave time to hear what's been going on at home; who is new, who's been gated out, who had something good happen, and who is hanging in there at Blue River. I wonder if we can get everything said on a single Saturday afternoon. I will need a list, and Mom and I will need a corner of the Blue River Common to ourselves. That's a tall order. Saturday is the busiest visiting day.

Zoey and I walk to the library. We've done this each day after school—except Monday when I had the bloody nose. It's just two and half blocks, but I secretly feel very grown-up walking on our own. We're allowed to eat snacks in the library, and so far, we've been remembering to pack something in the morning at the VanLeer house. If Zoey forgets, I remember. If I forget, Zoey is on it. Mr. VanLeer says we are a remarkable team. This morning he told Mrs. Samuels, "They're like a brother-and-sister act, huh, Robyn?" He chuckled. He chuckles all the time. He thinks he has to fill in the quiet parts.

Mrs. Samuels was quiet this morning after she heard that brother-sister thing. Zoey showed me an eye-roll from behind the pantry door where the granola bars are. For me, what Mr. VanLeer said feels like a little piece of something caught in the arch of my shoe. I don't know what it is. It's nothing much. But it hits a tender spot every once in a while and I wish I could knock it out of there.

At the library, we choose the History Room. We sit on spindly wooden chairs and hook our ankles on the rungs. It is not the most comfortable room in the library. That makes sense to me because Mom sometimes says that history is not always comfortable either.

We eat the granola bars and start our homework. There is a grandfather clock that tick-tocks at us in a serious sort of way. I lean forward to tell Zoey, "If that thing had fingers it would be shaking one of them at us." She squelches a laugh.

There's supposed to be no talking, no noise in the History Room. (Somebody forgot to tell that clock that.) The rule makes this room unpopular with most kids. Zoey and I whisper and nobody kicks us out. But we are not invisible. Mr. Olsen, who runs the after-school program, spots us. He knows that we have not signed up, and we are supposed to.

"Uh-oh," Zoey whispers. She barely moves her mouth. She sings to me, "He's looking at us . . ." She crumples her granola bar wrapper and stares down at her rainforest workbook.

I try not to let Mr. Olsen see that my eyes are seeing him. But of course that quadruples all this seeing that is going on. He comes right over to our table. He's got his clipboard tucked against his chest.

"Hello-odles, mighty eyeballers," he says. "Me again. It's the end of the week. You two haven't chosen a program. I'm here to apply pressure." We must be giving him twin looks, because the next thing he says is, "What a pair of pouts!" Then he laughs loudly right there in the History Room.

"All right, all right," he says. "I get it. Joining up isn't your bag. But listen to these fine offerings." He refers to his clipboard. "Board Games is very uncrowded. Young Water-colorists, now that's a noninvasive species."

I look at Zoey. She is biting her bottom lip.

"And there's still room for one—but I will make room for two—in the fiercely popular Computer Video Boot Camp." I think our faces must be blank. He draws a big breath. "Or . . . or . . . if you really want to be revolutionaries, you could be in my brand-new group called . . . Library Volunteers!" He sags. "Okay. I should be more creative about that title," he says. "Anyway, the volunteers schlep and shelve books, among other thrilling tasks. Or they will. When they start. If you start. Oh, please say you'll start," he begs. "We could use the help."

Zoey and I are silent.

"Puh-leese!" Mr. Olsen groans.

Zoey squirms from side to side. "Well, since Friday is already half over, can we give you an answer on Monday?"

"Deal!" he says. He retucks his clipboard, gives us a wave, and strides away.

When he is out of sight I whisper, "Do you think there is anyone else who hasn't signed up?"

"I get the feeling it's just us," Zoey answers. "We have to

choose. What do you want to do, Perry?" But before I can answer she adds, "I'm *not* doing Video Boot Camp. Brian and the line-butting lunchroom boys are all in there."

"Yeah, I saw that," I say.

The truth is, I would've liked to do it. I can only shoot short videos with the camera Zoey gave me. I would like to find out how to put them on the computer and string them together. But when I saw the swarm on that first day of sign-ups, I backed off.

A scraping sound tears through the quiet History Room. We hear a bump and a crash. A few feet away, a book cart has plowed down a pair of the spindly chairs. The books in their slippery bindings fall from the cart. *Fwap. Fwump. Fwap-fwap. Fwump!*

"Oh dear! Oh lordy!"

I know who says that. I pop out of my chair, calling, "Mrs. Buckmueller!" Then I realize that it's Friday. She should be in the Bucking Blue Bookmobile on her way to Blue River.

Fwap-fwap. Fwump!

The books keep sliding. Mrs. Buckmueller leans her whole self across the top of the cart. She looks like a chicken that's fallen down on its chest trying to protect its eggs. I get to her just in time to catch a book midfall. Zoey comes along and saves another.

Together, we pick up books and set them back on the cart. Mrs. Buckmueller gathers them, tucking them underneath her chest with her hands and elbows. When she finally stands straight again, the books are in a few short, perfect stacks almost as if she has hatched them.

"Phew!" She wipes her forehead with the back of her hand. Then she hoots. "Thank you, thank you!" Her voice fills the History Room air. "That was harrowing." She pats her rosy cheeks. For the first time, she looks right at me.

"Oh, Perry! My darling!" says Mrs. Buckmueller. "I didn't even realize that was you. I never see you in the library after school. I only ever see you over at the . . . uh . . ." She glances at Zoey. "At the . . . uh . . ."

"At Blue River." I say it for her.

"Over in Surprise!" She nods.

"I got taken out of there," I tell her. Meanwhile, I pick up one of the toppled library chairs and set it back on its skinny legs.

"Oh dear! Oh lordy!" She scrunches her brow. "Now, is that why they were all looking so down in the dumps over there on Tuesday afternoon? And here I thought it was the lack of contemporary titles I was hauling."

"By the way, this is my friend Zoey," I say.

"Hi there, darling," says Mrs. Buckmueller. "Thank you for the help."

"Anytime," says Zoey.

I look at the grandfather clock. The hands point to 3:50. "Hey, Mrs. Buckmueller, aren't you going to be late getting to Blue River?" I ask.

"Yes! Already am," she says. She gestures at the clock.

94

"Old Gramps there is a little slow. It's closer to four o'clock. I've been hunting down titles for the Leisure Library all afternoon. The bookmobile is a bit much for one person. But, lordy, I hate to disappoint, especially when the weekend is coming," she says. "On that note, I had better go load up." She pats her pocket, and I hear the truck keys jingle.

The tip of Mrs. Buckmueller's tongue sticks out and curls up on one side in a thoughtful sort of way. Carefully, she starts the book cart rolling. Carefully, she steers her way out of the History Room. She's going to Blue River, I think. I watch until I cannot see her anymore.

chapter twenty-four

BLUE RIVER
BOTTLENECK

Outside the Blue River Co-ed Correctional Facility, I'm craning and straining. The line of visitors is deep and thick. We're all trying to see in, and the residents are all trying to see out. I'm sure that Mom is waiting near the glass window with everyone else. I wish that I could get closer.

I've never been on this side of the Blue River bottleneck before, but I know it well. There are two sets of doors, and in between them, the security check. You have to get a badge, and you have to be counted. Blue River needs to know its numbers. It all takes a while. This is why I wanted to get here earlier.

I glance up at Mr. VanLeer, who is right next to me. He was in no hurry this morning. I was ready. I slept in my clothes right down to my sneakers. I made the bed in the closet, tucking the corners under, then the sides and the end. I like it neat. He made blueberry pancakes for everyone. He washed out the batter bowl and wiped the counters. Then he sat down with a tall stack and read the newspaper.

"Well, Perry, do you see your mom?" he asks. He clucks and chuckles as he looks around at the crowd. He acts as if he's brought me to a carnival. I am feeling ugly toward him. I push that aside. It's Saturday. I'm going to see Mom.

"It's quite a line," he says. He rubs his hands together then claps me on the shoulder. I fake a shoelace problem and slide away. I lean out of the line. I can't see far ahead of me, so I look behind me. Cars are still pulling into the lot. A scooter hums in; I watch the driver in her bubblegum-pink helmet. She leans into the turn then balances her way into a parking space. Who's that? I think to myself. But the truth is, I don't know all the visitors. Three more cars roll in. Well, at least we are not the last to arrive. There are plenty of families that come from farther out.

"Hello. Hi." VanLeer greets people who are waiting in line with us. He nods and says, "How are you this morning?" He doesn't get much for answers. I look all around. I pretend I'm not with him.

I spot Mr. DiCoco, well up in front. He'd never be late. He has flowers for his wife. He brings some every time he comes. Mrs. Rojas has brought her two little girls, Cici and Mira, and they all come running up holding hands.

"Perry!" Mrs. Rojas gives me a hug, and her purse swings

into Mr. VanLeer because he won't get out of the way. His lip curls. He stares. "The girls saw you from the back. We just wanted to say hello." Her voice dips. "We heard what happened. Jaime says he misses you so much!" She means Mr. Rojas, and I tell her that I miss him too.

The Rojas girls hold up their hands and say, *"Dame cinco!"* We high-five.

Mrs. Rojas laughs. "See you inside!" She rounds to the back of the line.

"Phew! I'm glad they didn't try to wedge in here," VanLeer says.

I look up at him with one eye closed. "Mrs. Rojas? She would never," I say.

I focus back on the big window. I can almost see inside. There is shadow and glare. I shade my eyes.

Mom! I nearly shout out. Her face breaks into a wide smile, and I know she sees me too. She covers her mouth with her hand. I grin and wave. She waves back. I see Miss Gina and Miss Sashonna wiggle and bump up against Mom. It feels good to know that they are probably saying, "He's here! Did you see? Perry is back!"

Big Ed stands near the women. Halsey towers behind them all, looking serious, like a bird on the hunt. It's unusual to see him in the common on a Saturday; Halsey doesn't get visitors. Maybe he wants to see me today. I face forward, jiggle at my knees, and mutter to myself, "Come on, line. Come on."

VanLeer and I finally make it to the doors. Fo-Joe is doing check-in, and when he sees me, he shoos me on through—doesn't razz me for one second. I don't even get a badge. VanLeer thinks he can follow, but Fo-Joe is stern with him.

"Whoa, whoa! Not so fast," he says. He blocks him with one arm and draws out the random scan wand. The wand will detect metal, like a pocketknife or a big clump of keys. You're not allowed to bring those things into Blue River. The random part means Fo-Joe decides to check VanLeer for no particular reason. Well, except to hold him up. I look over my shoulder and see Thomas VanLeer standing with his wings open. His face turns red while Fo-Joe sweeps the wand, slowly up one side of him then slowly down the other.

I am through the Blue River bottleneck. I dodge the crowd and sprint. Mom has moved into an open space. I hope she remembers . . . I hope she is ready . . .

And she is!

Six days with no practice, but she lifts me off my feet for a swing-around. I am twirling in the Blue River Common. I hear Big Ed calling, "There he is! There's my Morning Son!"

Through this long, long week, all I have wanted to do is fly—just like this.

chapter twenty-five

SATURDAY IN THE SLAMMER

We all talk at once. We laugh, we cry a little. Mom and I share a chair. She holds me around the shoulders, squeezes me like she is making sure that I am made out of the same thing I was when I left six days ago. Miss Gina, Miss Sashonna, and Big Ed are with us. There are a hundred versions of "I missed you!" and "So good to have you back!"

Big Ed says I'm skinnier. Miss Gina thinks I have grown taller. Mom wonders if I need a haircut, and Sashonna wants to know if I've brought digital pictures. But I tell her not this time.

I feel rushed to get things said. I haven't even brought out my list yet—and VanLeer is out there in the common. Somewhere. I figure he'll be in our faces in no time. He'll try to listen in like a bird on the line. I know that Fo-Joe can't hold him up forever.

"Don't worry about the district attorney, Perry," Big Ed says. (He can read my mind.) "We're keeping six for you," he adds in his under-mumble. "Keep six" at Blue River means you keep watch or create a distraction. Big Ed nods in the direction of the game tables.

I look and see tall Mr. Halsey steering Mr. VanLeer around so his back is to us. I can't hear them over the hum of visiting day, but Halsey is opening a chessboard. He shoves a chair into the backs of VanLeer's knees. He gives him a nice, friendly shoulder pat to help him sit down. When VanLeer tries to turn around to see where I am, Halsey spills out the chess pieces and sends a few into VanLeer's lap. Oh yeah. He's going to keep him busy.

Mom runs her fingers through my hair and asks me to tell her about life in the VanLeer house.

"First of all," I say, and I lean way forward, "did you know he's Stepdad Tom? I'm staying at Zoey's house!"

"I did hear that," says Mom. "I hope that's been all right."

"Shock of the century," I say. "But now it's the best part of this mess."

"Well good!" Sashonna pipes up. "'Cuz it's not fair, him not telling you that. He could have destroyed that friend-ship. Right, Jessica? Right?" Sashonna is repeating something Mom has said, I can tell.

I tell them all, "Zoey is still my best friend."

"Yeah, but that man"—Sashonna's arm punches upward— "that Mr. DA VanLeer, he should have been straight with you—"

"Shh-shh." Miss Gina pulls Sashonna's arm back down. "Let Perry talk."

"There's an idea. Let the boy tell his story," says Big Ed. Sashonna gives him a hiss. Mom looks down at me, gives me another squeeze.

I try to tell it right, but I go jumping from thing to thing.

"I couldn't sleep on the bed so Zoey's mom put a camp mat in the closet and that's lots better. But, Mom, there is no clock. I really need a clock . . . and then there is the shower. That thing is broken!" I say. "Nothing comes out up top and it's hard to get an armpit under that bath spout." I make a chicken wing with my elbow, and they laugh. "And trying to get your head wet? Forget it!" I'm talking so much my lips are sticking.

Mom listens. So does Big Ed. He is scrunching his fuzzy gray eyebrows and puzzling over that shower. Miss Gina flutters her inky lashes, which means that she is listening. Sashonna slithers around the back of our chairs like a gecko. She creeps around front then makes the trip again. Mom doesn't seem to mind. It's like it has always been. I'm her kid, but I kind of belong to everyone at Blue River.

When I hit a lull, I reach into my pocket. I pull out my list and turn to Mom. "These are the things I can't forget to talk to you about."

"Right," she says. "We should hit that before this day melts away."

Miss Gina gets up. "Come on, Sashonna. We're going to let Jessica and Perry be by themselves for a while."

"By themselves? Look around you. It's visiting day! You can't tell me to get out. I can be in the common. This is no infraction!"

"Shh . . ." Miss Gina pats Sashonna's arm. "Remember what I promised? I'm going to give you a makeover. How about a little glamour in the slammer? Smokey eye shadow with Midnight mascara? Want lip gloss too?"

"That Pink Pearl one?" Miss Sashonna asks. "Yeah, I want that . . ."

They go, and so does Big Ed. He wanders the common during visiting hours. He's another one nobody comes to see. It's hard to understand because he has made a lot of friends at Blue River. He says that's how he was before prison too—lots of friends. But he's far, far away from the old ones and it's been a lot of years. I see him sit down with the DiCocos. He tucks his nose into her new flower bouquet.

Mom sighs. "So, Perry. My Perry. Are you really all right? Tell me the truth."

I think for a second. I will tell her the truth. I just want to be sure what that is, and I want to give her the truest part first.

"I don't like it," I say. "I want to come home to Blue River. It was definitely the worst week of my life."

"Mine too! A godawful week," she agrees.

"Five minutes out of here, and I threw up in his SUV," I say. I jab a thumb toward the chess players.

"You got sick?"

"Yeah. And I had a bloody nose at school too."

Mom gasps. "Somebody should have told me!" She squeaks when she says it.

"There were some bad things," I say. "But look at me." I try to be funny, tapping my thumb on my chest. "I'm okay! We aren't going to love me living at VanLeer's. Not ever. But it's not forever. Remember all the people who have come through here?" I count a few off. "Mr. Mayer, Mrs. Cruz, Mr. Washington, Miss Dasha, Miss Jenn, and Mr. Solomon." I could go on and on. "They had catnaps to serve. Four or six months or something like that? And doesn't it seem like they weren't here very long?"

"But you shouldn't feel like you're serving any sentence, Perry. Always remember that you did nothing wrong." Mom's eyelids turn pink. Her nose is a little bit runny. Mrs. DiCoco would say she is weepy. I get it. She feels everything at once. She is sad and mad, but she's glad I am okay, and it's a relief to think we will be together again before long.

chapter twenty-six

THE LONG LIST

Mom and I pick our way down my list from our own corner in the busy common. It's strange to sit here, and only here. Usually, I roam around on visiting day like Big Ed does. I help serve coffee and cookies. But we're squishing a week's worth of everything important into part of one day.

"Hey." Mom tags my shoulder. "So tell me, who helps with homework?"

I shrug. "Mr. VanLeer bothered me about it for a couple of nights. When I said it was done he gave me a look, like I wasn't telling the truth. And that was after Zoey told him I was a pretty good student." I shake my head and think for a second. "But Mrs. Samuels is different. She's more . . . on my side about everything. She said she trusts me to ask for help if I need it."

"Good for her," Mom says.

"Zoey and I walk from school to the library every day." I tap a finger on my list because *library* is on it. "We get all our work done. But now we have to find an activity to sign up for." I tap the list again. "That's part of being in the after-school program."

I tell Mom about seeing Mrs. Buckmueller, how she crashed the book cart and had to protect the books like a hen. That makes me think of eggs. Thinking of eggs makes me ask about Eggy-Mon, who runs the kitchen, and I start craving "curds on whole wheat with a fresh-fried tweet." I would love to eat one with Mom—right now. I look toward the Blue River kitchen, where the serving counter is dark and quiet for the moment. I follow the red painted border from the top of the kitchen down the wall to where it meets the bright-red railing. The railing takes a turn and wraps up the stairs. The rope is hitched across the first step because of visiting hours. I used to be allowed to slip under that rope and dash up to the balcony above the common and into my room—

My room.

I look up. I see my door. Closed. I wonder what they're doing with it now that I'm not in it. Will they take the wall down? My eyes start to prickle with heat. I tuck my face into the elbow of my fleece jacket and press. I sniff hard and smell the VanLeer laundry soap.

"Perry, you okay?" Mom says.

I make myself sniff back snot. I squeeze my hot eyes. I

wipe my face hard and come out of hiding.

"Man, I thought I was going to sneeze," I lie to Mom. She offers me a tissue.

"So . . ." I blink to focus on my list and put my finger on the words *The Whopper Assignment*.

"Yeah, what's that?" Mom tries to be cheery. "It looks important."

"It is." I take a breath and say, "It's time again."

"Time for what?"

"The same old assignment with a different title. We did it in third grade. And fourth, and fifth. You know. There was immigration and westward migration, and traditions around the world." I take a breath and let out a sigh. "Whatever we're studying, there is always a personal narrative—something about us."

"Oh . . . yes," says Mom. "That assignment."

"This time it's supposed to be about how you and your family came to live and work here: Coming to Butler County."

"Oh joy," says Mom. "How perfect for us."

"The good part is Miss Maya is a cool teacher. We can write essays or poems, or do interviews. Kids are making bound books, maps, even videos. We have a lot of time. Six weeks or so."

"Right." Mom holds her bottom lip in her teeth for a few seconds. "But you have a dilemma."

"Yeah. Middle school seems different. I don't think Miss

Maya is going to pull me aside and give me a special assignment."

"Oh, you mean like instead of writing about your mother in jail, write a report on the state bird?" says Mom. She remembers. So do I.

"The western meadowlark," I say.

"Or the state flower."

"Goldenrod."

"State insect." Mom is nodding and smiling.

"Honeybee." We both laugh. "Or . . ." I cup my hand around my mouth to be secretive. ". . . how the teeny-tiny town of Surprise really got its name."

"Shh. Don't tell Big Ed!" Mom laughs.

"Anyway, I'm glad Miss Maya didn't change my assignment. I have an idea."

"Let's hear it."

I'm slow to get the words out. "Well, what if . . . I just told our story?"

Mom is listening, her eyebrows arched. I'm trying to decide if she is nodding just the littlest bit.

"If they know the truth, won't they have to stop inventing stuff? Like Brian Morris. I don't even think he means to lie," I say.

"No? Hmm. What do you think he means to do?"

"I don't know. He probably means to *ask*," I say.

"Right," Mom says. "And I bet you feel like all the Brian

Morrises of Butler are letting their imaginations work over-time."

"It's not just the Brian Morrises. It's me too." Mom looks up at me as if she knows what's coming next. "I know that we're here because you made a mistake a long time ago. I know you had a car accident and someone died. I know you got manslaughter." I stop to take a big swallow. We don't talk about this often. "I know some of that story. I want to know more—my *brain* wants to know more." Mom is jiggling one foot while she listens. "But if you still don't want to tell it, well, there are other things. It's like Big Ed says, 'How you got here is not the only thing you are about.'"

"But it is what the assignment is about." Mom's mouth tracks out to one side. She doesn't like this.

"The assignment is about coming here." I admit it. "But you have an important job at Blue River. You counsel other residents. You could tell that story if you won't tell the rest."

Mom's jiggling foot is going wild now. "So how would this work?"

"I want to do interviews. And not just you, Mom. Other kids are telling about their families. I have a Blue River fam-ily. I want to tell their stories too—if they'll agree to it."

She looks at me, eyes blinking. I wait for her to breathe. I wait for her to answer.

Then I hear Big Ed say, "You want a Blue River story, Perry? I'll tell you mine."

chapter twenty-seven

JESSICA

Jessica felt something like whiplash in her neck when Thomas VanLeer appeared so suddenly. Big Ed had just offered to tell Perry how he came to live at Blue River and boom! VanLeer was there.

"Time to go. Time to get on with the day," he said. He rubbed his hands together.

"But this *is* the day," Perry said. His jaw was slack with bewilderment. He got to his feet anyway, and Jessica knew then that she'd raised him to be way too compliant. Slowly, she pushed herself out of her chair.

She found herself staring at VanLeer. She noted the clean-shaven jaw and short, level sideburns. His face was pleasant enough—even handsome, to some, she supposed. But what the hell was making him tick—this man who was wreaking havoc on their lives, and who had just dusted her visit with her son off his hands like it was the nuisance of the day?

Big Ed coughed. "My story will wait for next Saturday," he said. "I'm not going anywhere." Then Ed looked at Van-Leer and added, "You'll need to plan to stay longer next week. Perry's got an assignment."

He may have said more. Jessica missed that because she took the last few minutes of the visit to make a mad dash to her room on Block C. She wanted to fetch one easy item from Perry's list.

As she stood in the common watching him go, she noted that he held her travel alarm clock to his chest like some precious ornament. It was sweet, and a little heartbreaking. The travel clock was finally going somewhere. She felt an ironic smile cross her own lips.

Perry hesitated at the first set of doors. She knew the posture; he had suddenly remembered something. He halted against Thomas VanLeer's hand, which was in his back. The man is a collie—an incessant herder, Jessica thought.

"Mom! I didn't see Warden Daugherty today," Perry said. "Where is she?"

Thomas VanLeer looked right at Jessica. Both of them knew the answer to that question. But even if she wanted to explain that mess to Perry here and now—and she did not—VanLeer would probably cut her off. So she didn't answer. She counted on Perry to know that he'd hit on something akin to a Blue River point of privacy, and instead, she kept her eyes on the man.

"Hey, he doesn't like that." She spoke plainly to

VanLeer—couldn't keep her index finger from poking into the air between them. He looked back at her, clueless. "Your hand," she explained, "pushing on my son's back like that. It's rude."

Perry looked at her and broke into a grin. He wasn't one to laugh out loud much. But she saw him gulp back a drop of amusement that perfectly matched the bright and knowing smile. She filled with warmth.

"Mom, tell the warden that I miss her, okay?" he called. With VanLeer up his heels again, Perry's sneaker-feet squeaked forward on the linoleum.

"I will. I promise," Jessica said, and she blew him a kiss as he stepped out the second set of doors.

Well, there went Saturday . . . and they'd left each other almost laughing.

Friends circled up beside her and behind her as the doors closed. She worried for her boy. Here she was with all their people. But where did that leave Perry, now that Van-Leer had him? He couldn't get to his own mother at will. Neither could he see his Blue River "other-mothers" as they sometimes called Gina and Callie DiCoco. Maya Rubin was no longer escorting him to and from school, though at least he saw her in class. But Perry had had no time with Jaime Rojas or Halsey Barrows; there had been precious little with Big Ed. None with Warden Daugherty.

Eventually, she'd have to tell him about the warden's suspension, and the investigation. Word had come to Blue

River that VanLeer was painting Warden Daugherty as a correctional system loose cannon, mostly because she'd let Perry stay all these years. There was no doubt she'd been creative when it came to fostering him. VanLeer wanted her dealt with. He wanted her out of Blue River.

But even worse for Jessica and her boy, as Butler County's district attorney, VanLeer had officially challenged her application for parole. He claimed she had been granted "unusual and questionable freedoms" for an inmate with a conviction as serious as hers. Jaime Rojas had sorted through the legal longhand with her.

"He's trying to suggest that you haven't truly served your sentence because you had the privilege of raising Perry on the inside." That's what Jaime had said. "Murky point," he'd added. "Bad news is, this guy VanLeer seems determined; he believes raising a kid at Blue River was a crime. He wants somebody to pay. Meanwhile, he's tying up your application, the skunk."

Jessica had a headache by late afternoon, her mind full of sharp-edged shards and returning worries. She begged Gina to keep Sashonna and her mosquito-like annoyances the heck away from her—just until dinnertime.

She focused her aching mind on Perry. She was proud of him for using Big Ed's mottos. "Way to cope, kiddo." She said it out loud. But she worried about that timeline. He wanted to put his sincere blue eyes on a prize: her release. She didn't know what to say to him about that. Not anymore.

Then there was the assignment. That whopper on his list. Maya Rubin probably had no idea how that one was coming down on Jessica. "I am *so* not ready to tell him . . . ," she muttered to herself. She gave her own temples a massage. She didn't blame him for asking—again. It was a thing that came up a few times a year, usually signaled with Perry confirming, "It was manslaughter, right? For both you and Big Ed, huh, Mom?" She knew he would not accept her off-handed "yup" forever.

Well, maybe the school project would be Perry's way of keeping close with his Blue River family. Big Ed had already offered to tell his story. He had guts. His story wasn't an easy one. Of course, neither was hers. She could never tell Perry all of it. But maybe it was time he knew something more. But how much?

"Hey! Hey! You're on mess tonight. Don't forget," Sashonna taunted as she stopped to show off her made-up face inside Jessica's door on Block C. "Eggy-Mon is gonna be looking for you."

"Yeah, yeah . . ." Gina followed closely, moving Sashonna along. With large soulful eyes, she blinked in empathy for all that Jessica was shouldering late on that Saturday afternoon.

chapter twenty-eight

RIGHT AFTER
BLUE RIVER

I sit in the VanLeer closet on top of the camp mat that I made up tight before the sun came up this morning. I cup Mom's travel clock in my hands, feel it tick. I open it up and stand it on top of the warden's suitcase. I hope Mom won't miss it. The clock fits next to the reading lamp Mrs. Samuels brought in here. The lamp has a flexible neck. It's a good reading light, but right now I am bending it so it shines on my timeline on the closet wall. I look at Saturday—today— and it feels over with. But I promised myself not to cross off any day until I come to bed at night, and we haven't even had supper yet.

I sweep the lamp light along the timeline, and it seems long. The last few days are folded into the corner where the closet walls meet. They look lost.

I've heard Big Ed say that a timeline stretches to its longest when you fail to count your wins. So I count mine. I got to see Mom today. My next thought is: the visit was too stinking short. That's not a win, so I try to shove it aside. But I cannot help knowing this: counting your wins doesn't mean that you don't know what your losses are. You do.

Still, I got to see Mom. I saw that she is okay. She saw that I am okay too. Win. Win.

I start a new list. I had a lot of things on my mind on the way home from Blue River today. Like the new intake, Mr. Wendell. I saw him standing by the front window, watching arrivals. I don't know if anyone came for him. I wanted to ask Mom or Big Ed how he's doing. But it slipped my mind.

Mr. Wendell would never know it, but I feel linked to him. We are new intakes in different places. I wonder if he's using the mottos. I wonder if he has made a timeline. I add it to my list; I'll ask about Mr. Wendell next week. But more than anything else, I want to start my Coming to Butler County interviews.

Zoey taps on my door, and we go down the hall together to set the table for supper. Mrs. Samuels is mixing ground meat for burgers, and for some reason I am dying to get my hands into that.

"Can I do that?" I ask.

"I bet you can, and yes, you may," she says. "Clean hands first, though."

Thomas VanLeer shows up with a paintbrush just as I

am finishing at the sink. I get out of his way.

"Well, aren't we all bustling around here tonight," he says. He pushes out a laugh. He tells us he is done painting the exterior trim around the garage. "Phew! That's what a Saturday is for, ticking things off the old chore list . . ."

He begins to talk to Mrs. Samuels then. "I'll light that grill as soon as I'm done cleaning up here."

She says, "I'm way ahead of you!" For some reason, that makes them laugh. Then all the VanLeers are talking about Zoey's dance lesson and a trip they took to the farmers' market in David City earlier today.

I pat the meat into burgers and line them up on a platter. It's a little bit like being on the mess team at Blue River. That's a rotating schedule. I remember that tonight is Mom's night. She will be working with Eggy-Mon. I should be in the Blue River kitchen with her, listening to food poetry right about now . . .

Instead I am watching Mrs. Samuels. She is weeping due to onions. She presses the back of her wrist to her nose and says, "Uh-oh! These are strong!"

Mr. VanLeer takes a tissue to her. He stops in front of her, touches the tissue to her cheeks, just below one eye and then the other. She sniffs. They laugh. He asks her, "Better?" He kisses her forehead.

I have seen him put his arms around her too. She does the same, or she leans in when they are standing close and then their shoulders touch for as long as they want. They do it like it's nothing more than another way of talking. Love looks different inside a house.

I follow Mrs. Samuels out to the patio. I carry the uncooked burgers, and she shovels them onto the grill with her spatula. There are two lawn chairs. She sits, so I sit too. The evening is gray and blowy but not cold. She tilts her face into the breeze.

"Maybe one of our big old Nebraska storms is coming through," I say.

"As long as it's not hail," she says. There's a little patch of quiet then she asks, "Good visit with your mom?"

Short. That's what I think but not what I say. "I was really glad to see her."

"I'll bet."

"She gave me her clock. I put it next to the lamp."

"Oh, nice . . . on the suitcase." She says this with the kind of nod that lets me know she is picturing everything in place inside the closet. "Gosh. Have you been missing a clock all this time? You can ask for things. I'm good at finding stuff." She grins at me. Then she says, "Something tells me you have the clock you really want."

I nod. "I just like that one because . . ." Why do I like it? It's an ordinary clock. I could tell her that it's because the clock has been around a long time. Or that I used to call it my pet turtle when I was little because of the way it folds into its own shell.

"Well, it's familiar to you," Mrs. Samuels says. "You've

got precious little in that room that feels that way. There's no denying."

We listen to the burgers sizzle and pop. I toe the patio. Mrs. Samuels swings her foot. The wind rushes through the trees and turns the leaves inside out. It seems okay with her if we just sit like this. When it's time to turn the burgers, she offers me the spatula and says, "Want to do the honors?"

And I do. Zoey comes outside, and the three of us sit in the breeze while the burgers finish. I think all of us are wondering if hailstones will fall.

At the VanLeer table, I pick up my burger and give it a good look. I have never eaten one quite like this—with the onion. What would Eggy-Mon say?

"A patty grilled nice, with a thick onion slice?" Or maybe he'd be creative. "A patty flipped twice with a fat crying slice?" I'm thinking that I stink at poetry, but I like trying anyway. I like doing this Blue River thing.

"Perry? Is that a grin I see?" VanLeer is looking at me.

Zoey flaps a hand at him as if she wants him to leave me alone. I think about mentioning the food poetry to the VanLeers. Then I think not. Not while Mr. VanLeer is here. He could say something that would take the good part out of it. I'm *seeking to understand* him.

I guess any new intake would say it: Some things, I get pretty quickly. Others are more work.

chapter twenty-nine

PICTIONARY THIS

While I am seeking to understand and helping to put dishes in the dishwasher, I learn that Saturday night is game night at the VanLeer house. Zoey says, "Pfft. We talk about it more than we do it. Playing with three people is dull."

I say, "Well, maybe with me as a fourth . . ."

"Yeah . . ." Zoey points back and forth between us and announces, "Yeah! Okay, Perry and I are a team."

"Okay, okay." Mr. VanLeer nods.

Mrs. Samuels says, "Uh-oh. We're going to get trounced."

Zoey gets out a game called Pictionary. She's on a mission, pulling out cards and pens and papers. "Have you played before, Perry? I'm psyched. We're going to wipe the floor with them."

I haven't played the game from a box. But when Zoey explains it I know that it is the same game we play on the dry-erase board in the common. I tell her, "No worries. We've got this."

We gather at a little square table in the VanLeer family room. Adults sit on the couch. Zoey and I are on big floor pillows. It's not long before we're laughing our heads off.

I smile as I draw a bloopy round head with two eyes and a tiny O mouth.

Zoey wiggles when she guesses. "Head. Face. Kiss?"

I draw just a few dots coming from the mouth and she shouts. "Spit! Spit! It's spit! Oh, sorry, I think I just spit a little."

"Aw, beautiful," says her mom. Zoey falls over laughing. I pull her back up by one arm. She's like a rag doll.

"Okay, okay. Our point. Tom, you're up. Mom receives."

"You kids are going to be tough to beat," Mr. VanLeer says. He takes up the pen and reads his word.

They try hard. But Mrs. Samuels thinks Mr. VanLeer's parachute is a mushroom or a flower. Or a tennis racket. They lose, but they lose laughing.

The best round is when Zoey draws nothing more than three spikes on a curve. "Dinosaur," I say.

"Right!" Zoey cheers. "Yes!"

"What? That's incredible!" Mr. VanLeer stares at the sketch. He looks at Zoey and me. He breaks into a very real grin. "How did you get dinosaur from that?"

"I just knew," I say.

"But there's nothing there!" he says, and they all burst

out laughing, especially Zoey. Her face is pink and bright.

When we get to the final point, we are way ahead. Mrs. Samuels draws while Mr. VanLeer guesses. "Stroller!" he shouts. His fist pumps the air. "No? Carriage?"

Mrs. Samuels groans. She puts up another shape, another line.

"What is it? A . . . wagon? No, wait!" Mr. VanLeer puzzles. "Is it baby bubby? I mean, buggy!" He's a different kind of Mr. VanLeer—on his feet, arms in the air. He thinks he has it. "Bubby! Buggy! Buggy!"

"Time!" calls Zoey. She can hardly speak. "Bubby! Tom, you said bubby!" Then falling over sideways again, she adds, "Twice."

Mrs. Samuels sags. "It was a lawnmower. Look at the wheels and the motor, Tom. Look!"

"What motor? Where's the motor?"

Everyone is in fits. Mr. VanLeer slumps back onto the couch, sighing. "Oh my gosh, oh my gosh . . ."

"Boy, we stink." Mrs. Samuels lets her pen fall onto the table.

"Victory!" Zoey says as we high-five. She stirs the scattered drawings with her finger. She picks one up and shows it around. "Spit. Now that's a classic."

"One for the fridge," says Mrs. Samuels.

"Put it next to the bubby," says Mr. VanLeer, and there is more laughing.

"I bow to the winners," says Zoey's mom.

"Good match," I say.

Mr. VanLeer sits forward with his elbows on his knees. "Isn't it great spending a Saturday night like this?" He tilts his head at me. I think he's looking at me like I am a Pictionary sketch. Time stretches. Mr. VanLeer scoots forward. "Perry, you're enjoying this, aren't you? This has to be a pretty awesome change for you, huh? I mean, you're really in a better place these days, finally living outside that prison."

An enormous beat of silence pumps through the room. Zoey lets a seething sort of breath through her teeth.

"And then . . . he does that," she says. Her nostrils flare.

Mrs. Samuels clears her throat and shifts in her seat.

Zoey gets to her feet.

For some reason my eyes meet Mrs. Samuels's eyes. I'm wondering if she is wishing what I am wishing; that a big old hailstorm would come right now. She blinks and speaks to Zoey.

"Tom just means that we're enjoying Perry's company—"

"That's not what he said." Zoey's face has turned from pink to red.

VanLeer squints at her. "Zoey, sweetie." He turns his palms up. "What is it? What's the matter?" He looks to Mrs. Samuels for an answer.

"Look, it's all okay," Mrs. Samuels says. She comes close to her girl. "Zoey, please don't—"

"No. No, Mom!" Zoey steps back. She looks at her mother but she points at Mr. VanLeer. Her voice gets loud. "He—he does that all the time. Just when everything is going fine, he has to say something about it. He kills it."

"How?" he asks. "How do I ki—"

"You say stupid things!" Zoey yells. "You say too much! You never just let things be!" She loses a breath, and I feel a hollow fill my own chest.

I know she's trying not to cry.

"Mom, don't you know what I mean? Don't you hear him do it?"

I'm afraid she's going to ask me next. I get how she feels, but I don't want to have to say it right here and now.

Mrs. Samuels puts her face close to Zoey's. She speaks softly. "Okay. What do you need to do here?" she asks.

Zoey swats at a few stray tears. She takes a shaky breath. "I'll separate," she whispers.

Mrs. Samuels strokes Zoey's shoulders. "Okay. Good job. You go, and I'll come by your room in a little while. We can talk." She gives her a hug.

Zoey nods. She leaves without looking at me. Of course, I am trying not to stare at her. I help Mrs. Samuels box up the game.

Mr. VanLeer watches. "That's too bad." He shakes his head. "I thought we were having fun. Zoey gets so upset sometimes." I realize he is telling this to me. "But we work on it. We work it out—"

"*Tom.*" Mrs. Samuels interrupts him, and it's like a karate chop. She gives him a hard look. He stops talking.

"Excuse me," I say. I think about telling them that if they want me, I'll be in the closet. Instead I thank them for supper.

Later, I am thinking about the way Thomas VanLeer is. I remember the ring he bought for Zoey—the one from their summer vacation. It was a gift. That's nice. But then he sort of told her how to like it instead of just letting her like it. Now, VanLeer thinks I should like being out of Blue River. But I miss home. I guess I don't get Thomas VanLeer. He doesn't get me either.

When I step into the hall on my way to the bathroom, Zoey's bedroom door is cracked open just the littlest bit. I hear talking.

". . . now he did it to Perry, Mom. He's trying to force him to feel good here," Zoey says. "But Perry wants to go home. So would I. Why doesn't Tom get it? Why does he think he can decide how everyone should feel?"

I wait, but Mrs. Samuels doesn't seem to have an answer for that.

chapter thirty

SPRAY!

There is a gurgling, sucking noise. Then a whoosh! I jump back, and nearly take the shower curtain with me. A full spray is falling from the VanLeer showerhead. Big Ed was right. He told me to look for a little pinlike thing, or a lever or a handle. He said, "Push it in, press it down, or lift it up. Experiment a little," he told me. "Show it you're the boss."

I step into the shower. In seconds, I am wet from head to toes. Ahh . . . finally. The best thing about a shower is the think-time. It's short, but you have it all to yourself. I need this time to think about the interviews.

There's a hard truth about the residents. I have heard Mom say it to her groups: "None of us is in here because we got caught sneaking sugar packets out of the diner."

The residents of Blue River have done some bad things. They're not murderers or kidnappers. Some are drug dealers; some are embezzlers. Some wrote bad checks or didn't pay child support. Sometimes I hear about it. Sometimes they tell me. I never ask. I rarely speak about what any of them did when I am on the outside. But now, I really want to. I know some rezzes would like to have their stories told. Then again, some have and probably wish they hadn't.

Mr. Krensky is Blue River's most famous resident. He perpetrated a colossal Ponzi scheme, which means he took a lot of other people's money. He pretended to invest it. But he really stole it. He bought himself boats and mansions and probably a whole lot of those tilapia fillets with honey-mustard glaze. Lots of rezzes are in for money crimes. But Mr. Krensky made the national news. By the time he got to Blue River a few years ago, we all knew who he was.

He arrived with the best-fed belly and the tidiest fingernails I've ever seen. He's thinner now, his hands are roughed up, and his hair has grown out into two poofy white clouds that sit just above his ears.

The first week he was at Blue River, I accidentally stepped backward onto his toe in the supper line. He swore and called me a little piece of . . . well, something nobody wants to be. Then he told me to get the hell out of his way, and I did. But Big Ed was right there. He caught me in a one-armed hug, pulled me close to his side.

He told Krensky, "Even the guilty recognize innocence when they see it. But you, Krensky, you must be in a place of ugliness all your own. Not going to be easy to rise out of that."

Even though he's famous, an interview with Krensky

doesn't interest me. He's no friend; he's a Cold One. The only reason to talk to him is if you need help in the law library. Mom has Mr. Rojas for that.

I pour VanLeer shampoo into my hand and smell mint. I slap it on my wet head and lather up. My eyes are closed, my scalp is tingling, and I think my brain is coming wide-awake. This is the way to scheme. I go at it. I scrub hard.

I'll need permission first. That's a given. Then I'll make a page for each rez I'm going to write about. I'll start with what I know, then check facts and fill in details on Saturday interviews. If I'm going to tell these Blue River Stories, I'm going to tell them right.

Blue River Stories.

I like the way it sounds. If someone doesn't want to talk, I'll have to scrap the story. But Big Ed already said yes. Mrs. DiCoco has always told it like it is. She hurt her back and got addicted to painkillers. "After a while, I couldn't afford them, so I stole money from the foundation I worked for. I'm an addict and a thief, but I'm putting those days behind me." That's how she tells it.

I think Mr. Rojas will talk to me about getting caught for his gambling ring. I'm not sure about Mr. Halsey. Miss Sashonna will want in because that's just how she is. But Miss Gina is the opposite. She won't want to tell, and I won't hurt her feelings by asking. Of course the story I want the most is Mom's story—the whole thing. She'll tell it to me now. She has to.

I realize that I've been scheming under the spray of the shower for quite a while. At home, our showers shut off after five minutes. I suddenly worry that Mr. VanLeer will rap on the bathroom door and speak to me about hot water usage. I kill the spray—exactly the reverse of what I did to get it going. Yes! I'm the plumbing boss!

I rub myself dry with a VanLeer towel, which feels as big as a bed blanket. When I wrap it around my waist it drags on the floor. I hike it up under my armpits. Fo-Joe would laugh if he could see me. I always cross the Upper East Lounge on my way back to my bedroom wearing a Blue River towel around my waist—only those towels are thinner and lots shorter. Fo-Joe likes to tease me. He makes his voice go high and says, "Pretty skirt, Perry."

I smile when I think how he held up Thomas VanLeer at the bottleneck so I could run to Mom. Fo-Joe has to walk a tough line with the rezzes. He has to be in charge. But you can always tell that he wants to see everyone rise up, the same way you would want that for a friend. I know he likes his job. So does the warden. I've watched them all my life. I realize something. They have Blue River Stories too.

In the steamy bathroom, I keep scheming. If I am going to do these stories, I am going to need more time at Blue River. I'm not sure how that's going to happen, especially when Thomas VanLeer's idea of a Saturday visit is, well, short. I slump inside the big towel. How am I going to get all the stories and still have time with Mom? I have a lot to figure out, and I'm going to have to do that without help from all the people who usually help me.

I open the bathroom door and a cloud of steam follows me into the hallway. I hear Thomas VanLeer's voice.

"Whoa there, Perry! Looks like we forgot to tell you to run the fan in here." He flicks a switch inside the door. The fan hums. "There. That'll clear the steam."

"Oh, sorry," I say. "We don't have that at home."

I see him wince but I'm not sure why. He puts on a grin, rubs his hands together. "I bet a hot shower feels good, huh?" He looks like he's about to say something more, but then he just nods a lot.

"Sure," I say.

He starts to go on his way, and I head for the bedroom I've been staying in. Then I stop. "Mr. VanLeer?" He turns back from the end of the hall to look at me. "I was wondering . . . could we plan for me to have more time at Blue River?"

He tucks his chin in. "Well, I . . . uh . . ." He looks at the floor and shakes his head.

"There's a school assignment," I say. "I need to talk to some of the residents for it." A silent moment stretches between us.

"For school, huh?" He makes a sideways sort of smile. He chuckles and looks at me like I'm some old liar. "Perry, the thing is, when you have a family, weekends are pretty darn precious. The workweek is long. This is when we do things together."

130

I wonder why he thinks he needs to tell me that. Mom works all week long at Blue River and she runs weekend meetings too . . .

Seek to understand before you seek to be understood.

"I-I don't mean to use up your family time." I say it quickly. "Maybe you could drop me off. You can come back here to your family and just get me later. Whenever you can. Also, Saturday is the main visiting day, but there are other hours—"

"I know when visiting hours are," he says. "But you're talking about multiple trips, Perry. That's more time away from home."

I look at Thomas VanLeer. *Feel furious* is probably not a good motto. I swallow hard. I stick to facts.

"The school assignment is real. You can check," I say. "I need a little more time at home. At Blue River." Then I say, "Please."

Behind him, Mrs. Samuels pokes her head around the corner. I wonder how much she has heard.

"We'll see, Perry," says Thomas VanLeer. "We'll see."

chapter thirty-one

LIBRARY VOLUNTEERS

It is Monday. Zoey and I are library volunteers. Mr. Olsen is smiling.

"This is splendid of you," he says. "Check it out." He flashes his clipboard. There's a long list with boxes next to each item. "I'm a fan of charts and graphs and boxes to check," he says.

I get that. I like drawing Xs through the days on my timeline in the closet.

"Now, I would never overwhelm a library volunteer. So, one task at a time, and never toil more than thirty minutes a day. Come. I'll get you started."

We weave past people who are bent over books or leaning toward screens. Mr. Olsen points things out. Really points things out. He swings his arm up until his elbow meets his ear. Then he drops his forearm across the top of his head and uses his index finger like a directional signal.

"This way to periodicals," he says. His finger straightens and curls, straightens and curls. He adds a sound. "Meep-meep." He takes a sharp turn.

Zoey twists her mouth to hide a smile. "Why is he meeping?" she whispers.

"He's trying to make it fun. He knows we have signed up for the lamest after-school program ever."

Zoey muffles a laugh and gives me a shove. I bump into a revolving rack of paperbacks, and I have to hug it to keep it from going down. Then I change a step to a skip to catch up while Zoey grins over her shoulder.

We reach the periodicals in their cloudy plastic bindings. The sight of them makes me homesick and happy at the same time. I know all these magazines because Mrs. Buckmueller brings the old ones to Blue River.

Mr. Olsen says he needs them organized. "Face-out in the racks. In order," he says. "Most recent month in front. Six deep. Anything older than six months gets shelved right around the corner." His arm goes up; his finger points. "Meep-meep." He shows us a long shelf piled with back issues. I figure this is where Mrs. Buckmueller picks from.

"You can sort on the wide table." He points again. "Remember, this is a remedial effort."

Zoey looks at me. She mouths the word. "Remedial?" I shrug.

"Every box you check will be a victory," Mr. Olsen says. "Thank you!" He leaves the list with us and we begin.

We make one giant heap of the magazines, then begin to sort into stacks. It's like a game of cards. Zoey asks me, "Got any *Consumer Guide*s from June or August, Perry?" She flaps July at me.

I tell her, "Go fish."

Soon, we get into a contest, slapping the plastic binders into stacks. We call out titles and months. I reach across Zoey. She pushes in front of me. Slap. Slap. A man looks up from his laptop to shush us.

I whisper to Zoey, "He has no idea, the sounds of progress."

"Yeah. And this is just one task. How are we going to get through everything on that list?"

"Not all at once," I say. "Mr. Olsen said remedial. Isn't the root word *remedy*?"

"Guess so. This is a sick old library," Zoey says. "And the remedy . . ."

". . . is us." We say it in unison then start to laugh. The shushing man shushes us again.

Zoey fans herself with an issue of *Sports Illustrated*. "Seen any of these? I can't find August?"

"Oh, *Sports Illustrated*. That's Mr. Halsey's favorite," I tell her. Zoey stops fanning to look at the cover.

"Oh yeah?" she says. She knows who Mr. Halsey is, that he's a friend.

"Yep. He grabs it up and goes through it cover to cover." Zoey is looking at me, and she's being very quiet. I tap a finger down on the September issue of *Modern Gardener*. "And this is Mrs. DiCoco's favorite."

Zoey thinks for a second. "She's the grandmother, right?" "Yep."

"Is there a lot of time for reading? At Blue River?"

"Well, after the workday. The magazines are supposed to stay in the common, but the rezzes sneak them back to their rooms for the evening." I go back to sorting. *"Money Matters*. September," I say. Then I can't help adding, "I know a guy who got his picture in this one. But not for anything good."

"Oh . . . Are you going to write his story?" Zoey asks.

"Nope!" I shake my head. "That's Mr. Krensky. He's unfriendly. He'd never give me his story. Besides, it's already been everywhere. I just want stories from people I've been close to."

I hear Zoey breathe out. "I hope you can get them, Perry. Mom thinks Tom should've let you stay longer on Saturday. She didn't say it. But she was super surprised when you got back so early."

I shrug. Now that I am living at the VanLeer house, Zoey and I don't talk about Stepdad Tom like we used to. I'd like to tell her that I'm sorry about the Pictionary game going all sour, and that I thought she was right and he was wrong. But it seems best not to complain about anyone that you have to live with—even if he is the person who seems to be ruining your life, and your mom's life, and making trouble for

Warden Daugherty. I wonder what is happening. Will the warden get yelled at, or will someone dock her pay? Or make her pay a fine? I don't really know what kinds of trouble a warden can be in.

Oops. I realize I'm not helping Zoey with the periodicals. I try to erase my brain for now. It's all going to work out soon. It has to. I turn and drop six months' worth of *Sports Illustrated* into the rack with a satisfying *thunk*.

When I turn back again Zoey is holding Mr. Olsen's list in her hand.

"Look." She leans toward me and reads, "Buckmueller for BR. And there's a question mark after it. She's the book truck lady, right? And what does BR stand for? Book run?"

"Or Blue River," I say. "Because she always takes requests from the residents."

"Exact-o-mento!" Mr. Olsen has come up behind us.

The shushing man heaves a sigh through the air and it lands on us. He closes his laptop and gets up.

"Oh. Terribly sorry! Did I disturb?" Mr. Olsen asks. "Oh dear. Try the History Room. It's quieter . . . ," he calls after the man. Then he looks at us. "So, Blue River. That's a no-go this week. But it will be critical next week and always ever after."

"Why is it a no-go this week?" I ask.

"Mrs. Buckmueller has to take time off. I shouldn't overshare, but since you'll be helping her anyway . . . she took a nasty twist getting out of the truck with the book cart on

Friday evening. Now her bad knee is worse."

"She was running late," I say.

"Yes. That job is too much for one person." Mr. Olsen shakes his head. "She's resting and elevating. She says she will be back next week, and she's going to need a lot of help from . . ." He winds up a bit before he lets it go. "Library volunteers!"

chapter thirty-two

THE DOORS OF BUTLER COUNTY

We sit in the SUV outside of Mr. VanLeer's office on Fifth Street in David City. The small car he drives went into the repair shop this morning so he needs a ride. I raise my camera, focus, and snap a picture of the door he will come out of. I'm taking photos for Mom this week. I have been to a lot of new places.

A picture of a door seems dumb. But the varnished wood and that brass handle are the sort of thing Mom sometimes talks about when she's looking for places to rent after her release.

Mrs. Samuels is up front behind the wheel. She leans on one arm and hums to the music on the radio. Zoey is just sitting. Me too. But I am also scheming. Again.

I'm thinking about the Bucking Blue Bookmobile. If we

are going to help Mrs. Buckmueller, I have to figure that means we will gather books and magazines, and maybe help load them into the truck. We'll have our hands on every issue. VanLeer is going to stick to his guns about his Saturday plans, I'm pretty sure. But if books and magazines move in and out of Blue River two times every week . . .

I feel a tap on my forearm. I look at Zoey. She's being very spylike and won't quite look at me. But she whispers. "You could use the magazines"—her eyes shift side to side— "to get word to residents that you want their stories. You could send questions . . ."

My eyes pop open. "I thought the same!" I whisper back. "How did you know?"

Zoey Samuels gives me a grin and a shrug. She says, "Pictionary."

"What was that?" Mrs. Samuels turns the radio down and looks up into her rearview mirror. She scrunches her brow. "Did you guys say something?"

Zoey calls up to the front of the car. "We're just talking about library volunteer stuff." She sits back, grinning. It's not a lie.

Mrs. Samuels flicks the radio off and pulls the keys out of the ignition. "Enough of this," she says. "Let's go up and rescue Tom from his office."

I'd like to touch that varnished door. So I pop right out of my seat belt. Zoey does a little moan and groan, but she follows.

The door is heavy. I pull it back and let Zoey and her mom go in ahead of me. "Thank you, Perry." Mrs. Samuels smiles the smile that I like. She appreciates a little thing like someone holding a door open.

Inside, the stairwell walls are painted deep green. The railings are varnished like the door. A light green carpet runs up the center of the stairs. Everything curves upward. It feels fancy, but not cake-frosting fancy; more like man-in-a-suit fancy. Zoey is looking up, and she's on a mission.

"Race you!" she says.

"Chase you," I answer, because I can't race her when I don't know where the finish line is.

She launches. I'm on her heels all the way to the top stair. We zip past the receptionist. The carpet muffles our thundering feet—more so than at Blue River. Zoey hangs a right, and we sprint past frosted-glass doors with names lettered in black-and-gold paint. We reach the last one. It's open, and Zoey claps her hand over the side jamb and swings herself to a halt. I crash up behind her. Two-kid wreck.

Thomas VanLeer looks up from a large wooden desk. At first his eyebrows are arched in surprise. Then he laughs out loud. Zoey's mom joins us at the door, and Mr. VanLeer rises. His chair rolls backward.

"Well who is this coming up to see me?" he says. "My family? Hello-hello!" He gives Mrs. Samuels a hug. "Hey, guys," he says to Zoey and me. "What a surprise."

140

"I'll bet you forgot that you don't have a car today," Mrs. Samuels says.

"Oh my gosh! I did!" He laughs. "Oh, and you've been waiting for me. I'm sorry. I was so involved here, I forgot the plan. Can you all give me a minute?"

"Of course. We can go find a distraction if you're really not finished here," Mrs. Samuels says.

"No, no. I can be done. Let me get it together." He begins to shuffle papers. He taps them on the desk to square them into stacks, begins to pack his briefcase.

This is one kind of Thomas VanLeer. He's happy that his wife and stepdaughter are here—in a real way. I look around the room. His desk is covered in papers, spread out so much he must need fly eyes to read them all at once. There is a bookcase behind him. I see rows of fat volumes like the ones in the law library at Blue River. The rezzes go there to look things up and to work on their cases. There is a long wooden table on one wall under a window. It's covered in boxes and stacks of fat folders. I guess it's true what he said. His workweek is long.

"Those are all open cases," he says when he sees me looking.

Stories, I think to myself. Each box and each folder must be all about a person. A person in trouble. I take a dry swallow.

On the opposite wall, framed documents hang. Some plain, some fancy. Thomas VanLeer has graduated from two colleges. He has a law degree, he passed his bar exam, *and* he won something called a Spark Award. I read the curly font: *Presented to Thomas VanLeer with gratitude from all who will pass through the Journey House Family Shelter.* The next line says: *When we serve our communities well, the ripple is felt throughout humanity.*

"That's the one that means the most to me," VanLeer says. He comes over to stand beside me. "That's the most important one."

"In what way?" I ask.

"It was an opportunity to make a difference. I volunteered legal services to families in need." He thinks for a second. "And that was a turning point for me. I knew I wanted to continue to make a big impact in a small place." He gestures toward the frame on the wall. "That award changed my career path."

For a few seconds I feel like I am listening to someone I know, someone like Mr. Rojas or Mr. Halsey. Or Mom. Mr. Thomas VanLeer is a person with plans. He's a guy with a timeline.

"Anyway," he says, "it's basically the reason I ended up wanting the DA post here in Butler County. I decided this was a door I needed to go through on my way to bigger dreams."

I look at the award and think about Thomas VanLeer. If I started to understand him, it lasted only a minute. If Butler County is his door, I can't help thinking that he has slammed it on our fingers. Mine, Mom's, and Warden Daugherty's.

chapter thirty-three

BIG ED'S STORY

As soon as we make it through the Blue River bottle-neck, I see Mr. Halsey. He's bridging a deck of cards in his hands. He gives me a quick grin. Then he corrals Mr. VanLeer. He turns him toward the game tables and asks, "You play cards? What's your favorite game, man? You play rummy?" He pats Mr. VanLeer's back.

Mr. VanLeer is stuttering and nodding. "Ye-yes. I play rummy. Er . . . I have played rummy." He takes double steps next to Halsey, who keeps sweeping him along. I have a funny thought that Halsey could probably palm VanLeer's head, same way he'd palm a basketball—or a head of broccoli. Halsey collapses Mr. VanLeer into a chair. He fits his own tall self into the one opposite and begins to deal cards. Game on.

Across the common I see Mom and Big Ed. They have staked a claim and circled up three chairs in an almost-

143

private corner. Mom waves me over with big arm circles. I grab the straps of my pack so it won't bounce, and I sprint. For the second week in a row she does not forget; she catches me for the swing-around. For the second week in a row, we hug and talk a blue streak, trying to get everything said in the first five minutes. It's going to be a short Saturday visit inside the Blue River Co-ed Correctional Facility.

Big Ed is about to tell his story. Mom sits and scoots her chair forward to close our circle tighter. She is Big Ed's support person for all things difficult. They do this for each other. Mom knows a lot of Blue River Stories. For sure, she knows Big Ed's. I've heard some of it. I know what he's in for. Manslaughter. Same as Mom.

I feel like a newspaper reporter, and maybe that's good. I have my camera in my lap just in case I get writer's cramp. It's not the fanciest, but it can record for a minute at a time if I need a break. I hope I can write fast enough. I hope that card game goes long. I open my notebook to the page I started for Big Ed.

Manslaughter is the crime of killing a human being without the intention or making of a plan to do it. I got that from the dictionary.

I look up at my old friend. Part of me doesn't want to ask him now. But another part of me thinks Big Ed wants to tell it. He offered. I say, "Start whenever you're ready."

Big Ed draws a slow breath. "Well, the first thing to know," he says, "is that I loved those kids."

He looks into the air, and it's like he floats to a space that is away from Blue River. A different place. Another time.

"I loved every last hood-ratty one of them. They started coming into the alley behind my bodega. Hmm . . . all those hot and muggy Florida afternoons when school let out," he says.

Florida. Now I know why Big Ed thinks of Surprise as being very snowy. I don't talk. I keep my pencil moving. Big Ed goes on.

"They were always looking for something to do; they were athletes, with nowhere to play until they picked that alley. They'd go running, hopping, launching themselves off the walls without stopping. Free running, they called it. They could swing from the fire escape, throw handstands up on the rim of the Dumpster. Then go full twisty-flips right off my back steps. Bunch of free-range acrobats." Big Ed smiles. "Take your breath away.

"I figured there was worse they could be up to. I put out a pair of sawhorses and some sandbags so they could set up a sturdy jump. I lugged an old futon back from the dump and padded up a rough patch of concrete in the wall there so nobody would sand an elbow off. I told Henry in the barbershop, and Lila in her consignment store, never mind they're climbing your irons. They're not street fighting, not getting mixed up with gangs." Big Ed nods. "Henry and Lila came around pretty quick, and the other shop owners did too. It got so we'd watch the show out our back doors and forget to tend store!" He laughs then he coughs.

"Those kids, they'd work up a sweat then come into the bodega. Get their snacks, soda pops. We'd sit and talk in the folding chairs. Cool off in front of the fan. I loved those kids." He says it again. "Most of them stayed good. Good kids."

Now Big Ed shifts in his chair. He tilts his head and sighs. "Then the trouble started. Somebody smashed the lock at the back door of my shop. It happened twice. Then a third time. Then one morning I found broken glass all over the floor of my storage room, and saw the little window knocked out.

"My apartment was right there—one flight up—and there were times I thought I heard things. I listened hard, but down in Florida I had a noisy old electric fan, and it hummed from Easter to Thanksgiving. So it was easy to think my ears were playing tricks on me. But I knew my inventory. I knew things were going missing. Then my cash drawer was jimmied and robbed two times in one month. I started pulling all the money outta there at night. One morning the whole register is gone. Been yanked clean out even though there wasn't any cash in it! I had to replace that. Those kids were still coming to play in the back, and they knew I was having troubles. I talked to them about it. But not like I ever suspected them. Not those kids. Not my kids.

"While I was so busy looking the other way I was losing money. I had trouble paying my vendors." Big Ed leans back. He shakes his head. "I had to do something. So I broke pattern. I waited there one evening after closing. I figured I'd catch my thief in the middle of the night—if I could stay awake. Humph. I didn't even have to wait that long. The sun wasn't even down before I heard the squeak of the new window in the storeroom and that skinny kid dropped down. His sneakers hit the floor like he was sticking a landing. He comes strolling through my shop stuffing his pack and his pockets like he's in his own mother's kitchen. I can see the shape of him, and I know him. He's one of my favorites. One of the ones I talk to all the time." Big Ed pushes his hands into his knees. He grimaces.

"Well, my favorite becomes my least favorite, and I get it into my head that I want to correct this whole thing." Big Ed's finger waggles in the air. Then he clenches his hand into a fist.

"I called out his name. He turned, and there he was, grounded in the glow of the setting sun as it came in through the front window of my store. Oh, that boy swore. Then he asked me what I'm doing there! Imagine it!" Big Ed says, and he throws both hands up. "So I said, 'You want to know why I'm here? To stop you! And you want to know why?' And I pulled my old gun out from the drawer under my register and I told him, this is why! I slammed that gun on the counter. His eyes went wide and scared, and I thought, yes. Yes! I want him scared—so, so scared. And I banged my hand down so hard next to the gun everything jumped—matchbooks, peppermints—even the gun jumped.

"I told that boy, 'Every shop owner for the next thirteen blocks has one of these. And the one that doesn't know you like I know you is the one that's going to pop a hole in you.' I picked up that gun to stash it—get it out of the way, because I don't even want to think about the badness—and the next thing I know, that kid is on the run, heading into the street. I ran after him. Not done making my point, is what I felt. He was young and fit and fast. I went yelling and wagging that gun in my hand—all full of righteous fight, I was."

Big Ed stops. My hand is stiff so I pick up my camera to record. I watch him on the tiny screen. He pulls at the corners of his mouth with his thumb and forefinger. He closes his eyes. Opens them again.

"I saw the skateboarder come—little kid in a hot-orange T-shirt. He jumped the curb, landed back on his board the way they do. Then he rode it right across the path of my thief. The bigger boy, he veered to avoid the little one. He went into the street. I can still see that. And I still feel how all that fight went right out of me the second I heard the screeching of the brakes and that—*thump*." He shakes his head. "My thief rolled up over the hood of that old sedan that just happened to be coming down the street. All these years, and I can't get rid of that." Big Ed squints. "I see the boy somersaulting through the air like he's playing acrobat. Except there is something sick about the twist of his body." Big Ed shakes his head. He wrings his hands. "Then that boy came crumpling down on the sidewalk with everything looking . . . all wrong."

I watch big Ed squeeze his eyes shut. His frown is heavy. He says, "I ran to him. But all I could do was hold him while he died."

"He died? That's who died?" I speak before I think. I look from Big Ed to Mom, then back at Ed, and at Mom once more. She nods at me. Her eyes are large and sad and knowing. She uses a knuckle to push away a tear.

"Um-hmm," Big Ed says. "Sure as I felt the life going out of him, I felt my own life empty out too. Yes. That fight leaves you and all you wish is that you could go back for a do-over. You want the moment just before the sedan came by, just before the little skateboarder rolled into the picture. And you want to see yourself staying inside your shop opening the candy boxes and filling up your Slim Jim bucket, and waiting for a lottery winner. You wish you could decide not to scare that kid with your damn gun. Just let him have whatever it is he wants. Even the money—because what's money but a bunch of old greenish-gray papers and some grubby coins? Let him have them. In my dreams I have done things one hundred ways different. But the thing is . . ." Big Ed clears his throat. "You can't rewrite your story."

chapter thirty-four

AFTER BIG ED
TELLS ME

"That fella Halsey, he's a bit of a master of distraction, isn't he?" Mr. VanLeer chuckles up into the rearview mirror. I watch the flat farmlands go by from the backseat. I've learned to sit behind Mr. VanLeer in the SUV. I feel less obligated to chat with anyone whose face I can't see. "Inmates become tight with each other," he says, in a know-it-all way. "Powerful system of doing favors," he says. "But it's okay. I expected that. And I don't mind a good card game . . ." More chuckling.

I hear him. But I'm in a not-listening state. I've taken in about all I have room for today, and if I listen to VanLeer, it'll be all the harder to hold on to the important stuff. Like what Big Ed said after he finished the story of how the boy died. I asked him how he got convicted of manslaughter.

"It's not like you shot him or pushed him into the road,"

I said. But Big Ed said the presence of the gun was the factor. "Menacing with a firearm," he said. "Resulted in a death— of a child no less. I was outside my shop, so no 'stand your ground' defense. That's what got me convicted. That, and the fact that I was filled with guilt and all out of fight."

VanLeer interrupts my concentration. "I trounced him," he says. Is it possible to hear someone looking in the rear- view? I think so. I don't look up. I'm still staring out the window, watching a dot of bright pink growing larger in the opposite lane. It's the scooter rider again, the one I saw in the Blue River parking lot last week.

"That fella Halsey," VanLeer says, "I beat him about like you and Zoey beat me and Mrs. Samuels at Pictionary the other night. And that's in spite of the fact that he's a sly player. Blue River is full of tricksters . . ."

I pull my notebook out of my pack and open it across my lap. I scan to the notes about Big Ed's sentencing:

Asked to serve time far away from Florida.

Take his shame with him. Never return.

Henry and Lila, others testified for him—not a danger.

My notes stop there. My hand was aching up to my elbow, and across the common the card game was breaking up.

I fish my camera out of my pack. I took five short videos in all. I scroll to the last one I shot. I watch Big Ed say, "I prayed the Lord my soul to take. But he wouldn't. Instead I had the good luck to land here in teeny-tiny Surprise, Nebraska." Mom leans forward then. She takes one of Big Ed's hands in both of hers and squeezes. The video ends.

VanLeer pipes up again. "How about you, Perry? Did they get you into their card games there at the prison?"

I glance up at the mirror but only for a split second. "You mean did they teach me how to cheat?" I let it out in an under-mumble way.

"What's that you say?"

"Mr. VanLeer, I don't mean to be rude, but I can't talk right now." I rustle the pages of my notebook so he will hear. "I'm working on my school assignment."

chapter thirty-five

COUNTING ON
BUTLER COUNTY

On Monday night, I am looking ahead to Tuesday. I've spent a lot of time organizing Big Ed's interview from my scrawly notes and the short videos. It's a job trying to turn it into one smooth-reading story. Especially when all I can think about is how something so sad could happen to Big Ed when he's one of the greatest people I know.

I've written down almost all the words. But there is something about watching Big Ed on the little screen. I can see his story—see the way he feels. It makes me wish I'd had the guts to sign up for Video Boot Camp in spite of Brian Morris and his friends. But being a library volunteer is going to give me an unexpected assist on the Blue River Stories. That's a win.

The part I worry about is time. If each rez thinks about

153

how to tell his or her story ahead of time, the Saturday interviews might go quicker. So I've written short notes to the ones I'm closest to. I've asked for their stories. That might sound easy, but like I say, I've never asked before. I know not everyone will want to tell me. But just in case, I gave them questions. Like, what did you do before you came to Blue River? What are you in for? (If you want to tell me.) How long will you serve? What are the best and worst things about Blue River? If you have your *eye on the end*, what do you see?

Zoey is going to help me get the notes and questions into the right periodicals. I wish I didn't have to feel sneaky about this plan. I don't know if anyone would care. But if there is a rule about not putting notes into magazines, I don't want to know it. I really need these questions to be on the Bucking Blue Bookmobile tomorrow. We have to do that before Mrs. Buckmueller leaves for Blue River—*if* she's going, that is. I hope her knee is feeling better. I hope so for her, and I hope so for me.

The VanLeer kitchen smells like a whole other country tonight. It happens a lot, and even though I miss Blue River meals, this is pretty awesome. Eggy-Mon would probably love to cook with the spices Zoey's mom uses. My mom would love to taste them. Tonight, something sweet and peppery is going into the skillet with the garlic and onions. But that's just the beginning. Zoey's mom has bowls of chopped vegetables and chicken pieces ready too. Mr. VanLeer will be late for supper, but we will see him right here in the Van-Leer family room; in about ninety seconds he'll be on the big-screen TV.

He's being interviewed on *Counting on Butler County* with Desiree Riggs. The segment runs every Monday evening during the news, and everybody around here knows about it because of Desiree. She has fancy hair and big-city clothes, and a gooey way of speaking that makes her sound like she's handing out cream-filled chocolates. Her voice goes low, and she melts her words together. All that just to interview the locals. I've watched her plenty of times on the set in the Blue River Common. She comes on just about the time we line up for supper there. I wonder if Mom and the others are tuned in now. I smile to myself when I imagine that we are doing the same thing tonight, even if it has to be in different places.

I can almost hear Mr. Halsey. He loves to get all breathy and call out, "Hey-yay! It's Deh-hezzz-ah-raaay!" That's how she says her name too, and it makes the rezzes laugh. But everybody does listen to her show. Chocolate cream sucks you in and sticks. Sometimes it sticks to Miss Sashonna so much that she tries to sound like Desiree all through supper. She's no Desiree. But I don't tell her that.

Desiree will interview almost anyone: a farmer with a bumper crop, a new businesses owner, someone with a blue ribbon recipe for chokecherry jam, or the winner of the Rising City Elementary spelling bee. But tonight, it's Mr.

155

Thomas VanLeer. And he's coming to us live.

"Mom, it's time," Zoey calls over her shoulder. She picks up the remote. "Mom, you better come in here . . . You're going to miss it." She adds a few bars of volume.

Mrs. Samuels clinks a spoon against her skillet and hurries around the countertop to be nearer to the screen. She bumps her hip on the way and says, "Drat!"

Zoey pumps up the volume some more, and there we are, all three of us, waiting to see Mr. Thomas VanLeer.

"This is Desiree Riggs for *Counting on Butler County*." There she goes, melting the butter, pouring on the cream. "Our guest this evening is our very own district attorney, Thomas VanLeer . . ."

I have never seen anyone I know on the television. It's strange to see VanLeer filling the screen, so big and close. I can see him better now than when he stands a few feet in front of me. He is VanLeer in high definition. VanLeer magnified. He's got a clean shave, but I can see all the places his whiskers will sprout from. They look like tiny grains of sand. He has no wrinkles in his skin, but there's a map of pale-blue veins at his temples. The camera moves out while the two say polite hellos. Desiree asks, "Mr. VanLeer, what brought you to Butler County?" Huge VanLeer fills the screen again.

"Well, Desiree," he says, "I was attracted to Butler County because I felt this was a place where I could make a difference as your district attorney. When I met my wife and her daughter, I knew within a few short weeks that I'd struck it lucky. I had a ready-made family. And I knew we were going to meet our challenges like every family does, and tackle our obstacles together. That's exactly what we have done, and our glue grows stronger with each hurdle . . ."

I look over at Zoey. She's sitting cross-legged on the floor, her elbow on her knee and her chin in her hand. I'm wondering if it is weird for her that her stepdad is talking about her. I wonder if he's making her mad. Her fingers drum her lip.

"Now, Desiree, you probably know that families and communities are built of much the same stuff," Mr. Van-Leer says.

I think of Blue River and decide that makes a lot of sense to me. I think of the award on the wall in Mr. VanLeer's office, and I figure this is why he won it.

"So, with an all-in approach"—VanLeer makes a little fist—"I thought, new family, new territory. I researched Butler and the surrounding communities—Rising City, and even tiny Surprise out there . . ." He chuckles. "These were precisely the types of areas I wanted to see better served. I'm a roll-up-your-sleeves kind of guy, and I'll give you an example. When I learned that there was a young member of our community—a boy the same age as our Zoey—who needed a . . . well, a suitable place to live, shall we say, I brought him ho—"

Desiree interrupts. "Now, you're referencing the boy from the Blue River Co-ed Correctional Facility?" There is no chocolate, no cream when she says it. I feel like I've been dunked in ice water. Thomas VanLeer and Desiree Riggs are talking about *me.*

I look at Zoey's mom. Her hand goes slowly to her mouth. She's losing color. On the TV screen, VanLeer dips his chin. He seems off-track now. "Uh . . . Blue River is a minimum-security facility. I am in favor of prison reform through the courts, and by that I mean reduced sentencing for the nonviolent. Now, I'm not at liberty to be specific here, but I am in the process of reviewing many, many cases. Now, when s-something . . ." VanLeer is flustered, trying to bail out. "An irregularity came to my attention, and I simply felt it warranted an investigation—"

"Investigation?" Desiree says. There might be some butter on that word. No. It's hot mustard, I decide, and she slathered it.

"Yes, there are . . . there is the appearance of impropriety. I'm concerned, Desiree." He spits it out. "About our community. The style of management at B-Blue River has been—"

"And would this be about the warden? Because you know, District Attorney VanLeer, there has been a long-prevailing sentiment in Butler—and outside of Butler as well, for that matter—that Blue River Co-ed Correctional is a progressive and effective facility with a recidivism rate of zero."

Wow. Desiree dipped that zero in caramel. The warden would love that!

"What's *recivi-difa-cism*?" Zoey nudges me.

I whisper the answer quick as I can. "Repeat offending. Returning to prison."

"Oh . . ." She nods.

"Ye-yes, but I'm not here to talk about that particular issue anyway." VanLeer puts up his hands and then taps his fingers on his palm. "Let's go back to the boy. We had to get him out of there, and with a very slim foster care system here in Butler County, I just felt I had to step up. I spoke with Robyn—my wife—and she agreed that we would open our home and our hearts to him."

I look up. Now Mrs. Samuels has her hand clapped tightly over her mouth.

"And we are doing that," Mr. VanLeer continues. "It is complicated. But for as long as he needs us, we will absolutely stand by him. We're making a difference. We are not quitters . . ."

VanLeer is stumbling on. Desiree is trying to wrap things up.

"I'm here to help him." VanLeer shifts awkwardly—lunging at the camera with just his left side. "I'll help him any way that I can . . . and he knows that." That's the last thing he gets to say. Desiree thanks him and starts talking her way out to the commercial break.

Mrs. Samuels breaks for the kitchen. Her spoon bangs. Pots clank and scrape in there. "Okay, I think that's over." She says it loudly. "Want to shut that down now, Zoey? Please."

"Yup," says Zoey, and she points the remote, kills the power. She looks at me. "That really stunk."

"Yeah," I say. "But yay you. You stayed cool." I'm looking for the win.

"Only on the outside," she says. "I've decided I can't spend my life in my bedroom." I grin, and she laughs. "Perry? Aren't you ever going to . . . I don't know . . . get furious?"

I shrug and don't really get the chance to answer. Something is going on in the VanLeer kitchen. Zoey's mom rattles the cooking skillet. Dishes clank. I figure she's going to sauté up a hailstorm. But when I glance in there, I see that she has pushed all her little bowls of chopped food to the back of the counter. She has shut down her burner. She clears her throat.

"Get your jackets, you guys."

"Mom?" Zoey looks over the counter at her mother.

"We're going out."

chapter thirty-six

JESSICA

"Oh no!" Jessica Cook shot out of her chair in the Blue River Common as if she had a rocket strapped to her back. "How dare he reference my kid on the air like that?" She stood pointing at the TV, her arm as straight as a stick. She listened to the whole Thomas VanLeer segment go further and further south, and when it was finally over she said, "That was excruciating."

"If there was any doubt before, he's proved it now. He's a horse's patootie," Big Ed said.

"Sure is!" several residents of Blue River chimed in.

"He should put a day-old sock in it," said Callie DiCoco. "In fact, I'd like to do that for him."

"Yeah! Because he shouldn't have done that!" Sashonna added her two cents, all the while channeling her inner Desiree Riggs. "Did you all hear him? You know what that's called? It's called uncouth!"

"And what's with Desiree?" Jessica whisked her hand in the air. "What was she doing perpetuating the conversation like that? 'The boy from Blue River Co-ed Correctional Facility,'" Jessica mocked.

"I don't know," Halsey Barrows said. "I thought she was sticking it to DA VanLeer, and I liked that part." He flashed a grin, grabbed a cafeteria tray, and twirled it over his head on one finger while Jessica considered that he just might be right. "Desiree was letting people know that VanLeer has done wrong by Perry. I say score one for Deh-hezzz-ah-raaay!" He pumped the tray out in front of his chest a few times and got the residents cheering: "Deh-hezz-ah-ray! Deh-hezz-ah-ray!" A smile loosened at the corners of Jessica's mouth.

When the noise died down, at Foreman Joe's insistence, Jessica said, "Is VanLeer's concern for Perry real? Or will he just do anything to raise his public profile? Is he using my kid to make himself look good?" The thought made her blood boil.

"If that's what he was after, I'd say it backfired," Big Ed said.

Jessica thought out loud. "Is he truly passionate . . . but also super-prone to putting his foot in his mouth? I seriously cannot tell."

"Hmm . . . I can't answer you that, Jessie," said Halsey, shaking his head.

Jessie. He had been calling her that now and then, and

she liked it. He passed her a tray and invited her to slip into the supper line ahead of him.

In the Blue River kitchen, Eggy-Mon tilted back his head, about to crow a poem. Jessica listened. She liked to share the rhymes with Perry.

"I wish I had some honey, to drizzle on this pork. Could make the meat taste funny, but it would glue it to the spork!"

She managed to give the Blue River poet a nod and a grin. But really he had only part of her attention. Down the supper line to her left, she could hear Sashonna being Desiree Riggs. The utterly unpleasant Harvey Krensky was reaching across her and three other residents to bang his knuckles on the steam table—a timpani-like assault on the ears.

Meanwhile, tall, kind, and handsome Halsey Barrows was close on her other side being, well, tall, kind, and handsome, which was a different kind of unbearable. But most of all that damn segment of *Counting on Butler County* was nagging her.

Jessica thought about skipping dinner and going off to air-swim a few laps in the halls of Block C. Rotary breathing and rhythmic arm strokes from her teenage swim team days still calmed her—no water required.

"Jessie, you have to eat," Halsey said, as if reading her mind.

"Yeah, yeah, yeah . . ." She thumped the back of her dinner tray against her own forehead. She let out a grunt, then put the tray up for Eggy-Mon to fill.

"Cheer up, lil' chicken!" the cook called to her over the serving counter, ladle in hand. "I mix my beans with sweet molasses, baked with love to please the masses!"

Again Jessica smiled. "I just hope Perry didn't see that segment." She said this mostly to herself, but then she tipped her head so her ear rested briefly on Halsey's upper arm. "Please tell me that he didn't."

chapter thirty-seven

A PAIR OF
ARGUMENTS

Before class on Tuesday morning, Zoey Samuels is in the school office dropping off an updated health form. It's taking forever. From the hallway I see a blob of blurred kids behind the pebbled glass door. I have think-time, and what I am thinking about is driving.

Last night after Zoey's mom abandoned her cooking project, she drove us to the Rising City Grill. We ordered burgers and fries and small milk shakes, but then Zoey's mom told the waitress, "Make them large."

We punched a whole bunch of songs into the jukebox at our booth and played a hilarious game of changing the lyrics—no teams, no losers. We stayed a long time. Then, instead of heading back to the VanLeer house, we took the rest of our giant milkshakes with us, and Zoey's mom drove way out on Route 92 past the turn for David City. Then at no particular place in the road, she turned around to head back to the VanLeer home.

I've heard of people driving in circles. But last night I realized that we can't really do that here in our part of Nebraska. We could drive in squares, I guess. But we'd have to choose either very small ones or super big ones. Mostly, it's long straightaways.

Anyway, there was a serious argument in the Van-Leer house last night. It started with low, low voices in the kitchen. Mr. VanLeer asked Zoey's mom, "Do you know what went through my head when I came home and saw this? My whole family gone and no note? No phone message? Robyn, I was scared to death."

"For that, I am sorry," she told him. "I am."

"Was this some sort of stunt?"

She said, "Stunt? You want to talk about a stunt? Come with me." The fight moved into the VanLeer master bedroom.

I don't know a lot about this kind of arguing—the wife-and-husband kind. At Blue River there's no getting married. I stood in the VanLeer family room with Zoey, both of us silent. Looking left. Looking right. Shuffling feet. It didn't feel right to stand there. But I wasn't sure where else to be. The new intake. "What do we do?" I asked Zoey. She shrugged and rolled her eyes.

"Hmm. Homework. Reading. Or just go to bed. It's

almost time anyway." So Zoey went on into her room, and I went on into the one I stay in. I sat in the closet looking at my timeline. I put an X on the day. Done. Through the closet wall, I could hear little bits of arguing, but all the words were fuzzed. I know that Mrs. Samuels was mad because Mr. VanLeer mentioned me on the television.

I found out that there is something sad about the way a fight fills up a house. They were fighting about me. I kept thinking about how they are Zoey's family, and how much things need to be good for her. All that food from the Rising City Grill lay in my belly and turned into a monstrous heap that didn't feel so great. I wanted that fighting to stop.

"Hey!" Brian Morris is standing in front of me outside the school office. I stare back and wonder how he got here. His tall friend looks on. "Saw you on the TV last night with Desiree," he says. His body waggles.

"No you didn't," I say.

He fluffs his hair like Desiree might, and I have to wonder, does everybody want to be Desiree? "The boy from the prison," Brian quotes her.

"That's you." His friend speaks and points a finger at me.

"I wasn't on the show." I say it plainly.

"Brian." Miss Maya comes out of the crowded hallway. The whites of her eyes gleam. "I'll just bet that you have somewhere you're supposed to be." She gives him a light touch on the shoulder, spins him toward the stairs. He gives me one more Desiree-type wiggle on his way out. Miss Maya sends his friend along too. She lets out a puff as she watches them go. The two of us step into one of the alcoves.

"How's everything, Perry?" Miss Maya asks, and I want to say that everything is ridiculous because of Brian Morris. "You know, I love having you in class this year, but boy, I miss our rides to school," she adds.

"It seems like a long time ago," I say. I think of the two weeks' worth of Xs on my timeline inside the VanLeer closet. Part of me thinks that should not seem so long. But that's half a month, and a month is long. "Miss Maya," I say, "I was at Blue River on Saturday. I didn't see Warden Daugherty."

"Yes." Miss Maya waits. Then she says, "My aunt's schedule there has changed." She pauses in that more-to-that-story sort of way. There is something she cannot tell me.

"Miss Maya . . . I already know that the warden is in trouble. She told me herself. She said it the day they told me I had to leave Blue River. And I know it was because of me."

Miss Maya has something on the tip of her tongue. But I can see her choosing something else to say. "Perry, if ever in your life you believe something for sure, let it be that my aunt wouldn't change any of the choices she has made. Especially not when it comes to you." She smiles and pushes back her long braids. It's a sure sign she's going to change the subject. "So, I heard you are at the library after school these days."

"Yeah," I say. I tug the straps of my pack. I've got my Blue River questions folded into my notebook in there. "It's been okay. I'd rather go home because . . . well, I've just always seen my mom right after school."

"Of course," says Miss Maya.

Here comes a wicked wash of homesickness. It's been like this the whole two weeks. I'm fine, and then suddenly there's an ache in my face, and I know the corners of my mouth are turning downward. My eyes start to tear. It takes me a few seconds to get rid of that. I look back up at Miss Maya. "But at least I get homework done at the library. I've been working on my Coming to Butler project," I say.

"Ah, good!" She pumps two little fists as if she likes that a lot.

"And today Zoey and I are helping Mrs. Buckmueller . . ." I shrug. Only Zoey Samuels knows my plan, and I decide not to mention it to anyone else—not even Miss Maya.

"Well, they're lucky to have you." Miss Maya looks at the clock. She gives me a sideways hug and says, "You're one of my favorite people in the whole wide world, Perry Cook."

chapter thirty-eight

BUCKING BLUE
BOOKMOBILE

"Piece of cake," Zoey whispers to me. She brushes her palms together.

I swallow a little harder than usual. We've done it; we secretly planted my questions inside the periodicals. It was easy because Mrs. Buckmueller sent us off to gather the magazines on our own. Together, we heft the loaded bins for Blue River onto Mrs. Buckmueller's rolling cart.

"Oh dear, oh lordy. I could not have done this today without you," Mrs. Buckmueller says. "Thank you, Perry. Thank you, Zoey. You both have such . . . such wonderful young knees!"

Zoey and I steer the cart toward the elevator. Mrs. Buckmueller leads, hiking one leg along as she goes. I catch just a glimpse of her knee brace. It looks like part of a bike frame or a lawn chair. It must be hard to have such a piece of equipment on you all the time. Mrs. B sighs. "I hope I won't need my bionics forever." She mops a little sweat from her forehead.

"Mrs. Buckmueller," I say, "can you drive? I mean, with your bad knee?"

"Oh yes!" she says. "That's when I forget all about it. I love to drive! It's the grunt work that's so difficult. I'm exquisitely grateful to have you two along today."

It sounds a little funny the way she says it, and Zoey gives me a squish-faced look. But we are along, I suppose. We push the cart into the library elevator. Zoey and I suck in our bellies and scoot the cart close to us to make room for Mrs. Buckmueller. She pulls her bionic knee inside. The doors close. It's a loud and jiggly ride down. The cart wobbles and so do we. Zoey Samuels is laughing out loud.

We are bending a lot of rules this afternoon.

For one thing, the old chugging elevator is for library employees only—so says a faded paper sign on the inside back wall. Second, we are not supposed to walk out of the library until five p.m. when a parent or guardian signs us out. Yet here we go—out to load the bookmobile. Finally, that bit of sneaking we did is on my mind. But it's just a page of questions. *And* a few notes, like the one I scribbled to Mr. Halsey saying I still want to play that game of one-on-one with him. *And* one to Miss Gina about my needing her to cut my hair again. Suddenly the notes seem a lot like pieces of mail. All the mail that comes to Blue River gets opened and checked before the rezzes get it. Oops. Another bent rule.

Outside, the cart bangs over every crack in the sidewalk, and we have to steady the bins. "Just head for the truck!" Mrs. Buckmueller calls calmly.

That's fine . . . until the sidewalk slopes. Suddenly the book cart seems heavier. It rolls faster. We are heading for the parking space that is marked with a sign that says Loading Zone. We are heading straight for the bookmobile. Zoey and I look at each other with wide eyes. We grunt. We grip. But we can't hold the cart back.

"Let it go!" calls Mrs. Buckmueller. We do. We can't help it. The cart thumps into the back bumper of the Bucking Blue Bookmobile. It's a miracle the bins don't go flying.

"Oops," says Zoey. She looks at me with serious sideways eyes.

"That's how it's done," Mrs. Buckmueller says. "That's what all that rubber is for." I see that the bumper has been padded up with strips from old tires. The bookmobile is an old ragtag mail truck that someone spray-painted blue—and missed a few spots.

Mrs. Buckmueller says, "Now then. This next part has to be done properly. You must secure all bins to the wall with the straps." She coaches us. "Hitch them in. That's right. Now tug each one to double-check. Perfection! Now, pull the cart in behind you, and secure it with the floor ties so it won't roll. Can't have that, especially with you two in the back."

Zoey scrunches her face at me. I scrunch back. We must be thinking the same thing; the book cart won't roll unless the truck is rolling. We'll be long out of there by then. Pulling it in behind us seems wrong. It's tight back here in cargo. We're going to have to climb out through the front cab. Still, we do what Mrs. Buckmueller asks. She rolls down the door at the back, and we hear it latch. I look at Zoey. She looks at me. We are blank as can be.

The truck wobbles. A spring squeaks. Up front, Mrs. Buckmueller is scootching herself onto the driver's seat. She pulls her bad leg in and turns backward to speak to us again.

"There you go, right there on the wall." She points with a flapping hand. "You have to pull them down."

"Pull them down?"

"They're called jump seats. Funny name. Couldn't tell you the etymology there," she says.

Zoey sees it first. She pulls. A little seat unfolds from the wall. She looks at me, her mouth in a big *O*. She turns, sits back like a duck, and settles onto the little square cushion. I look behind me and sure enough, I find my seat in the wall. I sit right across from Zoey Samuels.

"Buckle up!" Mrs. Buckmueller calls back.

We dig to find our seat belts. We click in and tighten the straps. Zoey still looks surprised, and I figure I do too. She calls up front, "We're in!"

"All aboard!" Mrs. B hoots.

The truck starts up with a few shakes and knocks. I lean forward in the tiny space behind the cab and whisper to Zoey. "I think we're going to Blue River." She wiggles and makes her feet do tiny stamping movements on the floor of the truck. I am sure I am matching Zoey's totally goofy grin.

Mrs. Buckmueller shifts. The truck bucks through its gears.

Soon we are on the road to the biggest thing you'll find in teeny-tiny Surprise, Nebraska.

chapter thirty-nine

ON THE INSIDE
WITH ZOEY

When we reach Blue River, Zoey and I are on a mission. We are out of our jump seats in a flash, unstrapping book bins and loading them back onto the cart.

"We're going *inside* Blue River, aren't we?" Zoey says.

"It sure seems like it."

"But will they really let me? Am I allowed?" she asks.

"I think so. You're a volunteer."

By the time Mrs. B and her bionic knee make it around to raise the rear door we have the cart ready. She sees it and says, "Oh lordy! Amazing! Come! Let's roll."

With just a little more luck and good timing on this crazy rule-bending day, I might get to see Mom. I might even get to introduce her to Zoey Samuels.

We roll up to the great glass doors. Zoey looks to me for

what comes next. I hit the silver call button, which is a little like ringing the bell on my own front door. I face the cam and wave to whomever is on duty. "They'll see us," I explain to Zoey. "Then they'll buzz us in."

"The door stays locked? All day?" she asks. I nod back.

There is no Blue River bottleneck on a Tuesday afternoon. Every foreman knows Mrs. Buckmueller, and the guy on duty today calls out "Perry!" as soon as he sees me. He logs us in and gives us badges. Zoey looks at hers before she clips it to her jacket. Then we push the heavy, clacking book cart on through.

Zoey's eyes are wide. She looks all around the inside of the Blue River Co-ed Correctional Facility. "Stick with me," I say. I want to show her everything that I've ever told her about the place. But in the quiet common she stops and looks at the red-railed stairway. Her eyes follow it upward to the Upper East Lounge and to the small door at one end. "Your room," she says. I nod. Blue River must look plain to her—even ugly. But I love the feeling that this is a place that *I* know. Zoey Samuels is in my house.

We set to filling the Pleasure Reading stacks. Few residents come through the common because this is an in-between time. But I know how Blue River works. Word can get around fast. Anyone who sees me will want to tell Mom that I am in the building. It's possible that by the end of the workday, everyone will know. I'm a *mouse in the house.* That's what they say when a kid comes to visit.

With Mrs. B directing, Zoey and I empty the carts quickly. We give each other sly eyes as we shelve the periodicals.

"Can you believe it, Perry?" Zoey whispers as she hands me an issue of *Sports Illustrated*. "You could've delivered the interview questions yourself."

"What a twist." I say it quietly and barely let my lips move. "But this is still the best way because I'm not sure who we're going to see today. But I do know who's going to pick up each one of these." I pat the last magazine into place.

Mrs. B is looking at the gray clock. "You've done all my work. What will I do with myself now?"

"Take a load off," I say. "I mean, sit and relax!" I push a chair over for her.

"I accept," she says. "I'll gladly rest this bad old knee. The residents can do a self-checkout today. Lovely," she says, and she settles with her own book to read.

Zoey and I stand around. I twist and look over my shoulder. Surely a rez will come through soon . . .

Mrs. B sighs. "Hmm. Not much more for you two to do now, is there? I don't like to see a bored child . . . much less a pair of them." She looks around the common. "Hmm," she hums. "I'd say you're free to roam . . ." She lets that last word float as if it has a little tiny question mark on it.

Zoey is waiting for me to take charge. I know that visitors are supposed to stay in the common. But the rules are different for volunteers, and we *are* library volunteers. Still, we can't go running the halls. I am trying to think where Mom might be this time of day. She's not up on the balcony in the Upper East Lounge. I can see that. So she's probably in a meeting room . . .

Suddenly, I hear the bin—the laundry bin—that muffled sound the wheels make on the thin carpets in the block corridors. It's coming . . . coming up from Block A. It rolls a little louder as it hits the linoleum at the front of the common.

Let it be someone I know . . . oh, please let it be . . .

"Mr. Halsey!" I call to him, then I cover my mouth. I wave my arm in the air. He sees me. His eyes and mouth open wide. I hesitate. I glance at the foreman who is studying a clipboard, probably doing a count.

I look at Mrs. B, and she is looking back at me. She has sly eyes too now. "Hmm . . ." She hums. Then her humming turns into words. "You know what time the truck leaves . . . and you know where I am if you want me . . ." Mrs. B adjusts her glasses and opens the book on her lap. She tucks her chin to read.

I grab Zoey's arm, and we head for Mr. Halsey, who is egging us toward him with hand circles. We reach him, and he pushes the laundry bin to one side.

"Perry!" He catches me in a messed-up cross between a high five and a sidearm hug. But it doesn't matter. "Well, damn! I mean, darn! Didn't my day just get brighter." He laughs.

"Mine too!" I say. "This is Zoey," I tell him. "She's my

best friend on the outside." I'm talking fast. I can't help it.

"Double bright, this day!" He gives Zoey a wide smile.

"Hi," she says. She smiles, but she ducks her chin and looks shy. "We brought you a new *Sports Illustrated*." She pokes her thumb back toward the stacks and manages to add, "Don't miss it."

"Love that!" he says.

"Mr. Halsey, do you know where Mom is?" I'm low-talking.

"Sure I do!" He looks left and right. "I'll take you to her."

"Well . . . I'm not sure what the rules are," I tell him.

He cranes now to look at the foreman, who is still busy. "It's not like you and I haven't done this before," he tells me. He offers me his arm, and I do what I've done since Halsey Barrows first came into Blue River. I jump and grab it. I pull up my knees, and he lifts. He deposits me into the empty laundry bin. He looks at Zoey and says, "Come on, girl, jump it up there!" And she does.

Zoey and I crouch in the bin and watch the ceiling go by above us while Mr. Halsey zigs us and zags us. Zoey has her hands clapped over her mouth holding in her laughter.

We come to a stop. Mr. Halsey puts his finger to his lips. Zoey and I stay low. We are just outside the main meeting room. I hear Mom's voice. ". . . so continue making deposits and build up that bank account. You'll be the better for it when you are relea—"

Mr. Halsey knocks on the open door and pops the bin

right over the threshold. "Hello, ladies!"

"Halsey? What are you doing here?"

I can hardly stay down. I'm dying to see Mom. Zoey is grinning from ear to ear.

"I must have gotten lost," he tells her.

I hear Mom sigh and the women laugh. "You are taking a wicked risk for a guy about to be paroled—wandering around the women's wing where you don't belong. Here it is, ladies," Mom says, "an example what you *do not* want to do."

"Come on now, Jessie, I just want to leave something off with you," Mr. Halsey tells her.

"What?"

"No, no!" I hear Miss Sashonna now. "We don't need a bunch of dirty laundry in this old meeting room. Already smells like bad cheese in here."

"Well then, how about seventy-five pounds' worth of a special delivery?"

"Seventy-five pounds?"

"Times two," he tells them.

I pop up, stand tall in the bin. Mom's jaw drops. The women gasp.

"Perry? Oh, Perry! How did you get here?" Mom is on her feet.

"We came on the Bucking Blue Bookmobile," I say.

"You're kidding. What do you mean *we*?"

Zoey Samuels shows herself.

"Oh look, a little girl!" Mrs. DiCoco claps her hands

at the sight of Zoey. "Seventy-five pounds times two! Oh, Halsey! Get them both out of that old bin!" she orders.

Halsey laughs and lifts us out the same way he put us in. I make a beeline for Mom, and she wraps me in a hug. "You're here!" she cries. She swings me in place then lets me go only so she can take both of Zoey's hands in hers. They smile at each other. "Zoey Samuels . . ." Mom sighs. "Boy, have I ever been dying to meet you."

"I've wanted to meet you too, Mrs. . . . uh . . . C-Cook . . ." Zoey suddenly stammers and blushes a little. She doesn't know what to call Mom.

"Jessica is fine," Mom tells her. Mom starts to thank Zoey for my camera and for being a friend but Mr. Halsey interrupts.

"Psst! I've got to go! Nobody tell!" He puts the laundry bin in reverse. "The mice are yours now," he says. I see Mom mouth a big thank-you his way. He nods, puts his hand up to wave, and whispers, "Later!"

"Well. Does anyone mind if we cut our discussion a few minutes short?" Mom asks. She is looking at a group of women who are sitting down at the far end of the table. They look at us, unsmiling. "Is everybody okay with some free chat time?" Mom asks.

Finally, one says, "Yeah. We don't care!" They start their own conversation.

Mrs. DiCoco reaches for Zoey. "Here, right here, honey. Come sit beside me. I'm Callie DiCoco, but you can call me whatever sweet thing you want. Now are you the same age as Perry? I have two granddaughters . . ."

I sit on the skinny arm of Mom's chair and feel tall as a king in his court. Zoey sits with Mrs. DiCoco. We tell about being library volunteers and stuffing the magazines with interview questions for my Blue River Stories.

"And after all of that, we ended up with a surprise ride to Surprise!"

Zoey tells Mrs. DiCoco, "We put a copy of *Modern Gardener* into the stacks. Especially for you," she says. "So make sure you see it."

"I will." Mrs. DiCoco glows. "And I'll look through it very carefully," she whispers, and winks. "Perry, you already know you can tell my story."

"I'll tell you mine! I will!" says Sashonna. She is being loud. But Miss Gina is very quiet. She keeps her eyes down, and I know that she doesn't want to tell her Blue River story. That's okay by me. I won't ask. Sashonna says, "Put those questions in a copy of *Glamour*, Perry." She pokes her pointer finger at me. She catches herself and curls it back into her fist. "Um . . . please," she says.

"Already done," I tell her. Part of me wishes I had my notebook and my camera with me now. But Zoey and I left our things back in the David City Public Library. I look at Zoey sitting with the women who are my family. I lean into Mom and say, "I can't believe I'm at Blue River today."

We know I'm not here for long. We start to talk back and

forth. We barely come up for air. This is how it goes ever since I had to move out. I remind Mom that it's her story I want most of all. "Can we do that on Saturday?" I ask.

"Saturday," she says with a nod.

Miss Gina braids Zoey's hair all the way around her head in a circle. "If you can get them, tuck flowers into the weave." Miss Gina blinks her dark eyes at Zoey. "It's easy."

Zoey pats the braid lightly with her fingers. "Wow! It feels so perfect."

"Gina's good! That won't come apart on you, little girl," Sashonna says.

"Don't say 'little girl.' Her name is Zoey," Mrs. DiCoco says.

"Okay! Zoey. Sheesh!"

Softly, Miss Gina says, "You can sleep in that braid tonight and wear it to school in the morning. I make them so they hold."

Mom is watching the clock. It's nearly the end of the workday at Blue River. When the halls fill it will be easy to sneak us back to the common. "I will have no problem showing my gladness today," she jokes. "I am *supremely* glad! I wonder . . . since the bookmobile comes every Tuesday and Friday, are you going to come with it? Two short but sweet visits midweek?" Mom asks. "I'd *beg* if it would make it happen. We could meet down in the common if the temp will just let me make a change to my meeting schedule—"

"The temp?" I ask.

"Temporary warden," Sashonna blurts. "That's what Foreman Joe is now. Just while Warden Daugherty is suspended."

"Suspended?"

Sashonna looks at Mom. Mom looks at Sashonna.

Sashonna says, "Oops."

Suddenly I understand how much trouble the warden is really in.

chapter forty

BUCKING BACK

"You know that I'm sorry about the warden, right?" Zoey Samuels has buckled up and cut to the chase. "And you know it's not your fault, Perry?"

"Hmm . . . it's because of me. I know that's not the same thing as my fault." I sit back and sigh.

The Bucking Blue Bookmobile waggles us back through Rising City. Zoey smiles a very soft smile. She looks toward the one small window in the rear of the truck. You can't really see anything out of it—not from where we sit—just a square patch of light sky. But Zoey doesn't take her eyes off it.

"I loved it," she says. She means spending time at Blue River. "They were so . . . nice. I thought I might feel scared." She admits it. "But then I wasn't." Her smile does a funny little thing—turns downward at the corners. Her bottom lip quivers. Her chin tightens like a little nut. Zoey Samuels puts up her hand to wipe away the tear that comes down her cheek. She won't look at me right now. She keeps her shining eyes on the square of light. A few more seconds and the soft smile returns.

I sit back and breathe out. I let my head sway with the rocking of the old bookmobile. I'm thinking about Warden Daugherty. I'm sick in my gut that she's actually suspended—all because she kept Mom and me together. I sort of love Miss Sashonna for finally spilling the beans. Mom said she was sorry for not telling me. She was waiting for the right time, but she admitted that she should've known it would never come. It would make plenty of sense for me to feel mad. But I don't have any mad in me; I just have this dull ache. I can't imagine Blue River without Warden Daugherty.

When we reach the library, everyone is waiting for us. Both VanLeer and Zoey's mom are standing on the curb right where the bookmobile gets parked. Our backpacks are sitting at their feet. She is calm. His arms are folded across his chest. His face is like a rock. Mr. Olsen is there, too, with his clipboard. He looks like a pale slice of cheese.

"Oh lordy!" says Mrs. Buckmueller. She limps and blinks while we push the cart. "What have we? A welcome committee?"

"Not exactly," says Mr. VanLeer.

Mr. Olsen looks at Mrs. B. He clears his throat. "Turns out we've had a little miscommuniqué . . ."

"These children were *never* supposed to leave the

library . . ." VanLeer starts in and doesn't stop—even when Mrs. B and Mr. Olsen try to apologize. "You took two children off the premises without permission!" Mr. VanLeer says.

Meanwhile, Zoey has tucked herself under her mom's arm while I wait in place with both hands on the cart. Next we hear about protocol, responsibility, and the "terrible fright" this afternoon has given everyone. He finally takes a break.

Mrs. Buckmueller speaks. "Why, if I made a mistake, I am unreservedly sorry. The way I understood it, I was meant to take Perry and Zoey with me. I had two library volunteers for the afternoon. I will say, their efforts were laudable. You should be very proud. They made a world of difference at the—"

"You took them to a prison!" VanLeer exclaims. "Children don't go on field trips to prisons!" He points at Zoey. "Look! She's been crying!"

"Tom, it's fine. She's fine," Zoey's mom says.

"I haven't been crying," Zoey says. "Not bad crying. Really. I'm okay, Tom." Her mom brushes her fingers under Zoey's chin. She touches the new braid.

"Pretty . . . ," she whispers, and Zoey nods.

"I want to go back again," she says right into her mom's face.

"Not possible," says VanLeer with a firm shake of his head.

I look down at my own feet. Scuff a toe. I think about Mom. I want Tuesdays and Fridays. I want them so much. What's it to him?

I hear Zoey being calm and cool. She says, "Mrs. B really needs our help."

"Splendid," says Mrs. Buckmueller. "Thank you, darlings." She takes over the cart, and with Mr. Olsen's help, starts up the ramp to the library.

I stand uselessly to one side. Mr. VanLeer is still shaking his head. Zoey's mom touches his arm.

"Look, all is well. Let's head home now," she says.

"Perry has been home," Zoey says. "This whole afternoon. You should have seen how happy they were to see him, Mom. They were even happy to see me." She puzzles. "I don't know what I thought it would be like. Perry has told me some. There is a sad part . . . and some of the residents seemed to turn away. But Perry's friends . . . well . . . they felt like new friends that you could meet anywhere—"

"Oh great, we have a sympathizer," Mr. VanLeer groans.

But Zoey's mom pulls her girl closer to her. "I think we have an empathizer." She looks at her husband. Softly she asks him, "And what's wrong with that?"

"What's wrong with any of this?" I ask, and I am a little on the loud side. "Isn't the bookmobile arrangement perfect? For everyone?"

chapter forty-one

VIDEO ROOM

On Wednesday afternoon, I'm in the video room at the library with Zoey Samuels. "Is it the right wire?" she asks.

"Well, it fits in the camera and the other end is in the computer port. So, yes, I think so." We're taking a stab in the dark. We signed up and we have this computer in the video room for thirty minutes. Then it'll be taken over by everybody-knows-who: Brian Morris and his friends. For now, we are tucked into the most private corner. Trouble is, neither Zoey nor I know what we're doing.

"All right. We're connected. See the icon for the movie maker program?" Zoey pushes me along. I click it. "Now let's see if it comes up," she says.

And it does. Six little squares of Big Ed lay themselves down in a row on the screen. "Yes! These are the short video segments from his interview."

"There you go! Now click one," says Zoey. She jiggles my arm, and I tap the pad. There is bigger Big Ed—from my tiny camera screen to the computer screen.

"Wow," I say. I've been scheming. Or imagining. I'd love to put the videos with the written story. Somehow. I'm picturing the Blue River Stories like mini documentaries. But I have no idea how to do any of that.

I click on the still shot of Big Ed to make it play. Zoey and I watch all six videos without speaking. Even though they are short, they tell the long, hard story. We hear Big Ed's raspy voice—the way he has to push out the awful words; we see the way his eyes look to a place far away. We see his fingers knot together in his lap.

"Oh my God, Perry . . . ," Zoey says when the last video ends. She leans on one elbow and presses her face all out of shape with her hand. "H-he didn't even mean to hurt the kid and—"

"Who is that guy?"

Our heads snap around. Brian Morris is right behind us. His mouth hangs open. He's staring at the stopped shot of Big Ed. I wonder how long he's been there.

"Hey! Get out!" Zoey Samuels is on her feet. "This computer is ours for"—she checks the clock—"fifteen more minutes."

Brian's chin juts toward the screen. "Who is that?" he presses. "Is he a prisoner?"

I wait. We are eyes on each other. He's asking questions

instead of making stuff up. "Well, we say 'resident,'" I tell him. "But also, he's one of my best fr—"

"Perry! Stop!" Zoey says. She puts her arms over the screen. "And don't let him see."

"I already saw," Brian says. "That guy killed somebody, didn't he?"

"Buzz off, Brian!" Zoey snaps. "Perry, what are you doing?"

"What are you going to do with the video?" Brian presses.

I shrug my shoulders because I don't know. I stand up, reach for the wire, and pull it out of the port. I gather up my camera. I tell Brian, "You can have the computer. We're done."

Zoey Samuels follows me out of the room. She's breathing fire at my neck. "Why would you even think to trust him?" she asks, and she goes on about it as we walk. "He could tell some messed-up version of Big Ed's story to all his lunch buddies . . ."

I turn around just before we get to the History Room. I tell her, "You could be right. But then again, people can change."

chapter forty-two

TWO WINS AND A DIG

On Thursday the VanLeer grown-ups go walking up and down the street after supper. They've been doing this a lot, especially this week. Zoey clues me in from the front window of the VanLeer house, where she holds the curtain back in one hand so she can see them. She says, "They call that having a discussion. I call it taking it to the streets. It's polite fighting."

"That's nice," I say. I don't mean to be funny, but Zoey laughs out loud. "I mean it's not the worst idea in the world, keeping it out there instead of inside the house where it makes everyone feel bad."

"You say it like it sticks to the walls or something, Perry." She drops the curtain and faces me. "They're going to let us do it," she says. "We'll be on the Bucking Blue Bookmobile tomorrow." She pops her fist into her palm like it's a done deal. We've both been waiting for the answer. Tomorrow is Friday, so it has to come tonight.

Zoey and I unload the VanLeer dishwasher. While we stack dinner plates and salad bowls into the cupboards I do some good hard hoping. I tell Zoey, "I want them to find a *yes* for us out there in the street. They can bring that inside and stick it to the walls."

Later, standing shoulder to shoulder with Mr. VanLeer, Zoey's mom gives us the news. "So, we're giving permission for the two of you to travel with Mrs. Buckmue—"

"Yes!" Zoey shrieks. She faces me. We slap ten.

Zoey's mom smiles hugely. Mr. VanLeer stays more serious. But I don't miss that there is a faint smile on his face too. He's watching us celebrate. He likes to see Zoey happy. Zoey throws her arms around her mom, then around Tom, crying, "Thank you!" Her stepdad cups his hand on her head, his fingers rest across the Blue River braid that has held up for two nights and two days.

I feel myself pull toward Zoey's mom. I think she almost reaches for me too. I could hug her, but I stop. I hold my own elbows. I smile and tell her, "Thank you. Thank you so much. This is going to mean a lot to my mom too."

"Just don't forget, you have a purpose while you're there," says Mr. VanLeer.

I still have my eyes on Zoey's mom. I know she went to bat for us. She is looking back at me with the same shiny-eyed look that Zoey had coming home from Blue River on Tuesday. She made this happen. But Mr. VanLeer did not have to agree. Yet he did. So I face him and say it.

"Thank you very much."

"You're welcome, Perry. I want good things for you. I do." He gives me a nod. "And really, it's a good thing you'll get to go tomorrow." He turns as if to get on with the evening. "That will make up for this Saturday."

We all twist to look at him.

"Tom? What does that mean?" Mrs. Samuels asks.

"Oh, I have to drive clear up to Abie to pick up a case file box. Inconvenient as heck," he says. "Sorry. A trip to Surprise is out of the question."

"What? But I have to go to Blue River." I hear myself blurt it. Then I think to myself, It's Mom's story! I need this! "Mr. VanLeer, I *have* to see my mom," I say. "I have an interview to do."

"Maybe get it done tomorrow, pal."

"But my mom works. We won't have time." I feel a hot knot in my chest.

"Tom . . . really?" Zoey's mom presses him.

"It's one of those impossible scheduling things." He raises one hand helplessly in the air. "I can't go up there tomorrow. I have a full day in court. These quirky little towns are understaffed. I don't like working Saturdays, but you know the story . . ."

"Wait, wait," Zoey's mom says. "No, I don't know, Tom.

We talked and talked." She gestures toward the street, and I wonder if they'll be going back out there again. "You didn't say anything about Saturday."

"Tom, Saturdays are your promise to Perry." Zoey speaks up. She pats his arm. He looks down at her.

"I have to work, Zoey. I have responsibilities."

"I'll take him," Zoey's mom says.

"No, no. You have Zoey's dance class, clear in the opposite direction, Robyn."

"I'll miss," Zoey says.

"No." Tom shakes his head. "Nobody has to miss anything. It'll be fine. It's just one week, and Perry will have had both Tuesday and Friday at the prison. That's plenty." He says this firmly.

"Well, we'll have to see. We'll see," Zoey's mom says. She's flustered and nodding her head a lot. "We'll see." If I leave maybe she can stop repeating herself.

"Excuse me," I say. I take huge strides, heels hitting the floor hard as I go down the hall and away from Thomas VanLeer.

In the closet I breathe and stare at my timeline. "What are your wins?" I ask myself. Tuesdays and Fridays. I take a pencil and circle them all the way along the wall, into the corner and out again. The Bucking Blue Bookmobile is a big win. But I'm furious about Saturday. If VanLeer can decide to skip one Saturday at Blue River, he can decide to skip more.

He doesn't get that this was the Saturday that Mom was going to tell me her story, or how long I've waited to know the whole thing. When VanLeer went on Desiree Riggs's show, he said he'd help me any way he can.

Canceling Saturday is nothing but a kick in the backside.

chapter forty-three

MOM'S STORY

On Saturday, Mrs. Samuels comes to the rescue, and so does Zoey. The three of us load into the SUV and drive out to Zoey's dance studio so she can attend an earlier class. Afterward, we stop for egg and cheese biscuits at the farmers' market to eat on the way to Surprise. Zoey's mom grabs a head of broccoli too. (I think she saw me looking at it.) I thank her at least six times for this trip to Blue River.

She says, "This is fine, Perry. Truly. I promise that Zoey and I will not crowd you on this visit. But I'd like to meet your mom."

They have brought books in a tote bag—things to do. When we get to Blue River, nobody has to make Zoey's mom play cards.

You are not supposed to curl up or put feet on the chairs in the common. (They're not that comfortable anyway.) But Mom does a sort of half curl. She gets one knee up where she can hug it. It's her favorite way to sit, and usually no one calls her out on it.

"So, Mom, can you give me a Blue River mini-bio on yourself before we get to your story?" I've decided to take a short video of the first part of each interview as long as it's okay with each rez.

She looks at the camera. "Well, I'm Jessica Cook. I arrived here twelve years ago. I had just turned eighteen at the time. So I have spent my twenties here." She dips her chin before she goes on. "Currently, I counsel other residents throughout their stays here, all in preparation for release. That's kind of ironic since I've never had the pleasure myself." Mom looks right at the camera and flashes a saucy grin. She makes me laugh, and I know that part of the video is going to look bouncy. "You have to keep your eye on the end," she says.

"I've had other jobs here. I was a greeter for several years. Before that I potted seedlings in the facility's greenhouse. I've done plenty of shifts in the laundry, and when I first got here I wrapped napkins around sporks in the kitchen. I still do mess duty, just like everyone else here."

"Okay, great." I set the camera down and pick up my notebook. It's a little strange to sit across from Mom. Even stranger to tell her, "Begin whenever you're ready. It's your story."

There is a stretch of silence. I don't breathe. My pencil is ready. I feel Mom switch tone, but she speaks to me.

"Well, you know what I'm in for," she says.

"I know what you've told me. You're in Blue River for two reasons. Because you told lies, and because your actions contributed to a death. I know you got manslaughter. Same as Big Ed," I say.

"And you know what it means," Mom says.

"Yeah. You didn't mean to kill, but you made a mistake that caused someone's death."

"Yep. I sure did."

"Who was it, Mom?"

"My father," she says.

I feel my eyebrow hitch upward. My fingers are weak around the pencil now. Her father would be my grandfather. I have never heard this before. I lean forward. Mom looks past me—but just to the back of my chair, not way off like Big Ed did.

"I grew up in a household that didn't have a lot of warmth," she says. Her mouth twists just a little. "Not that I ever wished either of my parents dead. I just wished they would love me—or love me differently than they did. I'm pretty sure my parents didn't plan me. I happen to know that an unexpected baby can be an incomparable joy."

I smile, but I keep my pencil moving, scratching down key words.

"But at my house it was just the three of us, and it's weird, but I felt more managed than loved. For a long, long time, I did my best at all the things that seemed to matter to them. I got good grades—great grades, actually—and good thing, because there was no room for flubbing up under that roof." She rolls her eyes. "You'd get no love for that. I worked hard at school, and I competed hard on the swim team. I had to win so I wouldn't have to see them turn their backs on me at the end of a race. By the time I graduated high school, I had won a nice college scholarship, and I think we were all looking forward to having me out of their house." Mom smiles just a little. "They had a rule, actually: out at eighteen.

"So one summer night we sat down to talk over some of my plans for the fall. I had changed those plans somewhat, and I was feeling assertive because it was *my* life and *my* scholarship. That didn't go over well. There was shouting and drinking—my father kept pouring one after the other. They were getting harder to talk to. Angry and exasperated. I was probably being a snot—I don't know." Mom sighs. "But things got very ugly. Finally I'd had enough of the shouting, so I picked up to leave. And that's when my father gasped and clutched his chest. I'll never forget it. He looked at my mother and said, 'Oh my god, Vivian, I'm in so much pain, I think I'm going to die.'

"We had to get him to the hospital. I was the one standing there with the keys in my hand. We got my father into the backseat. Mother got in with him, and we took off."

I set the pencil down and wiggle my fingers. I pick up the camera. Watch Mom through the window.

"Everyone thinks driving will be easy out on the straightaways. We sped along. My father had gone silent, but my

mother kept calling into the front of the car—hollering—
that we weren't going fast enough. Bad weather moved in—a
good old Nebraska hailstorm. I couldn't see." Mom shakes
her head. "My God, I was trying so hard to help." She lowers her eyes and bites her lip. "I made an awful mistake at
an intersection, and that was it." Her voice climbs up. "We
crashed."

The camera is off. I look at Mom, at her arms and legs
and her head where she is tucking her fingers into her hair.
I almost ask her, was she hurt all those years ago? But she
squints and picks up her story again.

"The rest is kind of a messed-up blur, Perry. Flashing
lights and stopped trucks, and feet slipping over hailstones
and crushing them. I could see my parents in the backseat—
neither one conscious." Mom's eyes water up. "I tried to open
the back car doors, but they were crumpled in. I couldn't
budge them. Couldn't get into that bloody nest of a backseat."
Mom wipes her eyes with her fingertips.

"I remember that the police were kind. I sheltered in a
blanket at the scene for what seemed like forever. A tow truck
came . . ." Mom shakes her head like she is trying to recall.
"The police put me in a cruiser. We followed the ambulance
with both my parents inside to the hospital. While the nurses
looked me over for injuries, I kept asking about my parents."
Mom waits a beat. "Finally, I learned that my father had died.
My mother had a head injury—something that was taking a
lot of stitches. I asked to see her, but the nurse just ducked her

chin and told me my mother was unavailable. A sad truth," Mom says. She clears her throat.

"When the police asked, I told them yes, I was driving. Then they said there was an obvious odor of alcohol at the scene." Mom shakes her head. She stares off for a few seconds. "The next hours were exhausting and confusing. The questions and the . . . pressure. I didn't know what to say. I felt like I'd dropped into somebody else's nightmare. They asked again and I told them again, I was driving. And finally, I told them that I had been drinking too. And then the next thing I know, I'm being arrested. My God, I was scared. I kept asking for my mother. I was told she would not come. At some point I realized that was her choice.

"I was alone and terrified. Bad advice was everywhere, but I didn't know enough to see that. Eventually, I pled guilty to the drunk driving charge. But then, because my father had died in the accident, there was the manslaughter charge too." Mom cocks her head. "Didn't see that coming. But I had done what I had done, and I had confessed. And a confession is . . ."

"A conviction." We say it together, though my own lips feel numb.

Mom is quiet, and I pick up the camera again. "Oddly," she says, "I don't consider that my Blue River story. That part would be about earning a degree in social work from the inside and my work here. But I think the part you wanted to know is what got me in, and I don't blame you. Being incarcerated is *not* something I would have chosen. But I found a new beginning here. I found out that life still goes forward even when you're inside."

I think Mom is finished, but then she adds something. "I thought my sentencing was ferocious—I felt I'd been made an example of. But I still had no real regrets about the confession—not until I found out about you, Perry. When I realized that I had compromised two people's futures . . . well . . . you bet I was sorry. I had a new biggest fear in the world, and that was being separated from you. We made it a lot of years before that happened," Mom says. She looks up at me and nods. "Coming here was a patch of good inside a blurry patch of bad."

chapter forty-four

JESSICA

Jessica Cook felt worn out on Saturday evening. She'd been determined to tell her boy an honest version of her story—but only one that both of them could afford. Every word had felt like a step onto a fragile stick above a tiger pit. Perry was earnest and trusting—open to believing the story. He'd been intensely focused with his little camera and his pencil. Afterward, he was respectful and loving, circling her with a hug that had gone deliciously long.

Perry was also smart. Jessica knew that her omissions were risky. She sighed as the microwave in the Block C kitchenette hummed and her bowl of broccoli went round and round. If he sensed gaps in her story, he could start filling them in with his own inventions . . .

Oh. Dear. She'd been so careful and now here came a flood of misgivings.

Well, if he has questions, he can ask them, she thought. She consoled herself as she pulled the steamy green florets out of the oven. She determined to swallow all her second thoughts along with them. The broccoli was a gift from one Robyn Samuels, who had blushed when she'd handed it over like a bouquet of flowers. "I was told this would be a big hit," she had said.

The woman had dancing eyes, a broad smile, and intriguing speckles of pale paint on her hands and forearms. How confounding that she had that arrogant thorn Thomas VanLeer for a husband!

Robyn Samuels had something else: respect. Not the kind some visitors to Blue River put on like a costume when they walked through the doors. Jessica had well-honed radar when it came to knowing who was genuine. She had glimpsed the mother and daughter from across the common while she and Perry were decompressing from her telling. Robyn and Zoey had alternately read their own books and chatted with various residents. There had been an origami lesson with the little Rojas girls, and Gina had come through with her rattail comb (and alcohol wipes) to weave new hair braids all around.

Jessica remembered something that Perry had said after his first week living away from Blue River—something about Zoey's mom being on his side. Today seemed proof enough of that. The way Perry told it, he would not have made it to Blue River with his camera and his pencil had she not stepped up. Yes. Robyn Samuels had warmth and compassion.

Now if only Jessica could get past the fact that Robyn also had Perry.

chapter forty-five

OVERHEARD

I'm looking at my notes from Mom's interview. I'm turning all my jottings into sentences and paragraphs. Every so often, I play a video from my camera. Zoey is right beside me at the long desk in the VanLeer family room. She's doing math problems.

Mr. VanLeer goes in and out the door from the kitchen to the grill. Each little gust of chilly October air brings with it something that smells good. Mrs. Samuels comes in from the garage. I hear water running and know that she's cleaning her paintbrushes at the kitchen sink. They either don't know or they've forgotten that Zoey and I are right around the corner from the kitchen.

"There you are," he says to her when he comes in again. "How's the paint project coming?"

"Great!" she sings. "Sorry to leave you to do all of dinner tonight. I really wanted to get that second coat on. It always takes longer than I think it will."

"Hmm . . . slow paint, slow food," he says.

"Yes, both so artful!" They laugh. Then they kiss. I can hear it. Zoey is multiplying decimals. She doesn't pay much attention to their kisses anyway.

"I don't know what it is about little round dining tables," Zoey's mom says. "It's not like we need another one here. But I couldn't resist bringing this ugly duckling in for a facelift. I'll find a good home for it."

"Absolutely. Somebody's going to love that table . . ."

Both voices trail off. The door bangs and all is quiet. They must be out at the grill together.

I look down at my notebook and rest my cheeks on my hands. The problem I am having with the Blue River Stories is that I want the stories to come from the residents—like they are speaking. But then I start writing down what they told me and everything slips out of their voices. Then I watch a slice of video and I begin to transcribe it and I hear the person loud and clear again. I work this around in my head. Then I think again about how perfect my project would be as a documentary.

"Ack!" I say.

Zoey snickers. I sit back and shake my head like maybe I can wake up my brain cells. Then I pull out a new sheet of notebook paper to try again.

So, what about quotes? I think to myself. I decide to give it a try. The back door opens again.

"Robyn, he would've survived without one Saturday visit." Thomas VanLeer is insistent—*and wrong*. I let my next breath fill my chest slowly. Zoey hums a low growl but doesn't look up from her equation.

"Survived, yes," Zoey's mom says. "But listen to yourself, Tom. Isn't the idea here for him to do a whole lot more than *survive*? How about we help him *thrive*?" There was a little jar banging then and even some quiet cussing.

Zoey looks at me and whispers, "Ooooh . . ."

I whisper back, "Everything was fine until . . ." I point to my own chest with my finger. Zoey shrugs.

"He *is* thriving, Robyn." Mr. VanLeer's voice is low in his throat—harder to hear. I catch something about the two trips a week in the bookmobile. Then he says it again. "He didn't need to go—"

"Yes! Yes he did—and he does!" Zoey's mom is loud and clear. I imagine her with one finger raised in the air between them. "I saw a different boy at Blue River. He was whole. I'm glad I took him, Tom. I'll take him again."

"Then you're reneging on the particulars of our foster care plan," he says.

"I call it taking a boy to see his mother."

"I call it you supporting the nonconforming policies of that warden who kept the boy locked up there his whole life."

"Oh, Tom! That's a stretch! He was *not* locked up. Look, we disagree about that, and you'll have to do what you think is right on that point. That's your job," she says flatly. "But—and I'm sure we'll disagree on this too—I have decided something else." She pauses. "I want to get to know his mother."

"Robyn, seriously?"

"Yes," she tells him. "Don't get in my way." She calls down the hall toward the bedrooms. "Zoey! Perry! Supper is on."

chapter forty-six

MISS SASHONNA'S STORY

On Saturday, we pull chairs together in our corner of the Blue River Common. No one has to make Mr. VanLeer play cards today. He has brought his own distraction—a fat folder full of papers. He's been dragging that to the VanLeer dinner table all week long. I'm glad when he sits down by himself to work in the common.

Miss Sashonna asked Mom to be her support person today. Miss Gina has helped her put on eye makeup. She looks at my camera and points. "You ready, Perry?" I try to keep the camera still while I nod yes. "Is that thing on?" I nod again. "You ready?"

"Yes!" I finally have to say it.

"Yeah, okay. I'm Sashonna Lee Lewis." She starts off sounding like Desiree Riggs, her voice all buttercream. She

211

taps her long skinny fingers on her chest. "I got put in here about six months ago. I got a long time to go. I don't even want to talk about that." She slips out of the Desiree voice quickly.

"So, I got put in here because of something I did for a stupid man—and it's not fair, what happened. Anyways, he was stupid, but I loved him. I was always doing what he wanted. And what he wanted to do was, he wanted to rob a bank. Just a little one. Because he owed a guy some money. I told Chaunce—that's his name—that his plan had a serious flaw in it." Sashonna's finger wags in the air. "Like, if he wants *me* to drive the getaway car then he better teach me how first. So, he took me to a big parking lot just before we went to the bank." She pretends she's holding on to a steering wheel. She sways. "There I am driving! I'm all, what's the big deal? This is easy! I got this!

"Chaunce wants to make sure I can drive real fast. I'm all, 'I know where the gas pedal is! I'm no chicken! I punch my foot on that"—she stops to laugh—"and Chaunce's head goes slamming back in his seat and he's screaming like a little sister!" Sashonna cackles.

"Chaunce had me wait outside the bank, and he says, 'Keep it running and make sure you keep all the windows open, baby! Got it? *Open.*' He gives me a big kiss before he goes into the bank. It's winter, so I'm sitting there like a Popsicle, poking at the radio, fiddling with the steering wheel.

212

Getting in some pretend driving practice." She wiggles back and forth. "I am ready to do my job. Then I look up at the little mirror and see some car coming up behind me. Closer, and closer . . . and holy crow! It's the Po-Po!" She claps her hands on her cheeks.

"They slide right into the space behind me and then—they sit there! So now I don't know if those police are onto what Chaunce is doing. But I do know, I gotta call this whole thing off! Chaunce can't rob that bank—not while the police are sitting right outside. So I think I can stop it if I just roll up those windows. So I do. Then I crank the wheel, pull the car out onto the street real careful. Then Chaunce comes running out of the bank—and it's like he's got a bear up his backside. He throws that duffel and it smacks into the window. Falls on the sidewalk. He grabs it up again—swearing—banging on the window. 'Open! Open it! Go, go, go!' So I'm pushing buttons and yanking that wheel trying to do everything Chaunce wants me to do. I get the window open and I think I'm doing good! So I push the gas pedal.

"Then the Po-Po puts on the blue-light special." Sashonna whirls her fist and rolls her eyes. "So now I'm scared! We're in trouble. I gotta get us out of there. So I hit the gas—real hard. Only thing is, I don't have Chaunce! So here he comes running alongside the car. He gets that duffel in the window—finally. So that's good and I punch the gas again.

"I know I should slow down. But the police put on the

213

sirens, and I'm scared. So I put my foot right to the floor. Zoom! That's when Chaunce tries to pitch himself in through the back window. But he only gets the top of him in. His legs don't make it. I can't look back there because— hello-o-o—I'm busy driving. Somehow he gets dragged back out of the car again. I'm still trying to go, go, go, and I feel the rear end of the car go over some bump. Well guess what? That bump was Chaunce.

"I keep going down the street before I look and see him in the back mirror. He's hurt. Twisting in the road, gripping his legs. I slam on the brakes because that's not what you want to see when you love some guy—even a stupid one. Next thing I know a security guard from that little bank runs up and sticks a knife in the tire. Man! So now I am afraid to try to drive a car with a flat, *and* I didn't learn about going backward in my *one* driving lesson. I try anyway. *Fwump-fwump-fwump—BAM!*" Sashonna bangs her hands together. "I go smack into some flower truck that must have come up behind me. Now I'm a mess. All I want is to be with Chaunce—ask him what to do. So I get out of the car and run back to him where he's lying in the road."

Miss Sashonna's eyes fill with water, and she pulls her knees up to her chest. She makes sounds like a kitten when it mews. Mom asks, "Sashonna? You okay?" She passes her a tissue.

"Anyways," Sashonna says, "here come the police. They don't even care Chaunce is run over. They slap bracelets on both of us. The only way I can tell that Chaunce is okay is he's swearing at me up and down.

"So he gets to go to the hospital to get his leg put in a cast. I get to go to jail and sit there. Can't believe that. I'm no bank robber! But I end up getting charged right along with him—and you know what else? I get more time than him!" She begins to count it off on her fingers. "They said I robbed the bank—so that's a federal crime. I got reckless endangerment with a motor vehicle, I drove without a license, no registration, *and* I left the scene of an accident when I ran back to Chaunce after I hit that flower truck." She shakes her head and says, "It's not fair."

Everything is quiet. Then Sashonna says, "Remember those questions—the ones you put in *Glamour* magazine, Perry? You asked me what's the best thing and what's the worst thing about being at Blue River."

"I remember," I say.

"Well, the worst thing is being in here with somebody else watching me and telling me what to do all day. I had enough of that on the outside. The best thing is Jessica—'cause she's been a good friend. Keeps me out of trouble. I like that—even though I know she doesn't like me so much."

"But I do!" Mom grins. "You're like my annoying little sister!"

"Yeah? For real?"

"You bet."

"Thanks for that." Sashonna takes her tissue in the heel

of her hand and rubs her nose in a big upward sweep. "Sorry," she says. "Sorry I got so much snot today. Oh my God! You didn't take pictures of that, did you, Perry?"

She laughs, and it makes all of us laugh too.

chapter forty-seven

STORM

In the History Room Zoey is reading Mrs. DiCoco's story. (I've pulled it together from a quick Tuesday afternoon interview.) She wants to read them all. But I wonder if I should be offering to help her with her own Coming to Butler County project. I know a secret: Zoey Samuels has not started her assignment. I haven't asked her why. Days go by slowly for me while I am missing Mom. But time must be racing for Zoey. Our projects are due in a couple of weeks.

"Aww . . . this is sad," she says. "Once you know the person, well, it makes you care. Can I see her videos too, Perry?" I pass the camera to her across the dark oak table. She holds it close, tilts her head while she watches the interview.

Outdoors a storm brings flashes of lightning and heavy drum rolls of thunder. The lamps in the History Room flicker under their green glass shades. The thunder builds until it is so loud that Zoey and I can hardly hear each other.

We take my notebook and camera and scrunch down side by side on the floor beneath the window.

"Mrs. DiCoco didn't tell about her trial," Zoey says. She taps her pencil on the page.

"She always keeps her story short," I say. "But also, she confessed. A confession is a conviction. So there was no trial."

"It seems like . . . she shouldn't have to be in prison," Zoey says with a scowl. "At least not for so long. Same for a lot of them. I mean . . . your mom? Big Ed? They made big mistakes once but would never do it again. They'd never do that *recivi-di-vis*—ack! What is it again?"

"Recidivism." I say it between rumbles of thunder.

"Yeah, that."

"Warden Daugherty calls it her goose egg," I say. I make an O with my hands. "Her big beautiful zero, because Blue River has zero percent recidivism. She says it's proof that the place works the way it is supposed to."

Zoey says, "You have a really good project, Perry. Telling the Blue River Stories . . . it's . . . important. The confessions get to me the most." She puts her hand over her heart. "When I do bad stuff, it's really hard to admit it."

"Yeah. But people want to be honorable. Own up, and start taking steps away from the bad thing . . ."

"And then there is Big Ed," she says. "Did he really even commit a crime? He said he had no fight in him. What if he had tried to defend himself at a trial? What if someone else had defended him?"

We stop talking and listen to the thunder as the storm moves nearer. I think about Mom. She confessed. She didn't get a trial either. I think about how she looks in the viewer of the small camera—how I recognize her as Mom but how there is also something different about her in the videos. Maybe it's like Zoey just said; it's hard to admit a mistake.

Still, something bothers me, especially as I hear more Blue River Stories from other residents. I flip back through the notebook pages until I get to Mom's interview. It is supposed to be finished; it's all written out. But it feels like pieces are missing. I look at the first note I made before she even began talking. She always told me that she ended up at Blue River because she contributed to someone's death and she told lies. Her father died. I know that now. But . . . the lies? I keep reading. Searching.

"Where's the part about the lies?" I say it out loud.

"Perry? What did you say?" A loud boom interrupts. Zoey crouches. "Whoa!" she says. She presses her hands over her ears as louder cracks of thunder sound. The History Room walls shake.

My mind races. What did Mom lie about? Did she tell me? Is it somewhere here in her Blue River story?

There's a flash of lightning. The sky beyond takes an enormous breath—I swear I can feel it from inside the library walls. *Ka-ka-BOOM!* The crack of thunder is deafening. Seconds go by. Then huge raindrops splatter against the History Room windows. They come in a rhythm like someone is throwing shovelfuls of cinders at the thick glass.

"So loud!" Zoey says, her hands still over her ears. I nod and close the notebook. I'll look at it again tonight.

When Zoey's mom meets us in the History Room, she says, "Tom called and begged us not to head home until this passes. I think he's right." She glances out the window.

The rain is still pelting the library, pelting all of David City, and probably Surprise too. It's not hailstones today, but I think about Mom—how she said the balls of ice crushed under her feet the night of the accident. What if that storm had not come? Or what if they had not gotten in that car that night? I'm standing in the History Room trying to change history. Everybody knows you can't do that.

In the closet at the VanLeer house I read every word of Mom's Blue River story. I even read it backward. I watch the videos again. I find the place in the beginning where she says that she told lies. I search every note I have. I see this:

They asked again and I told them again, I was driving. And finally, I told them that I had been drinking too.

Told them. But you can *tell* someone anything. You can tell them something that isn't true. I stand up straight in the VanLeer closet. I bump the warden's suitcase, and it tips. The little reading lamp and the travel clock hit the floor. My heart thumps. Am I wrong?

220

But why? Why would Mom tell them she had been drinking if she wasn't? Or driving if she wasn't? And if Mom wasn't the driver, who was? Her father? He was sick that night with his chest pains. Her mother? She said her parents were both in the backseat.

"Hey, Perry?" Zoey's mom taps on the door then pops her head in. "I heard a clunk," she says. "Everything all right?" She looks past me and sees the suitcase and lamp. Then she gives me a long look. "Perry? You okay?" she asks.

"F-fine," I tell her. My tongue will barely make words.

"Okay." She turns slowly. "Are you sure?"

I nod. She goes away.

I have to get back to Blue River.

I have to ask Mom about the lies.

chapter forty-eight

ERASER

On Saturday, Mr. VanLeer is still hovering after we are through the Blue River bottleneck. I look over the heads and shoulders of other visitors. A flash of bright pink catches my eye, like an exotic bird has flown into the common. I hear a jingle then a voice. "Hi, Perry." I raise my hand in return but I'm confused. It's Miss Jenrik from the school cafeteria, her pink hair in a tail and a pink motorcycle helmet tucked under her arm. She breezes by, all feathers and rings, and takes a seat across from a man with sad, sunken eyes. It's Mr. Wendell. He's the new intake. Not so new anymore.

Mom is waving from our corner of the common. I'm hesitating. VanLeer is sticking to my heels like a gooey piece of gum. I need to give him the slip, and I haven't been quick enough.

About fifteen feet from me, Cici Rojas is doing that thing

where she goes and stands on the linoleum by the vending machines with her arms folded across her chest. She swings her body and calls to Mr. Rojas, "You can't get me when I'm over here." He can't. Residents have to stay on the carpet during busy Saturday visits.

Mrs. Rojas scolds her daughter, "Cici! Respect your papa!"

Used to be I would go talk Cici off the linoleum. I was a Blue River helper. Used to be I could deliver cookies to Miss Jenrik and Mr. Wendell. Now I am shuffling through the common, trying to get to the resident I have come to see, *and* I can feel Mr. Thomas VanLeer's fingertips pressing into my back.

"Perry, my man!" Mr. Halsey slides in and greets me, palm up for some skin. I step forward and give it. He pretends to bounce a ball through his legs then weaves between Mr. VanLeer and me. I do a weave of my own and turn to put VanLeer behind me. I look Mr. Halsey in the eye and whisper, "Can you keep six?"

He bobs his head in a big slow *yes*. He spins back toward VanLeer and shoots his invisible basketball. He claps a hand on VanLeer's shoulder and tells him, "Man, have I got a new game for you."

"No, no. Thanks. I'm all set today." VanLeer is ready with his excuse. "I'm going to move along here and sit in on Perry's visit with his mo—"

"Naw, naw! You beat me solid last time. A gentleman lets

his opponent try again." Mr. Halsey jabs his pointer finger at the floor. "That's sportsmanship. That is how it is done, *sir*!" Mr. Halsey hooks VanLeer with one arm and reaches back to ruffle my hair with the other. Then he takes him away.

I miss Mr. Halsey. We are supposed to play that game in the yard before the weather turns cold. Before he gets gated out. "Two real dudes with a real ball," he has said. "You and me." But there has been no time for the game. No time to sit still for Miss Gina and her scissors. Most of all, I miss Big Ed—especially our Monday night suppers. I look around the common. I want to come back home to *stay*. But I have a strange feeling about Blue River now. It feels like something less than home. I don't know how that happened.

Mom eyes me as I walk up to her. I realize that I'm the one who forgets to launch for the swing-around. Or maybe it is both of us.

"Perry." She bends to speak to me. "What's up?" We have an awkward hug. "Is he being difficult?" She stands straight and sets her hands on her hips in a make-my-day sort of way. "Do I need to have words with Mr. VanLeer?"

"No." I shake my head. I have got to get the lump out of my throat.

My mom, the Blue River U-Hauler, pulls our chairs close together. "What's the matter, Perry?"

I hold up my notebook and wag it at her. "Your story," I say.

"Okay . . ." Mom nods slowly. I feel heat in my cheeks. "Will you let me read what you wrote?"

I hand over the notebook, and she bows her head to read. This takes minutes that feel like hours. I sit and bump the toes of my sneakers together. She finishes and tells me, "Nice job."

I ask her, "Did I get anything wrong?"

"You might be missing a comma or two." She smiles. "But the story is right."

"It doesn't seem right," I say. "I get the part about the death. I know that was your father."

"Yes."

"But you also said that you told lies. And I can't find a place in all my notes or videos where you say what the lies were."

"Right."

"Right? Mom! That's so bad! It's . . . it's like you tricked me!"

"I can see why you say that." Her eyes pool up. "But really, I didn't. Everything I told you is true."

"But there is more. Isn't there?" I say. Mom gives me a sorry look, and I know I'm right. "Is this one of those times when I have to respect your Blue River privacy?" I'm afraid she will say yes. My knees begin to jiggle. A lot. Mom reaches and puts her hands on them, holds them steady.

"Not entirely," she says.

"Okay. Then I'm asking. What were the lies?"

"I will tell you that." Mom draws a breath. "I lied to the police and the court." I watch her swallow. "The truth is, I was *not* driving the car. And I had *not* been drinking."

"But Mom! That was your whole confession!"

"Yes, it was," she says, and she doesn't even blink.

chapter forty-nine

JESSICA

Poor Perry. He looked like a fish hanging in midair after a daring leap from the pond. Or maybe it was she who'd turned his pond upside down and spilled it. Either way, Jessica wanted to surround him with water again, give him back everything she could that was familiar. But he'd asked that question, and she'd given him the answer. He caught his breath and asked another.

"Who was driving?"

For this, Jessica would do no more than shake her head. Sweat dampened the folds of her chambray shirt, and she began to peel a curl of skin from her own thumb.

"Were they drunk? Was anybody drunk?" He wanted his answers.

"Perry, this is the part I won't tell you."

"You *can't* do that," Perry said. He was on his feet—angry and maybe even panicky.

"I can do it, Perry. I'm a mom, and this is one of the things moms do. I've told you as much as I can."

"No. No! You're using that voice you use when you have to tell someone that they can't have something they want. Like when you tell a rez that a rule is a rule and there is no discussion." She watched him take two hurried breaths. "It's that eraser voice. You can't do that—not when it's us!"

This was a seldom seen version of her boy: offended and cutting free from his Blue River upbringing by way of this outburst. It was probably as good as it was awful, Jessica thought. If Thomas VanLeer continued to stand in the way of her release, she needed her boy to have some fight in him. But it broke her heart to see Perry's beautiful face wincing in confusion. When he cooled, would he remember that she loved him more than anything in this whole world? She swallowed, and it hurt like a throat full of toothpicks and bird feathers.

"I would never erase us, Perry," she said. "But you are right. There is no discussion. I confessed—years ago. I had my reasons. There is no point in looking back."

chapter fifty

WHAT THE
MEADOWLARK SAYS

On the way home from Blue River I press my forehead on the window and stare out at the grassy flats. The hug my mom pressed into me is still here like a strap around my chest and shoulders. I didn't want it. I struggled with her. But I think she put it there on purpose. Does she know that I feel like I'm *gone*—like I'm not made of whatever Perry Cook was made of before?

Up front, Mr. VanLeer listens to a radio show where adults tell political jokes. He laughs with the voices. I keep watching the fields.

A new thought climbs right up on top of me and sinks its claws in. For the first time in my life, I think that Mom should *not* be in the Blue River Co-ed Correctional Facility. I don't think she committed a crime—or at least not the one she's in for—not manslaughter.

But if Mom shouldn't be there, where should she be? Where should I be?

How can I not look back when the truth could change history?

Out the window I see the yellow chest and black bib of a western meadowlark perched on the fence post. His long beak is open—probably singing. My head makes up the words:

We were just kidding you, Perry! Just kidding that your mom is a convict! We were just kidding about your whole life!

That. That's what feels so bad. My eyes burn. The fields begin to blur into stripes and patches. Then huge sobs come up. I keep them silent, force them back, and it makes my jaw ache. I slide down into my jacket until only my eyes stick out of my collar. I do not want Mr. VanLeer to hear me choking. I have to get it together before we get back to Rising City.

When we pull up, we meet Zoey's mom at the open mouth of the VanLeer garage. She puts up her hands as if to say stop. She has four chairs lined up on the concrete floor. There are curled sheets of used sandpaper everywhere.

When I slide out of the SUV, I think my legs might not catch me, but they do. Mr. VanLeer kisses Zoey's mom. They stand shoulder to shoulder while she asks me about my visit. "How's Jessica—how's your mom today?"

"She's okay," I say. I can't really look her in the eye.

"I tried to join Perry while he was with his mom today,"

VanLeer says. "It would be nice to get to know her better." He sighs loudly. "But I was invited into a card game instead." I feel his stare, but that's small potatoes to me today.

"What are you sanding?" Dumb. It's so obvious, but Zoey's mom answers me anyway.

"Random chairs," she says. She and Mr. VanLeer laugh. "I hope they will look less random when I paint them all the same color. I'm thinking duck-egg blue."

"I like to sand," I say.

"Yeah? For real?"

I nod. "I used to spend Saturday mornings in the wood shop with Big Ed."

"Well, pull up a chair—ha-ha—and be my guest!" She laughs, and I wish I could laugh back.

Sanding is the perfect thing to do with the rest of this day. I stay hidden under a dust mask. I let my ears fill with the sound of the swishing and scuffing of the sandpaper. I sand and sand because a chair has lots of parts. I rub all the paint layers away down to the wood below. It's like Mom's story, I think. It's like all the Blue River Stories, the way you dig backward to find the beginning.

"Wow!" Zoey's mom startles me. "That looks ready for some primer and a new coat of paint. How about a break, Perry? Aren't you hungry?"

I stand back from the chair. "Not so much," I say. My stomach is quivery like the rest of me. "Can I start another chair?"

"Are you all right, Perry?"

"Yeah."

"Okay. Start another one, if you really want to. I'm going to wash up and make you a sandwich. Just a half. Sound good?"

"Sure," I say. I guess I will have to try to eat that.

Zoey's mom pauses in the garage. "Perry, if there is anything I can do to help you, you will ask, won't you? It's okay to ask for help."

I nod. But there is nothing she can do. While I work on the next chair I think about that. I want help for Mom. I need someone to look at her story—really look. I only know of one person who might be able to do that.

Thing is, all he's ever done for Mom so far is make a lot of trouble.

chapter fifty-one

A QUESTION
FOR VANLEER

All day Sunday, I just want to get back to Mom. It's hard to know what I know about her confession. The rezzes at Blue River talk about rising up, they also talk about reconciling with themselves. Mom has done that. But I haven't. I hate the badness between us. I know that I was yelling at her. Now I have to wait for Tuesday when the Bucking Blue Bookmobile will take me back to Blue River before we can talk again.

On Sunday night there is trouble in the VanLeer house. Zoey Samuels has a toothache. She makes it almost through supper, but then she is moaning. "Something's wrong," she says, and her jaw hangs. She leaves the table and goes to sit on the family room couch. She calls, "Mom, it really hurts. It's throbbing."

"Ugh. I'm so sorry," her mom says. "We'll get you through the night, and I'll call the dentist first thing in the morning." Zoey's mom gives her two pills and water to wash them down. Then she gives her a wet tea bag to bite on. I run down the hall to her bedroom and bring the pillow from her bed.

Mr. VanLeer sits beside Zoey. He's doing some stupid Stepdad Tom stuff. He's flapping his tie at Zoey and talking like a cartoon character. She squirms away from him and buries her face in the pillows.

"Are you kidding me?" The muffled version of Zoey groans. "This tooth is killing, and you're bugging me." She reaches one arm backward to swat him away.

"Oh dear," he says. "Robyn, this really isn't good." Mr. VanLeer strokes Zoey's arm. He tells her he's sorry.

"I just want to go to bed," Zoey says. She cups her face in her hand. "I want to sleep. Mom, what if I can't sleep?"

"Then you'll rest. Come on, let's see if we can get you comfortable . . ." They head down the hall together toward Zoey's room.

That leaves me with Thomas VanLeer.

"What do you say we tackle the dishes?" he asks. So we do that. I clear. He rinses and loads the VanLeer dishwasher. I take the damp cloth and wipe down the table. When I turn around I see that Mr. VanLeer has been watching me.

"You've been rather pensive today," he tells me. "Do you know what I mean by that?"

"Yeah. You mean you see me thinking about stuff."

"Exactly."

"There's a lot to think about."

"Perry, that sounds so heavy. You—you're young! You shouldn't have any worries. Why don't you tell me what's on your mind? Maybe I can worry about it instead." He faces me and waits.

"Well, for one thing, I've been thinking about what you said—that you'd help me any way you can." VanLeer looks back at me blankly. "You said it when you were interviewed on *Counting on Butler County* with Desiree Riggs."

"Oh. Right." He blinks. He rolls his shoulders like he's got a bug on his back. "And I will," he says.

"You know I'm writing stories for my assignment, right?"

"Yes, you're interviewing the prison . . . er . . . residents."

I hesitate. "I think there is something wrong with one of the stories."

"Well, why is that? Do you mean that you think you've uncovered something?" He leans at me, and I think he wants to hear something sinister. "Which story, Perry? Whose story?"

"My mom's," I tell him. He moves as if I have pushed a button on him—the squirm button.

"Perry, I know that you want to believe that your mom is innocent. That's perfectly natural. And I wish it were so. But it's not. Now, you know why she's incarcerated, don't you?"

"I know the charge was manslaughter."

"Exactly. I know that must be hard. I wish you never had

to know anything about her crime."

"Well, it used to be that I didn't need to know. But now it's keeping us apart. I need to find out everything I can. So, I know you have a lot of files in your office . . ." It's almost impossible to say the next thing. But I have got to do this. "I wondered if you can get my mom's file."

"I have her case file already, Perry."

"You what?" I am about to fall like a post.

He begins to explain. "See, it's my job to review her file before her parole date, and make a recommendation to the parole board. That's what I was doing when I uncovered your situation. You being raised at that prison."

I narrow my eyes. "But I thought . . . and Zoey thought . . . that you started looking after you heard that I lived there."

"I had asked for many files, Perry. Your mother's was one of them. I was pointed to it by what Zoey said."

"Well, if you want to know, living at Blue River was fine with me."

He smiles a little. "Well, it might have seemed fine, but it wasn't right," he says. "I wouldn't try to make you understand that, Perry, because that's the stuff we grown-ups have to sort out."

"Are you still looking at it? At her case or file or whatever?"

"I am."

"You'll do it in time for her parole hearing?"

"Your mom doesn't have a date," he says. "Her application

for parole is pending. That means it hasn't been accepted, Perry."

I'm staring at him, and he's staring at me. Then I know. *This* is why Mom was so low just before I left Blue River. It wasn't just that VanLeer was taking me out of there. This is why she never carries her New Start folder with her anymore. Mom knows she isn't getting out so soon. She didn't want to tell me. My insides begin to shake. I look around the spaces inside the VanLeer kitchen. How long, then? How long will I be here? How long away from Mom?

"You . . . ," I say to VanLeer, "you handed her a down letter. Didn't you?" I close my eyes for a second, but it makes me dizzy.

"I'm familiar with the term. It's what they say on the inside. But that's used more when it comes from the parole board at a hearing." VanLeer speaks slowly and evenly. "This—what I've done—is a request for formal postponement of the parole hearing to allow time for an investigation. So a little different."

"But it means she stays. She serves more time," I say. I've seen it happen to other residents. Not often.

"It's a postponement." He says it again. His tone is cool and easy.

I want to run from his house. But I make myself stay, and I ask him, "When does her parole hearing get put back on the timeline?" I can hardly pull in a breath. I'm trying to hide it from VanLeer.

"That hasn't been decided," he says. His eyes shift away from me now. "I have to get through her case. It's complicated by many factors, Perry."

"But it's all because I was living at Blue River, isn't it? That's the part you care about. You got the warden suspended too, didn't you?"

"Perry, it wouldn't be right for me to tell you more. The adults are taking care of it," he says. He steps toward me. I step back. "I promise," he says, "my goal is to help you."

chapter fifty-two

BRIAN

Zoey Samuels was up half the night with her aching tooth. I know because I was up too—boiling mad at Mr. Thomas VanLeer, and letting all the bad news chew a hole in me.

I wake up tired in the morning. I lie on the mat in the VanLeer closet and look at my timeline. Am I going to have to add to that, make it go all the way around these walls? I roll over and press my face into the pillow until my nose feels flat. I scream into it. Then I growl. *I cannot stand you, Thomas VanLeer!*

Zoey's mom is letting her sleep late this morning. They're going to the dentist later today. I tiptoe past her door and make a get-well wish for that tooth.

I walk into school alone. I look at my feet or at nothing way up ahead of me.

"Hey, Cook!" Brian Morris aims at me with both pointer

fingers. His friends look on. "The one-mile run. Coming up soon. Prepare to be crushed!" he says. "For the second year in a row."

I've got nothing to say to him. I haven't been thinking about the run. I haven't even been running. I stumble forward on tired feet. The boys laugh then scatter.

Then I see Miss Maya in the lobby coming to check in with me. She does it almost every day. I tell her about Zoey's tooth. "Oh, misery! Tell her I hope she feels better soon," she says. Then she asks me, "How're you doing with your Coming to Butler County project, Perry? I tried to make it all the way around the room on Friday. But I missed checking in with you and Zoey."

Miss Maya's question makes me drop my head. "Good," I say, and I manage to nod while I look at the toes of my shoes. "The stories can be hard. You know."

"I can imagine that it's very emotional." She is exactly right. I don't want to talk about the stuff I found out about Mom's story. It feels too private. Maybe not for Miss Maya, but for the school lobby.

"I've got the stories written out," I say. "I guess that's fine. But I have some video I took, and I keep wishing I could use that too . . ."

"Oh, sure," Miss Maya says. "That would be neat! Videography, right? You still have time. I don't know how to help you with that myself, Perry, but did you know there is a group of kids that meets at the library? They have a video club."

"Yeah, I know. I went to use the room once. But I don't know . . ."

"Go again! See what they're up to. Ask questions. Or look at the computer program on your own. There! That's your assignment for the day," she says with a grin. "Go check that out." She looks at the clock, gives me a nod, and heads off to her classroom.

I spend the morning trying to take extra-good class notes to share with Zoey when I see her tonight. I wonder about her tooth, and I miss her something awful, especially when lunchtime comes. I'm one of the last kids through the line.

"It's Perry!" Miss Jenrik says. She swipes my card with a jingle and a smile. She taps in my special code. I wonder if she will say anything about seeing me at Blue River. "No Zoey today?" she asks. She pushes her lips sideways to blow her feathery earring back from her cheek. I tell her about Zoey's tooth. "O-o-oh! Ow!" Miss Jenrik cringes. I think she's one of those people who cannot talk about tooth pains, the way some people cannot talk about spiders or snakes.

I take my tray past Brian Morris and his friends to get to my nook at the end of the table. It's weird not to have Zoey across from me. I look at the spaghetti, the breadstick, and the zucchini slices on my tray. I look at Zoey's empty spot while I eat.

It's not long before a balled-up napkin flies my way. I sit back and ignore the first one, but the second one lands on my tray. I look at the boys. I look hard.

"Where's your girlfriend?" one of them asks.

"It's not his girlfriend," another says. "She's his *sister* now. He got adopted."

"No I didn't!" I sit up and spin to face them. "I'm not adopted! I have a mom!"

"Well then, why did you move into Mad-Zoe's house?" The kid curls his fingers into claws. Brian Morris is being quiet. I wonder what's up with him.

"She's not Mad-Zoe," I say. "She's pretty calm now, in case you haven't noticed." Funny thing is, *I* don't feel calm and I think my voice sounds snarly. I look at my lunch tray. I don't want the food anymore. The napkin balls have spaghetti sauce on them—from someone else's spaghetti. That's a gross-out thing for me. Besides, I can't believe they said I was adopted—and they mean by VanLeer! I want a pillow to scream into.

Miss Jenrik's heavy boots come stepping over the bench across from me. *Clunk-clunk.* She jingles her way into Zoey's place. "Okay if I take my break here with you?" She tilts her pink head at me.

"Sure," I say.

She smiles at me while she shakes up a milk carton in one hand. She strips the paper off a straw. She looks at Brian and his friends. "Hi, guys. What's up? How's that *pee-sketty*?" she asks, and she points to the pasta on their trays.

"Good," one boy says, and he ducks his head a little.

"Yeah? Because it doesn't look that good." She points her shiny black fingernail at the napkin balls beside me and wrinkles her nose. Then she grins and the boys start to laugh. "Hey, Perry, do you need your spoon?"

"No," I say. I hand it to her. She uses the spoon to push the napkin balls back to the boys.

"Garbage," she says. "You guys are being a little bit yucky, aren't you?"

Brian Morris shrugs and snorts a little. "Yeah," he says. His face is red.

"Yeah," says Miss Jenrik. "You could probably cut that out." She sips milk up her straw, looks right at me. Then she says, "Hey, Perry, sorry I didn't get a chance to talk to you the other day at Blue River. The time runs short on visiting day, doesn't it?"

I feel frozen because of privacy—hers, not mine. Brian and his friends already know my mom is a resident. Miss Jenrik is looking at me. She has no fear.

"Will you be there next Saturday? I'll introduce you to my dad."

"Your dad? Mr. Wendell?" I whisper it.

She smiles. "Mr. Wendell Jenrik." She points to her name pin. She even turns just a little so the boys will see. "That's my pop." She says it plain and takes another sip of milk. "I miss him like the dickens."

I give her a small smile. I still won't be able to eat my lunch, and it's not like I'm happy that Mr. Wendell Jenrik is incarcerated. But I'm sitting across from a real friend. That's an unexpected win.

After school I walk to the library on my own. I start off in the History Room, but I only stay a few minutes. It's lonely without Zoey. I get it into my head that I will take another look at the video-editing program like Miss Maya suggested. It's not a Video Boot Camp day. So maybe, just maybe, one little thing could go right and I'll find that Brian and his friends are doing something else today.

The door is open so I step inside. I look over at the computer Zoey and I used a few days ago. I am staring at the back of Brian Morris's big head. Of course, he got in here first. I begin to turn away. But then I stop. On the screen in front of Brian, I see Big Ed. It's a still shot that zooms slowly inward for several seconds then stops. Brian Morris taps the track pad. He hits an arrow and the shot of Big Ed slowly zooms again, this time, while soft music plays.

"Hey!" I slice the quiet. "What are you doing?"

"Nothing!" Brian is up out of the chair. His cheeks turn red.

"Doesn't look like nothing. That's my file!" I'm loud. Brian glances out toward the library's main floor, looking nervous and guilty. There must be rules about privacy and messing with other people's uploads, and I bet Brian knows that.

"Okay, *not* nothing," he says. He tries to keep his voice low. "I—I was just doing some editing to show—"

"Show what? Show your napkin-thrower friends? Spread it around for no good purpose?" A speck of spit flies off my tongue.

"No, to show *you* how to—"

"Where did you get that photo anyway?"

"I extracted it from your video as a still. I put music with it but you could record your voice to tell the story." He's talking fast—too fast—like he's exploding with information.

"No!" I say. I must be crazy to have listened to him this long. Zoey was right about Brian Morris. I don't trust him. "Delete it," I tell him. "In fact, never mind. I'll do it myself!" I barge into his place at the computer. My fingers jitter along the track pad. "Idiot," I mutter as I click Big Ed away. I mean me; I'm the idiot for somehow leaving the videos on the computer. I don't know what Brian thinks. I don't care.

The computer shows me a box asking if I'm sure I want to delete the file permanently. I click Yes. I haul myself up and head for the door. I hear Brian Morris calling after me.

"Y-you could sign out the laptop and teach yourself the program. It's easy . . ."

I'm trying to get away from him. The strap of my backpack catches and drags me backward. I yank it. I take out a chair and have to stop to pick it up. Every person from every table in the library turns to look at stupid, stupid Perry Cook.

chapter fifty-three

A CHANCE MEETING

My heart is still pounding when I reach the circulation desk. Mr. Olsen is on duty. I have special permission today to walk over to Mr. VanLeer's office and wait there for a ride back to the house.

"Will you please sign me out?" I say.

"Leaving rather early, aren't you?" Mr. Olsen does his signature finger pointing—curl, release—at the clock. I can't believe it either—I'm choosing to go to Mr. VanLeer's office well before I have to.

"A little," I mumble. Thirty-two minutes is more than a little, but I won't point that out to Mr. Olsen.

"I guess there is no harm . . . as long as you go directly." He signs me out.

I cross the brick street at the corner and head for the building across from the courthouse—the one with the varnished door. I grip the brass handle and stand looking at the shining, honey-colored wood. I remember how I took the photo of this door because I knew Mom would like it, and she did. I think of her New Start folder again. Has she looked at that at all? Does she still keep her eye on the rental house on Button Lane? I don't think so—not after what VanLeer has done.

I puff an angry breath out over my lips and squeeze the brass handle. I shouldn't have come so early. The last thing I want to do is sit in his office with him. I decide to go in and sit on the stairs and read for a while.

I'm about to pull the door open when something makes me stop. It's a feeling—like the pull of a magnet through the air. I step back from the door. I turn my head and look at a spot several buildings down the street. I see my magnet.

"Warden? Warden Daugherty!"

Time seems to slow down as she looks up from her purse, which is dangling on her arm, rocking like a cradle. Her eyelids are lowered, but they slowly rise. Her head slowly turns. My heart spreads out under my ribs like a huge warm hand.

The warden's shoulders drop away from her ears. She straightens up tall. I watch her lips form my name. "Perry!"

We're in real time again. I run to meet her.

There is so much to say, and I go saying it all—fast as I can. Ever since I moved out of Blue River, I have had the feeling that the warden isn't supposed to see me. No one has said so. But here on the street I feel as if a hook will swing out of the sky, catch me by the shirt, and pull me away from her. That doesn't happen. We talk and talk. Warden Daugherty wants to know all about how I am. So I tell her.

When I get to the part about writing the Blue River Stories, she turns her face upward and takes a big breath. "Wonderful! So important, Perry."

"I wish I'd gotten your story too, Warden. You're so much my Blue River family . . ." It gets hard to speak.

"And you are mine," she says.

"I'm sorry about everything. I-I heard that you are suspended."

"Oh . . ." She seems surprised that I know. "Yes, but that's . . . well . . . it's okay," she says. "I've left your buddy Fo-Joe in charge, and I'm comfortable with that."

"But if you hadn't let me stay at Blue River . . ."

"I have no regrets, Perry." She says it soundly.

"Miss Maya told me you'd feel that way," I say. "Do you think you'll get to go back? Will you get to be the warden again?"

"Well, it could happen. But while things are being decided about me, I'm also deciding about things." She smiles. "I'm going to be just fine, come what may."

"Do you think my mom will be all right?"

"She will be." The warden's eyes narrow a little. She nods. "Your mom is a strong woman."

"You know what VanLeer did, right? He got her hearing postponed." I nearly choke on the words.

"Yes," she says, her mouth in a line now. She raises her

index finger. "He can drag out his investigation while he tries to make his case. But he can't postpone forever, Perry. That's against the law. You take comfort in that."

I do, because it's the first piece of good news I have had in days. I am dying to ask the warden how soon she thinks it could happen. When could we get it put back on the timeline? I almost tell her what else I know—that Mom's confession was a lie. We should have never been at Blue River at all. Then I wonder if the warden knows that too. All my life Warden Daugherty has known everything—everything in the whole world.

"I shouldn't keep you, Perry. I've got my errands . . . and I suspect you are supposed to be somewhere yourself." She looks past me, down the street toward the varnished door.

"Warden Daugherty . . ." I know she has to go, so I ask quickly. "When Mom does get that parole hearing, will you be there? Will you be allowed?"

She raises her eyebrow at me. "Let them try and stop me."

"Yes!" I say. She will speak in Mom's favor. We need that hearing.

The warden opens her arms, and we hug. "What luck, running into you today, Perry. I have missed you so much!" She steps back and looks me over.

"I still have your suitcase," I say.

"I don't need it back. It's your suitcase now."

I thank the warden in every which way I can right there

on the street, and I figure she knows it isn't just because she gave me a suitcase.

When she turns to go away I notice something. She moves slowly—a lot less like the wind-up toy on wheels, less like the warden that I've known all my life.

chapter fifty-four

ALONE IN THE
OFFICE OF VANLEER

After my surprise meeting with the warden, I go back up
the street to VanLeer's office and let myself in through
the varnished door. I'm not so early anymore. But my plan
is the same; I'm going to sit on the stairs and read until five
o'clock.

But when I look up the stairway, someone happens to be
looking down. She's the receptionist who sits at a desk in the
open space on the landing.

"Oh!" she says. "You're the boy from the . . . the boy
that . . . you're staying with the VanLeer family." She shakes
her head as if she has webs in her brain. "It's Perry, isn't it?"

I nod. I force myself to smile. At least she doesn't think
I've been adopted.

"Come on up," she says with a big sweep of her hand.

So I climb. With each step I am thinking, *darn, yuck, darn, yuck.* I'm going to be stuck hanging out with Mr. Van-Leer after all. I'm not sure I can stand it.

"You're early," the receptionist says. "Mr. VanLeer is still over at the courthouse. I don't expect him back for another twenty minutes . . ."

Good! I almost say it out loud.

"Hmm . . ." She checks her desk clock. "Four forty p.m. Mr. VanLeer told me to have you wait in his office if you arrived before he did. I don't think he expected you this early," she says, "but let's just stick with the plan." She motions. I follow her down the hall. "Sorry to say it, Mr. VanLeer is late returning from court more often than he's early." I don't tell her that it's fine with me.

The door is open. Mr. VanLeer's rolling chair is pushed back from the desk. I think about taking a running jump at it. I could ride it across the floor like I used to do with the warden's chair at Blue River. But the receptionist is watching, and I'd only make it a few feet before I'd crash into VanLeer's bookcase. Besides, I'm not sure I'm still Perry Cook who rides on chairs.

"I'll clear you a little space at the table." The reception-ist begins to push the stacks of boxes to the left. She gives a little grunt as she sets one up on another. "Whew!" She takes a breath. "Paper is heavy! Now, I bet you need a snack."

"Thanks," I say. "But I had a granola bar at the library." The granola bar makes me think of Zoey and her bad tooth.

There must be news about that by now. I hope she feels better. I hope she can eat. If only she'd been with me, she could have met the warden.

"Well, I'll be down the hall at my desk if you need anything." The receptionist gives me a little wave as she leaves.

I am alone in Mr. VanLeer's office.

I set my backpack down and pull a chair up to the long table. My eyes go straight to the boxes—first one and then another. They are all lined up with the ends facing out and each end has a label on it. They are like shoe boxes on a store shelf, only bigger. Inside of every one is somebody's story. Inside one is the story of my mom. I pull my bottom lip inside my teeth and bite it.

I look at the labels. Some are typed. Some are written by hand. But all have three lines on them: a case number, a name, and a date. Right in front of me, I see case number 1242-89. The name is HAYES, M. The date is 6-21-98. On top of HAYES I see PENDERS, then BROWN. I begin to scan every box on the table for the letter *C* for COOK. My heart jumps when I see COO. But the rest is PER for COOPER.

Where is COOK, I wonder? I stand at the table and do a slow full turn around the office. I see shelves and books and the documents on the wall—Mr. VanLeer's favorite, the Spark Award. He said he had Mom's file in his office. It has to be here . . . unless he lied. I go over to his desk. There are lots of papers there, but nothing that says COOK, and no box on the floor nearby, which is where it seems to me a box he's working from would be.

Liar, I think. He doesn't have it. He's not helping.

I give up and go back to the long table to start my homework. That's when I see more boxes. Lots of them. They're stacked on the floor underneath the left end of the table. There are three rows, stacked three high, and they are double deep, so eighteen in all.

I glance over my shoulder at the open door and wonder if VanLeer could be on his way. I feel like it hasn't been that long yet.

He's late more often than he's early.

That's what the receptionist said, and she must know. The office clock says 4:46. I read the labels in the front row. I find HOLMES, GOLDMAN, TARNOW, and six more names that are not COOK.

I've got to get to that back row. But what if VanLeer comes in? I'm supposed to be doing homework. I spill my whole backpack—books, notebooks, camera, pencils, a few crumbs, and a granola bar wrapper—onto the table in the space the receptionist made for me. I flip my notebook open. I toss my pencil to the floor. If VanLeer catches me moving boxes, I can say I was looking for the pencil. My heart pounds. I'm not used to lying.

I squat down to the floor and move the first stack of boxes. They're hefty, but they slide on the carpet. On my hands and knees I tilt my head to read the back row. ANGEL, JAMISON, MARTIN.

I slide the boxes back and pull the next row out. I'm looking at the first few letters only now. I see RO, TER, DUT. Still no COOK. *Darn!* I steal a peek at the clock; it's 4:50. *Move it, Perry! Move it!* Last row of boxes—last chance. I tuck myself below the table. KU, SO, SK.

No COOK.

My heart slides down to my gut. I shove the stack back into place and plunk down hard in the chair. I'm hot inside my fleece—and I'm mad. I thump my fist on the table. *Liar!* Somebody should know what a liar VanLeer is. Who is the boss of him, anyway? I kick my feet out. My toe strikes something that feels like another box. Did I really miss the one box that was closest to me all this time? Could it be . . .

I take a breath and think, Oh, please, please . . .

I slide down low in my chair. I lean sideways and look into the dark corner below the table. I squint and read: LAWSON. "A-a-ack!" I shove the box hard with my foot. I feel it jam up against something else, something behind it. I stretch my leg way under the corner of the table. I hook the LAWSON box with the toe of my sneaker. I push it to the side the tiniest bit.

I can see one last box. The last box in the whole world, I think. I swallow. I bump LAWSON again. On the last box, I see a *C* . . . and then an *O*. I suck a breath. I feel the dry air in the office rimming my wide-open eyeballs. I knock the box another inch and see another *O* . . . then *K*! Then I see the letter *J*—just like *Jessica*.

My forehead gets an amazing smack on the edge of that table when I dive down to the floor. I blink and shove the LAWSON box out of my way. I put both my hands on the one that says COOK, J. I feel like I'm touching dynamite.

The lid is free—a piece of plastic tape has been snapped. VanLeer wasn't lying! He has looked in this box. But then I wonder, when? How long ago? Probably back when he got me yanked out of Blue River. I squeeze my eyes shut and open them again. I can't stop to think about it now. I'm in the race of my life.

I poke my head out to check the clock. It's 4:52.

I pull the lid off the box and stare down at a stack of papers in the bottom. It seems like not that much—not when it's about someone's whole life. These papers, I think, are older than I am. But it's way too much to read in eight minutes—if I even have eight minutes—*and* I know the papers are full of giant words. This is the stuff the residents try to learn about in the law library at Blue River.

I jiggle the collar of my fleece to fan my sweaty neck. I have to do something before VanLeer comes back from the courthouse. *Think fast.*

I reach up to the table and grab my camera.

chapter fifty-five

FLIPPING AND SHOOTING

How can I hide below this table and shoot a whole bunch of photos? I can't. It's dark, and I will smack my head again. I need space and light. I use both arms to plow the mess from my backpack out of the way. I grab up the whole stack of papers from the box—about as thick as a skinny paperback—and set it on the table. I have the light from the window *and*—I can't believe I didn't remember this before— this window looks right down to the street! I can *see* the courthouse! I can watch for VanLeer.

"Yes! A win!"

I hover the camera over the first page. My hands are shaking. "Steady, steady," I whisper to myself. I put as much of the page in the viewer as I can and let the camera autofocus. I see mostly clean edges on the letters, and I take the shot.

I flip pages quickly, but I keep the stack neat. I see Mom's name, but I don't stop to read. I get a rhythm going. Shoot, flip. Shoot, flip. Look out the window, check the courthouse. Then shoot and flip two more.

It seems to take forever, but I make it to about halfway through and still no VanLeer. What if I missed him? What if he's through the varnished door and on his way up the stairs? No. Can't be. I've kept watch. I know I have.

He's late more often than he's early. The receptionist said so. I breathe and keep shooting. Six more pages. Ten more. I look out the window—there he is. He's on the courthouse steps. He is talking to a man and a woman. VanLeer loves to talk. I have wicked jitters, but I shoot two more pages—not just lines of type and big words this time. One is a photo of two roads crossing. The other is a sketch. No time to study them, I flip to the next.

I look outside again. VanLeer is stepping off the curb at the crosswalk. Two final clicks, and I make myself put the camera down. I gather the papers together and square them up. I set them back into the box. I pop the lid on top and slide the box deep into the corner behind LAWSON. I leave it like I found it. I look out the window again. I can't see VanLeer. He has to be down below. I imagine his hand on the brass door handle.

The seconds grind by. My heart thuds bass drum beats inside my body. I should sit down and pretend to work. But I can't. It's just a feeling, but I have to put myself far away from the box. I stash my camera in my backpack, leave everything else on the table. I cross the room and stand in front of the wall where VanLeer's Spark Award hangs. I stare at it. That's where I am when he comes through the frosted door.

"Hey, Perry," he says. He almost bumps into me. He sounds glad to see me. I feel a wash of guilt. "Have you been waiting long?"

"Not too long." My voice is jaggedy. I'm not sure he notices.

Mr. VanLeer smiles at me. "What are you looking at?" he says. He glances at the wall. "Oh, my Spark Award?" He's smiling about it as he sets his briefcase down and snaps it open. He shuffles some papers out and other papers in. He brings work home every night. He does work a lot. But that doesn't mean that he works on Mom's file. Who knows how long it's been sitting in that corner? I narrow my eyes. I wish there was a way to know . . . a hidden camera . . . a fly on the wall . . . a spy in the office of VanLeer . . .

I go back to the long table, stack my books and papers, and slide everything into my backpack. I stick my hand deep inside to make sure my camera is there. All the while I know that the toes of my sneakers are just a few feet away from the box that says COOK, J.

I shoulder the pack and cross the room again. I stop to look at the award on the wall one last time. Mr. VanLeer joins me. He sighs and says, "I see that award every day, and it reminds me what I'm aiming for, everything I have planned. It reminds me to dream," he says. "But of course, you can't just dream, you have to act. You have to practice and prepare. There were four years of college, then three more intense years in law school, then two years interning, and my year as the assistant in . . ."

My head is doing the math while VanLeer talks. I'm adding up his years.

". . . there's no denying, I've put in my time." He finally stops.

"But . . . that's . . . almost the same." The words fall from my mouth into the quiet office air.

"The same?" He looks down his shoulder at me.

I hesitate, then say it. "You've been working at your career just as long as my mom has been in Blue River." I look up at VanLeer. "It sounds like you're about the same age."

His eyelids flutter. "Well . . . perhaps. But our lives aren't at all the same."

"But they could have been. Maybe." I shrug, not sure that I'm right about that. "My mom earned a degree, and she gets the highest prison pay there is for her work. She saves and makes plans," I say. "And she dreams." I think about the New Start folder. "She wants a job on the outside and a membership at the YMCA. She wants to teach me to swim."

We stand in the quiet of the office for a few seconds. Then VanLeer begins to stammer. "Well, she made . . . well . . . you know she could be d-doing—"

"I know what you think," I say.

VanLeer scrunches his brow at me. "What's that?"

"You think that you're a lot different than my mom." I turn to lead us out the door. "And maybe you are."

Mr. VanLeer comes up behind me and puts his hand on the back of my neck to usher me along. I'm sure he's about to tell me he knows how tough everything has been for me and that he's here to help. Instead he says, "You feel . . . you're very warm, Perry." He tucks his cool fingers into my collar and it makes my shoulders pinch up. "And you're sweaty too," he adds. "Are you feeling okay?"

"I'm fine."

He starts to close the door behind us then stops. "Oh, almost forgot," he says. "It's Monday. The cleaning crew comes in tonight." He pushes the door back open, and we walk along the hall, past the receptionist. She's on her phone, but she waves.

Down on the street I toss my backpack into the car and climb in to sit in the seat behind Mr. VanLeer. He settles in and draws his seat belt out. I hear it click. He starts the car up and tunes the radio.

Then an idea lands in my brain. It's like a dart coming out of nowhere. Maybe there is a way to know—

"Wait! Mr. VanLeer! I think I need to use the bathroom," I say. "Like, right now. Can I run back upstairs?" I have the car door open and one foot on the pavement.

"Oh, of course, Perry! Go ahead."

"I'll be just a minute," I promise him. I hurry. Inside the

varnished door, I take the stairs two at a time.

The receptionist is still on her phone. I point down the hallway and mouth the word *bathroom* at her. She nods then turns her chair around to pull papers out of her fax machine. I hustle down the hall. At the bathroom door I look back over my shoulder. She's not looking. I slip into VanLeer's open office.

Smooth and easy, I think. I slide LAWSON aside and drag Mom's case box out of the corner and lift the lid. Then I go and stand in front of VanLeer's Spark Award and take a huge breath. Will this work? I'm not sure . . . but *something* will happen because of this. I have to do it.

I reach up with both hands, close my fingers around the frame, and lift the award off the hook. I carry it to Mom's box and lay it inside, right on top of the papers—it just fits. I cover the box and slide it back into the corner. I push LAW-SON into place.

At the door I feel dizzy. I puff two breaths then peek out into the hall. All clear. I slip into the bathroom, flush a toilet, and wash my hands with the squirty soap. Then I swing back out and down the stairs to the car where VanLeer is waiting.

He twists in his seat to look back at me. "Better?" he asks.

"Way better." I buckle up, dry my hands on the legs of my pants. Then I ask him, "Mr. VanLeer, how is Zoey? Have you heard?"

chapter fifty-six

WHERE ONE ROAD
MEETS ANOTHER

It turns out Zoey Samuels has a seriously bad tooth in her head.

"They gave us meds for the pain and said she needs a root canal." Zoey's mom is explaining it to VanLeer. "It'll take two visits."

"Oh my heck!" he says. "Zoey, honey. I'm so sorry."

"I don't care, I don't care. I don't want to think about it. I just want it over with," Zoey says. She slumps on the couch in front of the TV and tunes into Desiree Riggs's Monday evening segment. I think Stepdad Tom is going to play this right and leave her alone. Zoey doesn't want to talk to anyone tonight—not even me.

"And you have to go all the way to Lincoln?" VanLeer asks.

"Well, just outside the city. It's a hike, but she is one of the best oral surgeons for miles. *And* she had an opening for tomorrow."

"Good. That's the most important thing." Mr. VanLeer nods. "So what if I take the day off and go with you? Could we make a day of it? A little getaway . . ."

I am invisible this evening. I don't even have to sneak off—I just go.

I sit on my heels on the mat in the VanLeer closet. The camera screen glows. I look at pages and pages of tiny writing all about Mom's case. The parts I can understand seem to tell the story the way she told it to me. I see where she lied and confessed. But of course, it doesn't look like lying on these papers. It looks like facts. The court believed her. Maybe someone else could find important details in here— someone who knows what to look for, like VanLeer or Mr. Rojas. But I can't.

I advance the screen to the picture of the intersection. It's just a plain *T*. One road meeting another road. I zoom to one street corner and see a diner. There is a red-and-white sign that has a coffee cup on it. I zoom to the other side and pick out a square box of a building with gas pumps out front. It's completely ordinary except for one thing. There is an old truck parked up on the roof. It's the one funny thing about the picture, the one thing that pops out—red and rust against the sky.

I click to the next image. It's the diagram of an intersection.

Someone has scribbled *NE-79 and West Raymond Road.* There is a sketch of the way the accident happened. Vehicle A proceeded into the path of Vehicle B. There is a tiny graphic of a stop sign. A penciled arrow points to it. I flick back to the photo and zoom in to find the stop sign. So what? I think. I close my aching eyeballs and sigh. How can any of this help Mom?

"Perry, suppertime!" Mr. VanLeer hollers in the hall.

I shut down my camera and hurry to the kitchen.

chapter fifty-seven

A CONVERSATION
WITH KRENSKY

On Tuesday afternoon I tell Mrs. Buckmueller about Zoey's root canal.

"Oh dear, oh lordy. Poor thing. We'll miss her terribly on the truck today." Mrs. B leans over a pile of books and uses her hands, arms, and elbows to push them into a stack. When she's done, I pack the stack into a bin and heft it onto the cart.

"It seems sort of awful that a tooth has roots," I say. "When I think of roots I think of carrots. But I don't like the idea of carrots growing in my gums, and I don't like the idea of orange teeth."

This makes Mrs. Buckmueller laugh out loud. We are pushing the cart past the main desk, and Mr. Olsen puts on a serious face and shushes her. "This is a library!" he booms.

Mrs. Buckmueller hoots again as we go out the door. I do feel bad that Zoey isn't with us. Both her mom and Mr. Van-Leer went with her to see the oral surgeon. They said they'd have a "day date" while she gets the work done. They were laughing and sort of lovey about it. I think they both just want to be with Zoey.

It's a colossal win for me that VanLeer won't be in his office today. Time will stretch before he'll see that his award is missing. If he decides to work on Mom's case like he promised, he'll find it. If he asks, I'll have to tell him that I put it in there, and why. If that's a crime, well, I'll tell him I must belong back inside Blue River.

The Bucking Blue Bookmobile motors along, and I let out a tremendous yawn. I rub my eyes with both fists. I was up late last night in the VanLeer closet giving the papers another look. The good news is, the zoom makes everything readable. The bad news is, I need help to understand what it means. The worst news is, I know exactly who I have to go to for help, and I'm dreading it. The good news is, I know where to find him.

I hit the silver button next to the big glass door at Blue River and peer up into the security cam. They are expecting the Bucking Blue Bookmobile this time of day. The door clicks and slides open. Mrs. Buckmueller uses the cart like a walker to give her bionic knee an assist. I guide us slowly. The first person I see is Fo-Joe.

I raise my hand, and he slaps it. "I heard they call you

Temp-Joe now." I want to congratulate him. But I feel so bad about Warden Daugherty.

"Somebody's got to play the part," he says.

Mrs. Buckmueller chimes in. "You're a good man for the job."

"Warden Daugherty said so herself," I say. Then I ask, "Do you know where Mom is today?"

"Yep. She's up in the main meeting room . . . where I am sure she has been moving all the furniture." He rolls his eyes. I grin. He checks the gray clock in the common. "They're scheduled to go until four thirty today. But she knows you're coming. She'll make it down before you leave."

I have another question for him. But one of the forewomen shows up, and they begin flipping through papers on a clipboard. I shuffle my feet. Mrs. Buckmueller is tilting her head at me like she knows something is up. Fo-Joe and the forewoman keep talking. I know I can't interrupt them, and I can't hold up Mrs. B. I sigh and shrug. We rev up and push the cart through the common.

We unpack the book bins. As I finish filling up the magazine rack, she stands close beside me. In a low voice she asks, "Where is it you need to go today, Perry?"

"Oh . . . uh . . . law library," I say. "I need to see Mr. Krensky. Do you know him?"

Mrs. B makes wide eyes and clears her throat. "Um-hmm, um-hmm, I do. Unpleasant as the day is long, that one." Mrs. B starts to hum. She draws the copy of *Money*

Matters magazine off the rack. She collects a short stack of books and winds a rubber band around them, still humming away. Then she reaches into her bag and pulls out a fat marking pen and a notecard. I smell the ink and listen to it squeaking along the card. She writes: KRENSKY—LAW LIBRARY. She tucks the notecard under the rubber band.

"Perry!" she says, and her voice rises into the quiet common. "Be a darling and deliver this up to the law library for me, will you? It's *urgent,*" she says. She thrusts the package at me. Her arm hinges open, like a wing, her sweater sleeve draping. She points up the stairs. She whispers to me, "I'll ask for forgiveness later. You go."

So I do. With the book bundle under one arm, I hoist myself along the candy-red railing, all the way up the stairs. It's strange to walk past my Blue River bedroom, past the warden's office with no warden in it, and it's strange not to run the Block C corridor to Mom's door. But she wouldn't be there anyway. I take the turn toward the law library instead. At the door, I steel myself then step inside.

It's quiet here now. It'll fill up in about an hour with residents who want to work on their cases. But I see the law library's constant occupant. Or rather, I see the two white poofs of his hair. Mr. Krensky's back is to me, he's looking down, probably studying a case for someone—someone who will owe him a week's worth of bed making or personal laundry service or gifts from the commissary. I wish I could talk to Mr. Rojas instead. But he's Mom's good friend, and I don't want either of them to know what I've done.

I walk around to the other side of table and stand in front of Mr. Krensky. He looks up—when he pleases. I get the feeling he's seen my feet and has identified me by my sneakers.

He speaks. "Well, look who's back. Not to stay, I hope."

"Hi, Mr. Krensky," I say. "Mrs. Buckmueller sent me up." I set the book and magazine bundle down in front of him. I try not to let him see that I'm nervous.

His mouth tracks out on one side, a complaining sort of straight line. "Right. You and I both know I would've stopped by the common on my own later."

"Well, I guess that's true—"

"No pleasantries," he says. "Cut to the chase. You want something."

I'm going to have to get him to forget that I'm Perry Cook, the kid he hates to have underfoot.

"I-I need your help . . . with my . . . with a case—"

"Too busy," he snaps. He looks down at his work. I take a breath, but I don't let him hear it.

"I know you don't like me," I say. "But you don't have to. This is business." I try to sound like one of the residents.

"Too busy," he repeats. But I hear the tiniest break between the two words. He is listening to me.

"Never mind," I say. I take one step back from the table.

"Hold on," he says. "I happen to want something from the outside. I'll take it as payment *if* you can get it."

"What if I can't?"

He turns his palms up and makes a sour face. "Then I guess you lose," he says. He goes back to his reading.

"What do you want?" I ask.

"Fish," he says. "Sardines." He points a finger at me like he's putting me on a skewer. "Three cans of Wild Planet sardines, California caught, packed in one hundred percent virgin olive oil. No substitutes." He looks over his wire glasses at me.

"No second choice?" I ask.

"Were you listening?" A tiny spit ball lathers at the corner of his mouth. "If you don't bring me Wild Planet, I don't give you that case analysis." He stares at me a second then goes back to his reading.

"I'm in," I say. I unzip my backpack and pull my camera out. I hesitate. I've saved all my photos and videos on memory cards. But this camera means a lot to me. Krensky could keep it. He could sell it! I'd never see it again. With a leap of faith, I set it down in front of him.

"What's this?" he says, giving me a cranky, closed-eye look.

"Everything is on the camera. Well, almost everything. I couldn't shoot it all becau—"

"What? You bring me *part* of a case and expect me to read it from a two-by-three-inch screen?"

"I-I got most of it. And you can zoom in."

"Baw!" Krensky puts his hand over the camera. He slowly slides it across the table back to me. "You give me a headache just thinking about the eyestrain, you little piece of—"

"Fish!" I say. "I'll pay you in fish! For any advice you can give me—"

"I don't give advice. I analyze."

"Fine. I just need anything you see here that doesn't look right. Three cans of Wild Planet sardines, California catch, in olive oil." I say it so he'll know that I intend to get it exactly right.

"Double compensation," he says. "For the pain of eyestrain."

"What's compensation?" I try not to blink.

"Payment."

"You're doubling your order of sardines?"

"You heard me."

"But as long as I get the fish, you'll put the case in plain English for me?" He sneers but he dips his chin twice as if to say yes. "Done," I say. "When do you think you'll have it?"

"When can you deliver my fish?"

"Friday," I say.

"All up to you," Mr. Krensky says. "Now, do me a favor." He sticks his pinky finger in his ear and gives it a twist. He says, "Get lost!"

chapter fifty-eight

A QUESTION FOR
ZOEY'S MOM

"It feels better because of the medicine. But it's like I have a chunk of cement in there now." That's what Zoey tells me when I ask about her tooth.

"You do sound like you have a mouthful of marbles." I tell it to her gently.

"One thing is for sure," she says, "I wish I could have it all done in one appointment. I don't want to go back."

"Oh . . . not so sure about that, Zoey," her mom says. "There's a reason the surgeon breaks it up into two appointments."

"It's quite a procedure." Mr. VanLeer nods. He's chopping and mashing Zoey's supper. He's been changing out her compresses to keep the swelling down. If she feels well, she can go to school tomorrow. She'll see the oral surgeon again next week. I've caught her up on homework—except for her Coming to Butler County project. Miss Maya gave us all of fifth period to work on the projects today, and Zoey missed it. They're due next week. Kids are talking about presenting them. I should talk to Zoey before the project becomes real trouble for her. But tonight I think we all just want to take care of her. It's good to see her slowly eat her mush. I make a scene of smashing up my supper too. She laughs from her lopsided mouth. Then the adults mush up their food too.

Later, I help Zoey's mom carry the freshly painted duck-egg blue chairs from the garage to the cellar. She's put three coats of paint on them. They look new, but not new. Recycled, I guess. Together, we move some boxes out from under a little round table. The boxes make me think of VanLeer's office. My supper goes a little cold in my belly. Zoey's mom has no idea how many boxes I've moved recently—and that's not all.

"You okay, Perry?" she asks.

"Sure." I add a nod.

"Okay, let's just push the chairs right up to the table." She lifts one, I lift another. We get them all in place. She stands back looking at the arrangement.

"You almost have a dining room in your basement," I say.

"Ha! I was thinking the same thing." Zoey's mom laughs.

I point to some broken-down bed parts and a little couch with curly arms. "A bedroom and a living room." I keep the joke going because I like to hear Zoey's mom laugh, and she does again and again.

Together we pack things in a little tighter. "Because who knows what I'll be bringing home next," she says. I help her slide an old trunk against the wall. "Good muscle!" Zoey's mom says. She dusts her hands off. "Hey, I didn't even ask you, how was your mom today? Was there time to see her?"

"Yeah . . ." I have to think to remember how the afternoon went. "I visited with another resident while she was finishing up her meeting. But we got to sit in the common with Mrs. Buckmueller for a while."

"Oh, that sounds nice." She tilts her head.

"Yeah . . . except Mom is low. She wants that new parole date." I catch myself. I shouldn't talk to Zoey's mom about this.

"Hmm . . ." Now Zoey's mom looks sad to me. "She will get that date, Perry." She sits down sideways in one of the duck-egg blue chairs. She folds her hands over the high back and rests her chin on them. "In the meantime, is there anything I can do for you?" She waits then says, "I know I keep offering, but you never ask for anything." She gives me one of her sweet, soft smiles. The moment stretches, and my jaw begins to ache a little.

"Fish!" I say. "Could you help me get some special sardines for a . . . for one of the residents? He has expensive tastes," I warn. "But he wants them so much."

"Sardines? Sure. We'll run out tonight. We need to get

Zoey some pudding and oatmeal anyway."

"That would be great," I say.

"If fish is your wish, I can grant it," she says. She draws swirls in the air with one magic-wand finger.

I have to smile. She's become a real friend.

chapter fifty-nine

WHAT MR. KRENSKY SAYS

"Show me the fish," Mr. Krensky says. I lay the six cans out in front of him on the table in the law library. "Ah . . . yesss . . . ," he says. He traces his fingers all the way around the top seam of one can. For about two seconds, Krensky looks happy.

"May I please have my camera back?" I say. He slides it over, and I breathe a great sigh of relief. It's only been a few days, but I have missed it. I wait and hope Mr. Krensky will have something important to tell me, and I hope he'll say it plainly.

"Well, you're right. There is something wrong with the case. Several things."

I slide my notebook out of my backpack and open it. He's

going to talk fast, and he won't repeat anything, I just know it. I grip my pencil.

"Putting it simply . . . she refused counsel and confessed," he says.

Six cans of fish and he's telling me something I already know.

"There's something wrong with that," he adds. "I'll get back to it in a minute. As near as I can tell, the driver of that car was technically at fault."

The driver. I repeat it to myself. I don't interrupt. I already know this too.

"Only an eyewitness can dispute the description of what happened at that intersection," he says. "The car pulled left into the path of the truck. The diagram of the accident clearly shows. I'd be interested in intersection records. The history. This looks like a supremely bad one." He stuffs his fingers into his hair and scratches his head. "Now about the fatality—the man that died—looks like he was your mother's father . . ."

"Yes," I say. I already know this. *Come on, Krensky!*

"Well, unless it's on a missing document—and it might be"—he holds one finger in the air then points it at me as if to blame me for not photographing every page—"nothing in the report says he died of injuries sustained in the accident."

"You mean he didn't get hurt by the car crash?" I think for a second.

"I don't know." Krensky shakes his head. "It doesn't say.

That whole report is full of holes." He flicks his hand. "See, counsel would've dug into that," he says. "*If* she'd had counsel." He drums his fingers on the sardine cans. "She refused a defense *and* she pled without a Breathalyzer test to check for alcohol. It's practically inexplicable," he says. He wipes his lips with his fingers. "But debacles like this happen with mind-boggling frequency."

I'm thinking about what Mom told me—that she didn't see the manslaughter charge coming.

"Wouldn't they make her do that?" I ask. "The breath-a-thing?"

"Should have. That had to be somebody's mistake. Can't tell you what happened there," he says. "But I do know that the courts love a guilty plea. A confession is . . ."

"A conviction." I say it.

"Correct. Thing is, I hadn't pegged your mother for an imbecile, even young as she was." Krensky goes on. "I can tell you this, refusing counsel and confessing usually means one thing." His eyebrows curve together like two furry white caterpillars meeting head to head. He makes me wait, like he's not going to tell.

"I got you your fish," I remind him.

He nods. "My guess is . . . she was protecting someone."

When he says it, it comes at me like a surprise, but not a surprise. It's more like a jolt that wakes up something inside me. "The driver," I say. I'm talking to myself, but Krensky nods.

He says, "Look, kid. A mess was made of your mother's case. I see a girl with no representation, a dangerous intersection, bad weather . . . list goes on." He shakes his head. "But I've asked around and—"

"You didn't ask *her*, did you?" I can't hide my panic.

"I didn't have to!" he squawks. "You know this place is full of voices. Your mother's trouble over her parole hearing is *not* because of the incident that got her put in here." He fixes his eyes on mine and cocks his head.

"It's about me," I say.

Krensky nods. "So all this digging around in the past probably isn't going to help her."

"Even if she should've never been in here in the first place?"

"She's already served." He sounds annoyed with me.

"But I-I have to keep her from getting more time," I say.

Mr. Krensky's lips are in a tight line. I want him to say something more, give me a piece of advice—anything! But he sits there, tapping his old split fingernails on the cans of sardines.

"What do I do?" I finally ask him.

"You count on justice," he says. "Good luck with that. If you ask me, somebody's going to have to pay."

"You mean pay for me being at Blue River," I say. I don't need Krensky to tell me that I'm right.

chapter sixty

THE BIG NIX

On Saturday, I tell Mom that I'm finished with my Coming to Butler County project. "The Blue River Stories are all written," I say. "Everything I know . . ." I mumble the last part. I'm not going to bother her about it. I just want us to play a game and have a normal visit—whatever that is. Besides, we've got a bird on the line: someone is listening in.

Thomas VanLeer gave everyone the slip today. He is sitting close by. Mom and I have put our backs to him as much as we can. He keeps snapping open his newspaper pages behind us while we play a round of the memory game on one of the small tables. The game was my birthday gift from the warden when I was five. We have worn the pictures and blunted the corners of the cards. But it's a favorite.

"I have to print and bind the stories the beginning of this week, because we're presenting on Thursday. I made a cover. It's mostly a big blue sky with an outline of a building that looks like Blue River. I cut out shadow shapes of the people and put them on the inside."

"Oh . . . silhouettes," Mom says. "Nice."

"I still wish I could have made a video for the presentation day. But each of us gets a turn to stand and give an oral summary of our projects." Behind us, VanLeer shifts. I go on. "We're going to move all the desks to the edge of the classroom. Miss Maya is giving us an entire class period to walk around and see the projects close-up and personal—"

VanLeer scoots his chair, and it's noisy. Mom and I both look over our shoulders at him. He looks back at us like he's going to speak, but then his mouth just hangs open. I wonder if he knows that Zoey hasn't started her project. I'm not going to tell him. I turn my back to him again. I flip over two cards. No match.

"We're having make-your-own sundaes afterward in the school cafeteria. That's our culmination celebration." I grin. "So it's almost like an afternoon off."

"Oh, I bet you love that!" Mom says, poking a finger at me. We go back to turning up cards two at a time. I love it when I know that I've seen the same picture twice. Then I love it more when I remember where the match is. I get a pair—the red bird on a branch. Then Mom snags two in a row. I hiss. Mom laughs. Later, Big Ed joins us for the second round. It is a quiet Saturday visit at Blue River.

In the late afternoon, I walk into the VanLeer kitchen

where the grown-ups are talking. I hear Mr. VanLeer say he has to *nix it*. "First thing Monday morning," he says. "I'm going in to talk to the principal." They go silent when they see me.

I look at Zoey's mom. Her face is red and she is wiping down the countertop like there's been a poison spill. This has to be about the Coming to Butler County projects. They know time is almost up, and I'm guessing they know that Zoey hasn't done her work. It's not my business, but I hope they'll cut her some slack. That bad tooth is a good excuse. She's a little bit off the hook anyway—in a sad way. She's going to miss the presentation day. It's the same day she goes back to the oral surgeon. I feel six kinds of sorry about it. For one, I'm nervous about presenting my Butler County project without Zoey there as my support person. But not being there is probably better for Zoey Samuels, who has not done her work.

On Monday it happens. Miss Maya calls Zoey into the hall. This makes my palms sweat. I keep watching the door. I'm dying to know what Miss Maya is saying. When Zoey comes back in, our eyes lock. She makes a tight little *O* with her lips like she's going to whistle. She rolls her eyes toward the ceiling. Then she breaks into a relieved sort of smile. It's the face that Mr. Halsey and Mr. Rojas make when they *almost* get caught playing the jump game in the common. Zoey Samuels is getting away with something. She slips into her seat next to me. She whispers, "Miss Maya gave me an extension on the project . . ."

"Perry." Miss Maya waves me toward her.

I put my finger on my chest. "Me?" She nods. I follow her into the hall.

"Perry . . ." Miss Maya looks at me. She bites her bottom lip then she sighs. "I feel terrible about this, because I know how hard you've worked, and how much it has meant to you . . ."

I cannot imagine what she's about to say, and yet my face is turning hot.

"This doesn't come from me, but . . . I'm afraid we can't have you present your Coming to Butler project with the others."

"What?" I am sinking.

She shakes her head sadly. "I just got the message this morning. It seems that the topic becomes sensitive because of . . ."

"Because of Blue River," I say. "Because it's a prison."

Miss Maya puts her hand on my shoulder and gives me a gentle jiggle. "A concern has been raised about privacy," she says.

"But everyone gave me permission!" I throw my arms wide.

"I know. You did everything right. I'm truly sorry, Perry." Miss Maya shakes her head. "We will still bind the stories, and when you turn the project in to me I will read every word. I know that I'm going to see A-plus work."

What good is that? I think it to myself. Miss Maya's eyes are getting all pooled up. Now mine are burning too. I give her a nod, and we go back into the classroom. Sometimes you just know that everyone is looking at you. I feel it as I walk down the rows of chairs. Everyone can see me blinking my dumb eyes all the way to my seat. I park it, put my elbows on the desk, and set my forehead into my palms. A second ticks by. Zoey leans close.

"Perry? What happened?"

I can barely whisper back. "Tell you later." I stare at the top of my desk.

"What's with him?" Brian Morris says. "Is he in trouble?"

"Whatever it is, it's not your business," Zoey Samuels tells him.

Up in the front of the room Miss Maya is about to begin a new lesson. I shake my head. I look up and try to listen. "Before we begin," she says, "I want to remind you all that you'll be taking the timed one-mile run in gym class this afternoon . . ."

Oh brother. I had forgotten about that.

"It has to happen before the first snowfall!" She says it like she's joking, but it's true. Then she warns us, "I expect good sportsmanship all around."

I'd like to be first across the line for the one-mile run. But right now, I feel like I can't win anything. I can't share the Blue River Stories. I feel low; Miss Maya feels low. I think how it's going to be with Brian Morris after that run. Some-body is going to feel bad about that too. I sink my face into my hands again. I'm sick of everything. But most of all, I'm sick of Thomas VanLeer.

chapter sixty-one

THE ONE-MILE RUN

Ihave seen both men and horses kick at the ground before they race. I have plenty of reasons to want to kick something today. I scratch up the surface of the school track. The boys are running first. The girls are waiting on the bench. The air is chilly, but I feel heat around my nostrils. I also feel Brian Morris staring. He's been doing that ever since Miss Maya pulled me into the hall to nix my Blue River Stories presentation. Either he wants to know what she said to me, or he's just thinking about how he's going to bury me in the next seven and a half minutes.

"Come on, Perry. Make it your best mile yet," I hear Zoey call to me. Then Brian's friends call out and cheer for him. They're a lot louder. At least nobody says, bury Perry!

Mrs. Snyder gives us the ready-set-go. Brian and I move right to the front. We run shoulder to shoulder. I remind myself to stay on my own pace. Soon, he's ahead of me. My feet make a crunching sound on the cindery track. I huff a breath out every time my left foot strikes, the way Mr. Halsey taught me. I hear him in my ear saying, "Hoo-hahh, hoo-hahh . . ." I keep the rhythm. I think Brian is going to burn out if he keeps the pace he's on.

At the quarter-mile mark Brian is well ahead. I don't have my mind on winning. I'm on automatic pilot, and I'm thinking about Thursday. If I can't share my project, what am I going to do? It'll be worse! I'll stick out like a sore thumb, thanks to VanLeer. Heat surges through me and goes to my legs.

He didn't have the guts to tell me he was nixing my presentation. He's a chicken for making Miss Maya do it. That *hoo-hahh, hoo-hahh* rhythm in my ear changes to *darn-you, darn-you.* Then it's *Darn-you, Van-Leer!* I might be pounding the track a little harder now.

At the three-quarter-mile mark, I am still behind Brian Morris. He looks over his shoulder. I stretch my stride. Little by little the gap closes. The final hundred yards, I come up beside him. I have a kick for the finish. I'm sprinting toward Mrs. Snyder with her ticking watch. Brian tries to match me. I go on by—

"Seven ten!" Mrs. Snyder calls out as I cross over the finish line. If I could smile, I would. That's a personal best. My legs chug to a stop. I lean forward and rest my hands on my knees and breathe.

"And . . . seven fourteen!" I hear the call and turn to see

Brian Morris pitching to the ground at the side of the track.

"Excellent times, both of you!" Mrs. Snyder calls to us. Then she turns her attention back to the track to call out the next finishers.

Brian gets to his feet. He comes up to me and bumps his shoulder into mine. Both of us are huffing and puffing. "You drafted me!"

"I wasn't close enough to draft," I say. "Until I passed you."

"Race you again," he says with a sneer. I think he's out of his gourd! I'm pooped, and I bet he feels worse. "One more lap," he says. He taps his fingers on his chest. "Come on. Take me on."

I should give him a chance if that's what he really wants. I look at Brian. Slowly, I crouch into runner's stance. He says, "Go!"

I ache. Everywhere. Especially in my lungs, which crave normal breaths about now. I hear Mrs. Snyder shout at us to halt. But we're gone, pounding our way around the gritty track. We pass the slowest runners—kids who haven't completed the mile yet. That's when I understand that this was not a good idea. It's mean. But it's too late to stop. I focus on matching Brian. We run. Hard.

This time the finish is a blur of people. Most of the boys are standing at the line. The girls are on their feet. Mouths are open—shouting and cheering. I have the race—I know I have it—

My head and chest break the invisible thread of the finish line. But am I first?

"Aaarrrgh!" I hear the sound come from Brian's throat as he follows me in. There is a dull thud when he rolls onto the ground. His friends moan in disappointment. Brian is laid out flat, his chest rising and falling, rising and falling. When he can speak he calls out, "Uh . . . you beat me, Cook!" Funny thing is, he doesn't sound mad. Kids are hanging around saying it was close. Somebody says we are both the best runners in the class.

Zoey Samuels gives me a grin and a fist pump. My legs feel rubbery as I begin to walk it off. I watch the late finishers coming in with red faces. They're ready to collapse. I offer a high five, and two of them tag my hand. Mrs. Snyder calls out their times down to the final finisher. She compliments them on their effort, and for sticking to it. Then she turns to Brian Morris and me.

"That was poor form," she says. "Very discourteous, very unsportsmanlike." All I can do is look down at my shoes. She sends Brian and me to the end of the bench where we will have to sit—together—until the girls finish their run.

We are a hunched pair of losers, trying to catch our breath. I don't know about him, but feeling ashamed makes my heart beat faster. We watch the girls move onto the track. Zoey always does fine on fitness tests. Today she's mid-pack.

"So hey, sorry." Brian finally speaks. He keeps his gaze out at the track. "I challenged you. And I got you in trouble."

I shrug. "I didn't have to take the challenge."

"Yeah . . . but if you hadn't . . . well, that would have been pretty dorky."

I snort a big snort. It just happens. That makes Brian laugh, and he snorts too. I never thought I'd be sitting on a bench snorting with Brian Morris.

"Seriously, why are you so good?" he asks.

"One of my friends is a super-athlete." I'm thinking of Mr. Halsey. "You could say I trained with him." I like the way that sounds. "And my mom was a swimmer, so maybe competing is in my genes." I look out at the school track and see that Zoey Samuels is losing ground. I keep my eye on her, but I ask Brian, "What about you? Why are you so good?"

"Older brothers," he says. "I'm always either chasing them or running away from them." I snort again. A few seconds later Brian asks, "So why did you get taken into the hall today?"

"Oh, that." It all comes zinging back at me. "I can't—they won't let me—" I hesitate. Brian will find out anyway. "They can't let me present my Coming to Butler County project with the rest."

"What?" Brian sits up straight and turns toward me. "Why not?"

"Too much private stuff," I say. On the track, Zoey has slowed to a walk. She is holding her cheek in her hand. It's the bad tooth.

"That stinks," Brian says.

"Yeah . . ." I get to my feet. "Mrs. Snyder! Mrs. Snyder!" I point out across the track to Zoey, just as she drops to her knees. "Runner in trouble!"

"Oh goodness!" Mrs. Snyder says. "Hurry out there, Perry. Walk her in," she says. I get up and start sprinting. I'm surprised when Brian Morris follows.

chapter sixty-two

A PLACE OUTSIDE
OF LINCOLN

On Thursday morning, I dress and make up the camp mat bed. Then I take a minute to scan my timeline on the closet wall. This is the day I was supposed to share the Blue River Stories. That plan has changed because of Thomas VanLeer.

On my way to the kitchen, I stop in the hallway. I hear low-talking.

"Why don't you ask him, Tom?" Zoey's mom sounds squeaky. And mad.

"Well, I'm trying to give him the benefit of the doubt. Even though I know it had to be Perry. I mean, think of the influences. I'm crushed. I really thought being here with us was doing him some good."

"Tom, he's not a criminal!"

"That's not what I'm saying . . ." Mr. VanLeer's voice fades. Then I hear him again. "I'd just like to see him come to me about it."

"Don't hold your breath. You don't know that he took it." She says it firmly.

"Robyn, what would a cleaning staff want with a framed award?"

"What would Perry want with it?" She throws it back at him. I stand in the hallway and feel like dirt.

"Boo!" I jump and knock my elbow on the wall. Zoey apologizes for the scare. "What are they talking about?"

"Nothing!" I say. "I don't know!"

"Don't bite my head off."

"Fine," I say. "Sorry." I change the subject to the only thing I can think of. "Hey, so now that you got that extension, when are you going to start your Coming to Butler County project?"

"Oh. That." She shrugs and says, "You don't know. Maybe I already have." She slinks past me and announces herself in the kitchen. I follow and there are good morning greetings all around. I pretend that I don't see Mr. VanLeer's glances, the ones that say Thief Boy.

"Hey, Zoey. All set for root canal part two?" VanLeer asks. He rubs his hands together and gives her a big grin.

Zoey rolls her eyes. "It's not like I won concert tickets, Tom. I just want to get it over with. I can't even run without making it throb." She looks at me. "That was miserable. And now I have to take a makeup mile."

"How about you, Perry? What's up for you today?" Van-Leer wants to know.

"Not much." I say it slowly. I can't believe he asked. "You know . . . I had a project to present today. But not anymore." Talk about miserable.

But the day brings a surprise. By late morning I am doing something I have never done before. I'm leaving school early—before lunchtime, and before our class presents the Coming to Butler County projects. I'm making the trip to the oral surgeon with Zoey.

Zoey's mom made this plan. She always knows what's up. In the school office she signs me out right along with Zoey. "This way, you'll be out for the afternoon," she says. "Then one more day and the weekend comes." She draws loops in the air with two fingers, showing me that time will stretch. Kids will forget that I didn't present my project.

From the window of the VanLeer SUV I watch the farm fields. The first frosts of the year have made the grasses go pale. Miles roll by. Funny, instead of being in school talking about home, I'm looking back over my shoulder wondering how many miles I am from Surprise. How many miles from Blue River and Mom?

Mr. Krensky said the past didn't matter now. But I can't keep the questions from filling my head. Who was Mom protecting with that confession? I asked her who the driver was. She wouldn't tell. I've wondered if it was her father.

But he was doubled over in pain. How could he have gotten behind the wheel? Besides, he was in the backseat after the crash . . . and if her mother was with him . . . and if they're both dead now, who is left to protect?

I shake my head. I keep chasing these thoughts, but I end up with no answer. It's like there was an invisible driver.

It must be an hour later that I begin to see buildings instead of sleepy wheat and sorghum fields. The roads are crowded with cars and trucks. If it's this busy outside the capital city, what's it like inside? When we get out of the car at the surgeon's office, I notice that there is less quiet. Airplanes fly low overhead, there is vibration on the ground. The sidewalks sparkle in the late October sun.

Inside, we sit with Zoey until the receptionist invites her in. Her mom gives her a hug. I put up my fist, and we knock knuckles. "Good luck," I tell her.

"You'll be done before you know it." Her mom is being cheery. Zoey fakes a grin and disappears down the hall. Her mom looks at me and says, "She'll be at least an hour. Shall we go on a treasure hunt?"

We go walking along the busy streets. Zoey's mom likes it here. She looks in every window. She takes phone photos of painted floor tiles, rugs, artwork, and a new little table made from old pieces of wood. I dig into my pack for my camera and take the same shot so I can show Big Ed and the guys from the woodshop.

When we come up on a YMCA I snap photos of the sign

with its huge block letters. "For my mom," I say. I know that she grew up near Lincoln. I smile a little when I think that it could've been a place like this.

"Your mother was quite a swimmer, wasn't she?" says Zoey's mom.

"Yeah," I say. "She really was. She had a scholarship. But then she had the accident."

"Boy, one small moment," she says. Her voice is sad and drifty. She puts her arm around my shoulders, and we turn down the next street to circle the block. We don't want to be far away from Zoey.

Her mom takes more photos. I follow. She says, "Sorry, Perry. This probably doesn't feel like a treasure hunt to you. I just love being in busy places. I always lived near cities. I miss that, and I lap it up whenever I can."

"Why did you leave?" I ask.

"Oh, because Tom got the job in Butler County." She smiles. "He wanted it so much."

I think of Mr. VanLeer and his office. And the award. And what I did with it. For about the hundredth time, I have to swallow down my guilt. I remind myself that he has not helped *and* he has not looked inside that box. The sidewalk sends up shiny flecks of light. I walk on with Zoey's mom.

When Zoey comes out of the treatment room she is wearing a one-sided smile. The first thing she says is, "Mom, I'm so hungry."

"That's a good sign! We'll stop and find you something

soft to eat on the way home," her mom says. "I think we're all hungry."

The receptionist says, "If you're heading back toward Butler County on 79, look for Toni's Corner. Twenty minutes after the airport. Best grass-fed beef burgers in the county, and they serve a custard that'll be perfect for Miss Zoey's tender tooth."

Zoey Samuels is so glad to be done. The medicine is covering up the pain. She's talking up a storm. In minutes we are back on the straight and empty roads. We find the place called Toni's Corner. Zoey is out of the SUV in a flash. Inside, the waitress seats us. When our food comes, Zoey has a challenge. "My left lips are useless," she says. She pinches them in her fingers like she is lifting them aside.

"Your left lips but not your right lips?" Her mom laughs.

I take big bites of a grass-fed burger. Zoey spoons her custard and tells me, "Perry, take a picture of me trying to eat! We can show it to Tom." I do that, and we laugh as she tilts the spoon in under that useless lip.

I finish first because I gobbled that burger. This is a late lunch. I excuse myself to go find the men's room. Restaurants tuck the restrooms out of plain sight. I have noticed this since living on the outside. Before that, I hadn't been to restaurants much. I ask our waitress, who slips out of the kitchen with Zoey's second dish of custard. She directs me around a corner just past the cashier.

The men's room sits right beside the women's room.

While I am being careful to get the right door, I notice something on the wall between the two. It's a big color photograph of an ordinary stoplight. I see the word *victory* written across the bottom. Framed newspaper articles hang all around it.

I'm curious, but I hurry into the bathroom so Zoey's mom won't worry about me. On my way out I just have to stop and look at that victory wall again. I see an award that says *Toni's Corner Wins Best Burger in Lancaster County*. I see that they sponsor a girls' softball team—all in blue T-shirts. But underneath the stoplight that says *Victory* on it, I see newspaper articles and some photos of car wrecks. I read the headlines. One says: Third Accident in Six Months. Another says: Diners Narrowly Escape Injury—Toni's Corner Damaged in Crash. There is a picture of a tow truck beside a car that is half in and half out of a building—this building! There's a grainy photo of another car that got folded around a pole, and one more article showing Toni's having a grand reopening after repairs. In the background is a plain white building with a rusted red truck parked on top of the roof.

I get that feeling—it's like the memory game—matching pictures.

I bend closer to get rid of the glare on the glass. I reach for one of the frames, lift it, and hold it in my hands.

I'm Perry Cook; I take things off walls.

chapter sixty-three

INFAMOUS INTERSECTION

The smell of coffee curls around me.

"Uh . . . may I help you?" I look at the waitress who stands beside me. She has silver hair like Mrs. DiCoco's. She holds a steaming pot in her hand. "Do you like our little local history wall?" she asks. She seems pleased.

I tilt the frame toward her. I ask, "W-where is this?"

"Well, it's here, honey. Right out there." She nods toward the road out front.

"But . . . where am I?" My lips feel cold and I'm confused. "Is this the intersection?"

"Yes. That's right out front," the waitress repeats. Her tone is sweet, but she's looking at me like I'm not too bright. "You must not be from around here." She points outside the large glass windows and says, "That's the *infamously dangerous* intersection," she says. "Or it used to be. The crossing of Nebraska 79 and 55—better known as West Raymond Road It looks different now than it did when those photos were taken."

"Infamous . . ." I step back and look out the glass front of the diner. I see the roads—the place they cross. NE-79 and West Raymond Road—I know this! This is the picture from Mom's file—the red truck on top of the building. This is the place! About a hundred grass-fed cows thunder through my gut.

The waitress gestures at the picture in the frame I'm holding. "See how it used to be off center? Dips down off thataway? It was deadly. Come dark of night? Bad weather? Forget it! I can't even tell you how many times we called 9-1-1 over the years. It took years of petitions, but the state finally straightened the crossing. More important, they gave us the traffic light. See there?" She points upward, and I happen to catch the light across the way going from green to yellow to blazing red. "We are coming up on six years with *no* accidents," she says.

"Six years . . ." I close my hanging mouth. I turn back to look at the framed articles. "Do you know which one?" I ask.

"Which one what, honey?"

"Oh, sorry. Nothing," I say.

The waitress hurries away with the pot of coffee. I feel like there is fog all around me. I place the frame back on the wall so it won't slip out of my fingers. I scan the articles for the name Cook. I don't find it. Still, I know what I know, and I know it with all my heart.

"Oh! Perry! There you are." Zoey's mom is glad to see me. Her purse hangs open on her arm. She draws out her wallet to pay the bill.

"S-sorry," I say, and I mean it. My short trip to the bathroom was long.

Zoey pushes my backpack at me. I grab it to my chest. Then I stand there wondering if my legs are going to hold me.

Zoey's mom turns from the cashier. She's closing up her purse, belting her jacket, ready to leave.

"Hey," I say to both of them. "Y-you won't believe where we are."

"Toni somebody's," Zoey says. She puts her hand on her cheek and winces.

"But also . . . this is where the accident was. The one my mom was in. It happened here," I say. I point outside.

Zoey gasps. Her mom says, "What? Oh no! Can't be." She sees the wall and starts to read and so does Zoey. Their mouths hang open just like mine.

"Mom, look. It was a bad corner."

"I see . . . but Perry, what makes you say it happened here?"

"It happened just outside of Lincoln," I say. "And these are the route numbers—I saw them—"

I freeze. I didn't mean to tell her that. I breathe. If I have to admit that I went through my mom's case box in her husband's office, I will. If I have to tell her I moved his award, I will. Being here is so big I don't care about much else.

Zoey's mom doesn't seem to notice anyway. She leans closer to the frames. She reads. I hear her say, "Hmm . . . ," then "Well . . ." like she isn't quite sure.

"Well, at least shoot it, Perry!" Zoey Samuels tugs at my pack. "Get your camera out. You have to show your mom. She's not the only driver to make a mistake here. It was a bad setup and they changed it. Don't you want her to know?"

With shaky fingers I take a shot of the wall and then try for a few close-ups of newspaper articles. Zoey's mom still isn't sure about all of this. She is reading and thinking. Her eyes narrow just a tiny bit. But I am sure. It dawns on me that there is proof right inside my camera—the photos from Mom's file. Still, I won't say it if I don't have to.

"Honey." The silver-haired waitress comes back by and touches my elbow. She glances at Zoey's mom. "You seem . . . you *all* seem so interested. If you want to talk to somebody who remembers every bit of history from this old corner, well that's Bosco over there at the gas station." She points across the road, to the plain-box building with the red truck parked on the roof. "He drives the tow truck," the waitress says. "He's been doing it for years."

chapter sixty-four

BOSCO TOW

Zoey's mom agrees to go. "We need to gas up anyway," she says. Then she sighs. "And if there is a Bosco, or Mr. Bosco, there, Perry can . . . I don't know . . . test his memory, I guess."

"Yes! Yes! Ow . . ." Zoey grabs her face and says, "I think the novocaine stuff is wearing off. Oh . . . Mom . . . I think I had too much custard."

"Then you need to sit tight and rest," her mom says firmly. "The prescription will be at the pharmacy. We'll pick it up before we go home." She pulls the SUV up to the pump.

"Perry, you have to tell me if he says anything important," Zoey says, and she manages to tag me in the arm as I unbuckle.

Zoey's mom and I hop out together. "Perry," she says. She's tilting her head at me in a sorry sort of way. "You know this might not amount to much, right?"

I nod. I know what she means.

"I don't want you to be disappointed."

"I'll be fine," I say. "And I'll be quick."

"I'm on empty," she says, grabbing the nozzle from the pump. "But we also have to get Zoey home." She gives me a nod and a smile. I slip away.

Inside, I smell oil and rubber, and maybe cat litter. I call out. "Hello?"

"Yes, sir!" A man with a thick brown beard and a cap rolls out of a tiny side room on an office chair. I can tell he's gotten a good push off something—maybe from the cluttered metal desk inside. It looks like he makes nests out of papers. Behind him, the office walls are covered with hubcaps and keys on string tags, rusty license plates and loops of wires.

"Are you Mr. Bosco?" I ask.

"You found me," he said. "What can I do for you?" He glances out toward the gas pump, probably wondering if something is wrong.

"Well, we're filling up," I say. "But I have a question. A waitress at Toni's Corner said you might remember an accident that happened at this intersection. It was a long time ago."

"Hmm . . . okay . . . so try me," he says. "Tell me what you know."

"It was twelve years ago."

"Twelve. That's about the time I took the place over from my pop."

"It was August. Nighttime. There was a hailstorm," I say, and I watch his eyebrows rise.

"We get those," he says. "Car? Truck? Big? Little?"

"Car." I think hard. "Three people inside. Two older and one would have been a young—"

"Oh . . ." He breathes and squints like he might be seeing into the past. "There was a girl . . ."

I nod, but I wonder if he's guessing or playing fortune-teller with me.

"Hmm . . ." Bosco pops out of his chair and hauls open a rickety drawer in an old file cabinet. A great fat cat is startled to her feet on top of the cabinet, and she in turn startles me. She balances while Bosco tugs and the cabinet sways. "I probably don't have the towing record anymore . . . but . . ."

I lean left then right trying to see around him. He is shuffling through bunches of cloudy plastic zip-top bags. They look like they have trash in them—curls and wads of paper, and I can't tell what else. He mumbles something. I think he says, ". . . the watch bag . . ." He reaches way back— the drawer swallows his arm—and he pulls several bags out. He drops them on the office desk and pokes through them. "I'm thinking . . . this one," he says. He taps it with his finger.

I'm thinking that I wasn't really looking for bags of trash—and Zoey's mom will not want me to bring one into the tidy VanLeer SUV. I can't even take one just to be polite. Maybe Zoey's mom was right; maybe this is disappointing.

"I remember them for different reasons," Mr. Bosco says. "This one, because of the girl. She was wrapped in a blanket when I pulled the truck up."

He has my attention now. Mom said the police gave her a blanket.

"She was all alone, ankle-deep in hailstones and staring off almost like she was expecting to see something come out of the roadside fields." He waves a hand through the air. "I thought she might have lost a dog that jumped out and ran off after the crash. But this girl wasn't calling out." He ducks his head. Then looks up at me again. "I remember reading later . . ."

"Someone died." I say it for him.

"Yeah. Tough," he says. He scratches his bearded jaw. "I hope it wasn't somebody close to you. You're very young," he says, as if he has just noticed that.

"I wasn't even around," I say. The cat jumps down from the file cabinet and tiptoes over the mess on the desk. It hops to the floor and slinks out of the office. I hear it meow somewhere near the entrance. "Mr. Bosco . . . I don't understand about the bags of garbage," I say. I can't stop eyeing the one he has picked out for me.

"Oh, not garbage," he says. "Well, that's debatable, I suppose." He reaches and pops the bag open for me with a snap. He looks inside and gives the contents a shake and a rattle.

He dumps it out. I see receipts and gum wrappers, a Chap-Stick and a few coins. But something heavy slid out too. I heard it hit the desk. "My job is to clean up the scene after the police are done," he says. "Big stuff. Small stuff. I save everything in case the police ask for it. But nine times out of ten, they don't."

"Really?"

"If there's no investigation, no lawsuits or legal stuff, they don't take the time. Then I'm supposed to call the car owners to come get it, and I do. But I've seen a lot of wrecks go right to scrap. Sweet old cars somebody once loved." He grins slightly. "I sweep them out before they go, but like I say, most of the time nobody comes for, as you say, the garbage." The cat lets out an impatient yowl. Bosco says, "Anyway, kiddo, I'm ninety-eight percent sure that this is what I've got from the night you're asking about. It's yours if you want it."

"You can just give it to me?"

"I'm supposed to throw it out after four years," he says. "But as you can see, I'm not much for getting rid of things." He steps out of the office to tend to the cat.

I should hurry. The gas tank of the SUV is probably full, and Zoey is hurting. I give the pile on the table a stir with one finger. I catch something—a strap. It's bright orange and bendy. I pull on it and uncover that one heavy thing that slid out of the bag. It's a sports watch with a face like a dashboard but it's smashed—and I want it. It's just that it doesn't feel like it belongs to me. A picture! I need my camera! But my backpack is in the SUV.

"Sure. He's inside," I hear Bosco say.

Then I hear Zoey's mom. "Hey, Perry? You ready?"

"Yep!" I close my hand over the watch and tuck it up into the cuff of my fleece.

chapter sixty-five

TIMEKEEPER

At the VanLeer supper table, Zoey feels better again. She's had her medicine. She eats oatmeal and tells about our trip. ". . . and my tooth was the least of it, Tom. This was sad but amazing," Zoey says. "We were actually *at* the intersection where Perry's mom had that accident, and it turns out that—"

"What? Where did you go?"

"We went to the oral surgeon." Zoey's mom pushes those words out. "We *think* we had lunch at the intersection where it happened. It seems like maybe it was the place."

Wow, I think. She's still not sure. Even after I told them in the car, "Bosco remembers." That's what I said, and I showed her bright eyes from the backseat. Then again, she never saw the photos from Mom's file like I did. She doesn't know about the watch. I'm keeping that to myself—I'm dying for a better look at it. So far, I haven't dared. I haven't even taken off my fleece jacket. I'm sitting right here at the Van-Leer table with the watch still tucked up inside my sleeve. I try not to look down at my wrist.

"Perry talked to the tow truck driver," Zoey says.

"He wasn't a witness to the crash," I say. "But afterward he saw a girl wrapped in a blanket staring at the night. That's how my mom told the story to me."

Mr. VanLeer seems squirmy. He looks at his wife and shakes his head. She is silent. I push my food with my fork. I'm not that hungry after our late lunch.

Then Zoey says, "You can't get mad at Mom, Tom. Nobody can plan a coincidence."

Boy, do I love that. Zoey Samuels is right.

After dinner, the VanLeer adults excuse us from cleanup. They ask us to go ahead to our rooms, please. On the way down the hall, Zoey whispers to me. "I bet they take it to the street," she says, which means the adults are going to argue. About me. At least they will be busy.

Inside the closet, I kneel beside the warden's suitcase and switch on the reading lamp. I slide the watch out of my sleeve and turn it over in my fingers. There's a white starburst crack in the glass that makes it hard to see the face. I see three circles under there. Must be for different functions. The clip on the watch is broken. The orange band is still bright after all these years. On the inside of the band someone has written with black pen.

For Flip, my timekeeper for all time. Love, J.C.

My heart stops beating. J.C. *has* to be Jessica Cook. Who is Flip? And what is this message about a timekeeper? Of all the voices in this world I hear Mr. Krensky telling me that Mom had to be protecting someone.

I whisper in the closet. "Who is Flip?"

chapter sixty-six

JESSICA

Jessica Cook looked down into the common from the Upper East Lounge. Halsey Barrows stood with a duffel strung across his body. He was dressed in street clothes—no chambray. A few more minutes and he'd be gated out—gone. She'd had to distance herself from him these last couple of days—no other way to bear the impending separation. Perhaps he felt the same; he'd been moving around her rather than to her. Even now, she kept back from the railing just in case he'd look up and deepen the crack in her heart.

She saw the small assembly: Big Ed as his support person, one foreman, and the temp. So often Perry had joined these small sendoffs. This was going to crush him. Halsey had been one of their special ones. She watched the taxi pull up in the circle. She saw Halsey hand Big Ed two . . . *envelopes* . . . she was fairly sure.

At the end of the work day, Big Ed put both of them into

her hands. One was addressed to Jessie, one to Perry. The supper line was forming, and the common was too busy for the delicate business of letter opening. So she hiked up the stairs, took a chance, and tried the door to Perry's old bedroom at the end of the Upper East Lounge. To her surprise it was unlocked. Inside, she sat on his stripped-bare bed and gently worked her thumb along the triangular flap of the envelope addressed to her. She slid the folded paper out, and when she opened it, several bills fell onto her lap. She felt herself blush as she packed them deep into her palm with her fingers. Then she read:

Jessie, I tried and tried to write you something that would tell you all the things I want you to know. I failed again and again. Sorry. But you're quick, and you've got a read on this whole world like nobody I've ever known— and isn't that ironic given the long years you've spent on the inside? (I hope you're smiling.) Point is, I think you know what's in my tongue-tied heart. Stay strong. Do it for you; do it for Perry. I'm leaving my gate money for you and your boy. I don't need it. I've got an honest gig— pretty far from here—but it pays well.

Love, Halsey

Jessica dumped herself onto her side. She pulled her knees up and curled around them. She wept convulsively.

314

When she could, she took her salt-burned face down to a late supper, where Eggy-Mon put up a serving for her. He cooed softly, "I saved you a biscuit—crumb and flake, and a bowl of split pea—the best I make. Birds fly high and birds fly low. When birds fly out, we watch them go . . ."

He came around the counter, took Jessica's tray, and walked her to the table where Gina, Callie DiCoco, and Sashonna Lewis sat. From inside his apron pocket Eggy-Mon produced a napkin full of oatmeal raisin cookies, which were met with squeals of approval. When the women broke the cookies, the smell of cinnamon filled the air, and Jessica leaned toward the warm shoulders of her friends.

chapter sixty-seven

THE ENVELOPE

On Friday at school, I dodge a few questions about missing the Coming to Butler County projects. It's pretty likely that Brian Morris has filled people in. I don't care. I have something bigger on my mind—a job for the library volunteers.

Before we get into the Bucking Blue Bookmobile, Zoey helps me slip messages into magazines—again. I'm going to need the rezzes to keep six for me on Saturday like never before. I'm waiting until then to ask Mom about the watch. Friday afternoon is never enough time, and for this, we've got to be alone.

"So why do you need them to keep six on Saturday?" Zoey asks. I think about the watch with the orange band. I have it stowed in the interior pocket of the warden's suitcase in the VanLeer closet.

I tell Zoey half the truth. "I need to talk to my mom about the coincidental lunch at the infamously dangerous intersection," I say. "Your stepdad isn't cool with what happened. So . . ."

"Oh! Right! And you have the picture to show her!" Zoey's thinking of the History Wall at Toni's Corner. I'm thinking of pictures I took of the watch because it seems more important. "You need Tom out of your way," she says. "And if I see your mom today, I won't mention any of it," she says. Zoey Samuels is the best friend in the world.

At Blue River, Mrs. Buckmueller settles in her chair. Zoey and I empty the bins. As we stack the periodicals, I am so focused on the notes inside it about knocks me over when I feel a tap on my shoulder.

"Mom! You're so early today."

"I asked for permission," she says. "I wanted more than a few minutes with you." She gives me a tired smile, and I wonder what's up. When she excuses us to a far corner in the common, I am sure she has bad news.

She holds out an envelope. I take it between my finger and thumb. It feels warm from being inside her pocket. "From Halsey," she whispers, and instantly I know that he is gone. *Released.*

"Should I open it here?" My voice is small.

"Up to you," she says.

I peel the envelope open.

Dear Perry,

Blue River is gating me out today. I'm glad about that. But it means I'm going to miss saying good-bye to you, and we're going to have to take a rain check on that game of one-on-one. I wanted to give you my story, so here it is:

I am a pro player. No joke.

Once, I had everything in place for a crazy-good life, but I messed it all up. Not proud of that. But that's my story. That's how I ended up at Blue River trying to figure out how to rise up again. I'm on the comeback trail. I'm suspended from playing in the US for a while longer. So I'm off to train with a team in Germany. I hope to see you again one day. In fact, I'm counting on it.

Until then, you keep listening to your mom. She knows it all. Thanks for being around, Perry. Thanks for raising me up.

Fraternal love,

Halsey

"Well, we knew he was getting out," I say. My throat is a little sandy. "Good for Mr. Halsey." I blink but I won't cry because a good thing has happened—same thing we want for Mom. "We'll see him again," I say.

"I hope so," says Mom.

"I know we will," I tell her. "He promised me a game."

chapter sixty-eight

THE WHOLE TRUTH

On Saturday morning my rezzes have my back. Big Ed comes to distract VanLeer.

"There's our district attorney!" he says. "How about you drink a cup of coffee with me? You'd like that. Sure you would." VanLeer is looking over his shoulder at me.

Mr. Rojas comes up the other side of VanLeer, saying, "Coffee. Yeah! Yeah! This is a man . . . this is a man who loves coffee. Needs coffee!" So VanLeer is squished between Big Ed and Mr. Rojas, and he's not getting out of there. They take him to a table where some of the rezzes are serving sweets to the Saturday visitors.

I walk up to Mom. We skip the swing-around. She says, "Perry, what's up? You've got everyone keeping six." She sticks her chin out toward the common. "Is this about Halsey leaving?"

"No. Mom, we need to get lost in Blue River today. Way away from VanLeer."

She's confused, but she's with me. We circle around the common and find Fo-Joe. I've never had to ask him for a favor this big. "Please," I say. "Can you let us go upstairs?" I beg him. He rolls his eyes like I'm asking for the moon. Fo-Joe can be like that. "You're the temp," I tell him. "You can decide."

"Yeah, yeah." His lips barely move. "Back it up this way," he says. His eyes scan the common while we shuffle back toward the bottom of the stairs.

Across the way, Miss Sashonna is chirping at Mr. Van-Leer. "You'll like that cookie. Oh that's a *good* cookie!" She holds the oatmeal raisin in a set of serving tongs. She pushes it at him. He's already holding a very full cup of coffee in the other hand.

"That's your cookie," Big Ed says. "Take that cookie." He points. But VanLeer is not taking it. He's trying to turn around.

Sashonna gives us wild wide eyes. She reaches out and gives VanLeer's hand a slap. "COOKIE!" she repeats. He draws the hand back. His coffee sloshes. There are people up his back now. He's taking the cookie. I think he's afraid to take his eyes off Miss Sashonna or she'll swat him again.

We back all the way up to the stairway rope. Fo-Joe unhitches it. "Wait . . ." He checks on the refreshment table. VanLeer is occupied. "Go!" Fo-Joe says. Together, Mom and

I take the stairs two at a time.

"Your room! Your room!" Mom says. Her hands steer my shoulders. We duck into the room at the top of the stairs just off the Upper East Lounge. It's the first time I've been inside my old bedroom since I left Blue River.

Mom breathes. "Perry, please. You have to tell me what's so important."

"I have to show you something." I pull out my camera. I find a picture I took of the smashed watch face. I hand the camera to her. She takes a look but shakes her head at me like she doesn't understand. I take the camera back and advance to a close-up shot of the writing on the orange band. I show her.

Mom's breath goes into her lungs, and it sounds like a cry from an animal. She brings her voice back to a whisper. "Perry! Where did you get this? My God, tell me where?" She looks at the shot again. She is shaking and frantic and now I don't know what to say.

"Mom, it was a coincidence," I tell her. "I met the tow truck driver. He collects stuff after crashes. Nobody even comes for it—"

"It's not possible!" she says. Her eyes fill, and she sits back hard against her chair. She drops her face into her hands. I look at the picture again, at the words in black pen.

"J.C. is for Jessica Cook, right, Mom? Who is Flip?"

Her shoulders are shaking. It's real crying, and Mom doesn't do that. "Perry, why did you do this?" I fight to hang on, but then I start to cry too. She leans forward, hugs me hard, and then holds my hands. She squeezes them tightly.

"I didn't mean it like that. No, no. Don't you be sad," she begs me. "It's okay, it's all right. I'll tell you everything. Right now. No pencil notes, no videos." She wipes her face on the inside elbow of her chambray.

"So, I once loved a boy," she begins. She sniffs hard. "You're probably not surprised to hear that, because, well, here you are." She manages a tiny smile.

"I know the biology part," I say with a shrug. "Everybody has a father."

"Yep. I called him Flip. His initials were FLP, and he had the quickest flip turn and the best push off the wall of any swimmer in the state. I gave him that watch. We used it to time each other during practice. We did everything together . . . and he was with me that night.

"We were trying to talk to my parents. We'd both won swim scholarships at the same school. We had decided to live together off campus in a co-ed house with some other swimmers. We wanted my parents' blessing, and of course, they wouldn't give it—quite the opposite. They were angry and drinking, and they said horrible things to that boy that I loved. I fought with them. Flip was better. He tried to be reasonable. He defended me.

"But it went on and on. We gave up." Mom's face twists up. Her voice pitches high. "I told my parents this was good-bye. Flip and I got up to leave, and that's when my father doubled over with chest pains. We wanted to call an ambulance—how I wish we had. But my mother refused. She got his heart meds for him. But his pains continued. Like I told you, I was the one with my keys in my hand that night. How they ended up in Flip's hand instead, I can't remember. My mother and I struggled to get my father into the car—so maybe it was then. Anyway, Flip got behind the wheel."

A breath goes over my lips. I understand now. Mom looks at me. She nods.

"In so many, many ways, Perry, I am to blame for what happened. I pushed him to go fast, and so did my mother, screaming from the backseat. So he did, even when we drove into the hailstorm. When we got to that intersection, he slowed to take a left. He would've come to a full stop just like he was supposed to. The hail was beating down; my adrenaline was through the roof. I looked to my right and saw this silver sheet of hail with lights in the distance. I thought we had time, and I told him to go. I *made* him go. He trusted in me—and I put us right in the path of an oncoming truck." Mom shakes her head.

"So what you told me is true," I say. "You made a mistake at the intersection."

"Yes, I did. Flip probably saved my life by speeding straight across instead of trying to make the left. It was a split-second decision. We got nipped hard in the rear quarter instead of dead on the side. We spun out and stopped when we smacked into a pole."

It makes me cringe. I look at Mom. She could so easily be gone . . .

"Everything stopped." She says it slowly. "Frozen moment. I raised my head, turned to see if Flip was okay. He looked right at me. We were both okay! I reached to hug him, and that's when I smelled his breath, and I knew he'd been drinking."

"Wait. Drinking with your parents?" I ask.

"No, no. He drank before we sat down with them. He knew it would be tense and awful. He was scared, and he thought a drink would take the edge off."

"He made a mistake too," I say.

"He did. I saw both my parents, unconscious in the backseat—terrifying. I asked Flip how much he'd had to drink—and this was all in a matter of seconds. He was afraid it was too much. The police would know." Mom sighs and presses her hands out along her knees. "I couldn't let him be caught. This was *my* fault. So I told him to run. He didn't want to leave me. But I reminded him about school, and how he'd lose his scholarship. His life would be ruined. I convinced him that I'd be okay—I was sober. It was just a bad accident. I made him go. Later, I told the police I was driving. I figured I'd be in some trouble, but I thought it would all work out.

"The rest is like I told you, Perry. Within hours I learned that my father was dead. My mother froze me out. I knew that she would never forgive me, and I would not forgive myself. Those were the loneliest hours I've ever known."

"But didn't Flip come back?"

"Oh yes. He tried. More than once. He talked about turning himself in. But I wouldn't have it. I pushed him away because . . ." Her face drops, and she can hardly talk again. "The more things went wrong for me, the more I wanted him to be free. My father's death was my fault. That haunted me. But the thought of Flip paying for it, well, that would have been unbearable. I cut off communication. Finally, he put all the money he had into my commissary account. I know because the deposit was exactly the amount we each made lifeguarding that summer." She smiles a little. "It was all he had to give me, and all I would take from him. And you should know, Perry, he never knew about you. Several months went by before I realized you were coming. You were my sign—my reason—to go forward. I figured if there came a time when I couldn't have you with me, I'd make the next plan. But our Warden Daugherty made things work for us." Mom cups her hand around my head. "For a very long time."

I squeeze onto her chair to be beside her. It's a chair for one, but we fit. "I'm sorry, Mom. You lost so much," I say. "I thought I knew. But I didn't really know."

"Of course you didn't. I didn't tell you."

"But now I get why you didn't tell me," I say. "Sorry, Mom."

"Don't be sorry," she says. "You know, I was always afraid my mother would come forward and say that Flip had been driving. But she didn't. Then a lawyer sent word a few years after you were born saying that my mother had died. That hurt. But mostly because she'd left me long before that." Mom rests her cheek on my head.

We sit in the quiet as if a bubble has dropped down over us. If someone walked in right now—even VanLeer—I think our calm would be unbreakable.

"Mom . . . what if the watch is the one thing that could get you out now?"

Mom shifts. She says, "Perry, keeping secrets is hard. I know. I'm an expert. I believe that no good purpose would be served by telling anyone. I won't bind you with a promise. That would be wrong. But I hope with all my heart that you won't try to use what you've learned. It scares me that the watch is even out there."

"But I do promise." I hold the camera where we both can see it. I delete one photo then the other. I wonder if I should tell her that the watch isn't out there—that it is safe inside a pocket of the warden's suitcase, deep inside the VanLeer closet. Mom squeezes me like she feels better for having seen the photos disappear.

"Mom," I say, "there's something else. You'll want to know this." I show her two more pictures—the intersection, before and after.

"Oh . . . look at that." She breathes. "They fixed it." Her voice is hoarse and squeaky. "A traffic light . . . thank goodness."

"It was a really dangerous spot, Mom. It wasn't your fault."

"Thank you, Perry." She puts her lips to my head and whispers into my hair. "You know, he saved you that night too," she says. "Tiny, tiny unknown being that you were. Your father saved you."

"Yeah, he did," I say. We sit curled together a little longer in the peace of my old bedroom up above the common.

When we slip back down the stairs, we move through the visitors to the refreshment table. Mom gets a coffee. I'm not hungry. But Miss Sashonna has saved the last oatmeal cookie for me, and I know better than to refuse it.

We sit down at one of the long tables where Mr. and Mrs. Rojas and Cici and Mira are visiting. They have crayons and photocopies of family pictures. Mrs. Rojas likes to bring them. I see the photograph of Mr. Rojas with his girls—the one I took at the Fathers and Daughters Dance—how many weeks ago? I was still at Blue River. Everything was different.

"*Hola*, Perry! *Hola*, Miss Jessica! *Dame cinco!*" The girls put up their hands. Mom and I give them high fives.

Mr. VanLeer sits down beside me. We all get quiet. But Mira Rojas is little. She looks up at him with big eyes. She smiles, puts up her hand for him. VanLeer smiles back, and claps his palm against hers. "We're making art," she tells him.

"I see that," he says. "Nice job." Mira offers him a crayon, and he takes it.

I'm nibbling the cookie. Mom is slowly sipping coffee. She's still upset and sniffling. Mrs. Rojas passes her a tissue. We watch the artists put borders on their photos. I think to myself that it is a comfort to have a mouse in the house, and even better to have two.

But soon VanLeer looks itchy. He tells me, "Time to wrap it up, Perry."

Mom leans up and says, "You know what? He's going to eat his cookie." Then she tells me, "Perry, take your time."

"Fine. Fine." VanLeer rests back in his chair.

Cici climbs onto her father's lap. She draws a box around the picture from the Dads and Daughters Dance. She adds a roof and a chimney. She writes *home* at the top. Mr. Rojas picks up a purple crayon and adds more writing at the bottom. He reads it to us. *"El deseo de mi alma."*

"What does it mean?" Mom asks.

I can feel VanLeer leaning in to hear the answer.

"The wish of my soul," says Mrs. Rojas. "It's an expression."

"Aw, that's beautiful!" says Mom. She thumps her fist to her heart.

I take a mouse-size bite from the cookie. I'm going to make it last.

chapter sixty-nine

JESSICA

After Perry left, Jessica found an empty chair in the common and folded herself into it. She watched the crowd of visitors slowly thin. She missed him so much. Again. But today there was a certain sort of warmth at her core— something akin to peace, or contentment, or, this time, relief. When he'd asked to write the Blue River Stories, Perry had made the case that it was easier to tell the truth than to step all around it. He was right. Jessica felt like her long, awful secret had moved out. A much better feeling was filling the space.

This morning, she couldn't have guessed she'd end up revealing the whole story to her boy—that amazing boy. But he'd pushed her into it. Oh, he was a brave info-digger. Now that he knew, he seemed to understand. Maybe she should credit his weird life at Blue River for preparing him. Perry, she thought, was an excellent student of human nature.

How else could he have done the one thing she'd craved all these years—to have someone hold her and say, *It wasn't your fault.* She caught a flood of hot tears in her fist and held onto them close to her chest. How badly she wanted to make a home on the outside for Perry.

At Jaime Rojas's urging, Jessica had pressed again for information on her parole hearing. "They can't put it off this long." He'd said it purposefully. "They have thirty days to get it back on the calendar after a postponement. They've gone too long on you. They have to at least grant you the hearing. After that you just have to hope. And I have plenty of hope for you, Jessica. This has to go your way."

"But there's VanLeer," she'd said. She heard his name the way a hammer drives a spike—and not for the first time.

"Not today," she told herself as she rose from the chair in the common. She determined *not* to let thoughts of Thomas VanLeer eat wormholes in her soul on this amazing, wrenching day. She climbed the stairs, paused just a second to look at the door to Perry's old room. Then she air-swam all the way down the Block C corridor to her room.

chapter seventy

A QUESTION
FROM VANLEER

The first week of November slides by quietly. The frost-
ier days remind me that Mom was supposed to be out
weeks ago. Things are standing still. I don't know how to
make them move. I keep my promise; I hold on to Mom's
secret.

On Sunday evening I walk into the chocolate-colored
bedroom I am using in the VanLeer house with Zoey on my
heels. When I see Mr. VanLeer standing there, I stop so fast
Zoey bangs into my back.

"Umph!"

VanLeer turns quickly. He's got the warden's suitcase—
my suitcase—wide open on the bed I never sleep in. My
short stack of shirts is spilled out on the bed.

"Tom?" Zoey is advancing to have a look. "What are you

doing? Whoa! Are you packing up Perry's things? Are you unpacking them?"

"I . . . uh . . . no." He folds his arms across his chest.

I know what he's doing. He's looking for something, and I'm scared cold that he may have found something else. I think of Mom. My breath turns shallow.

"Everything is okay here," VanLeer says. He presses both palms out in front of him. His hands are empty. That's good.

"But why are you in Perry's stuff?" Zoey says.

VanLeer lets out a sigh through his nose. "Zoey, would you please leave us alone a minute? Perhaps longer, actually. Perry and I need to talk."

"Why can't I stay?"

"Zoey." He says her name sternly.

"Okay, okay. Whatever." She shows me wide eyes on her way out.

I head for the bed and my suitcase. I lift the stack of shirts back inside. I secretly brush my hand along the baggy inside pocket. I feel the watch. I close my eyes and breathe in relief.

Mr. VanLeer shuts the door behind Zoey. There are two small hard chairs in the room. He lifts them high and sets them facing each other. He motions for me to sit, and I do. He sits across from me.

He leans forward, out-turned elbows on his knees, and his hands clasped together. His face is in my face. Anybody would want to back away. I hold steady. I see him like I saw him when he was on the television, on *Counting on Butler County* with Desiree Riggs. I see the tiny pepper dots on his skin—the places where his whiskers grow from. I watch his upper lip. It shines.

"Perry," he says, and I feel the pop of his breath on that letter *P*. It hits me right between the eyes. "Do you know why I'm in here? Do you know what I'm looking for?" He doesn't wait for me to answer. "There is something missing from my office—an award that was on my wall." He pulls at his chin with his hand. "I think you know the one."

"The Spark Award." I say it.

He nods. His eyes narrow. "Perry . . . did you take it? Because it's okay if you did. This can be made right. I-I want you to know that I understand—"

"I didn't take it," I tell him.

I'm not going to listen to him tell me how much he understands me—how I grew up around bad influences at Blue River. I won't let him talk dirt about the people I care about. I look him in the eyes. I see his whites and the few tiny red vessels that sit like little curls of red thread there.

"I moved it," I say.

"Y-you moved it?"

"Yes." I swallow and my ears pop. "I needed to know something. That was the only way I could find out."

He tilts his head at me. "I don't understand. How does stealing—or moving something—give you information? What do you think you found out?"

"That I can't count on you."

"What? Perry . . ."

"You said you'd look into my mom's case."

"Yes! Perry! That file is in my office right now." He turns up his palms.

"I know it is. But your word is no good." I don't like saying it to him. "You said you'd look at it. But for three weeks now, you haven't touched that box."

"What? I-I absolutely have . . . done . . . that . . ." Mr. VanLeer draws his chin back so hard his chair squeaks. He opens his mouth, but no words come out.

"If you had looked at my mom's file—inside the box in your office—you would have found your award," I say. I watch one of his eyebrows tick upward just a little. "That's where I put it. Three weeks ago."

He lets out a noise—a huff or a gulp. He covers his mouth with his hand. Then he's out of his chair and crossing to the door.

"I know you're really busy," I say. "But time is important to me. I couldn't wait for you any more. I want to be with my mom. So I had to try to do something to help her." I stand up and start to refold my clothes. "Check the box that says COOK," I tell Mr. Thomas VanLeer. "I'm sure your Spark Award is still in there. You can hang it back on your wall."

I fill the suitcase and pull it back into the closet. When I turn around, Mr. VanLeer is gone.

chapter seventy-one

A TIME AND A DATE

It happens at the end of a Blue River Tuesday. I'm packing up the book bins with Zoey and Mrs. Buckmueller and worrying that if Mom doesn't come down in the next minute or two, I'm going to miss her. She's running so late. All the residents are coming in to the common, even the ones who should have been in her meeting. They shake hands, show their gladness, and the sweet smell of wood shavings surrounds us.

"Perry! Hold up!" Mom waves from the balcony in the Upper East Lounge. She comes down the stairs so fast her feet barely touch down. "Hi! Hi!" Mom hugs me, then Zoey. She touches Mrs. B's hands and begs her, "Can I have Perry for just a couple of minutes? Please! It's important."

"Of course. Perry is *yours!*"

Mom hurries me to a spot beside the window. We plop into the chairs with a little table between us. She reaches across and takes hold of my hands.

"The date came through," she says. "My parole hearing is scheduled."

"Wha—"

"I know. All of a sudden!" she says. "Well, all of a sudden after all this waiting." She laughs and tugs at my hands. "I don't know why, but it all jiggled loose."

"Whoa, Mom! This is the best news! How soon?"

"It's this Thursday, in the morning."

"Thursday, the day after tomorrow? That Thursday?"

"Yes, yes! I couldn't wait to tell you." She takes a big breath now, and I see that she is hiding her worry behind the smile. "I'm hopeful, Perry. But I think we have to be prepared. We might not get the news we want. Because that dirtbag—sorry, District Attorney VanLeer—knows how to make a strong case for what he wants. He thinks it was wrong that I got to raise you here. And he wants to make a big loud point about it."

"He wants someone to pay," I mumble. I remember what Mr. Krensky said. "But he's not the only one who gets to speak to the parole board, right? Warden Daugherty will be there?"

"And you, Perry."

"Me? I can come?"

"Open to the public! Anyone can come."

"But what if VanLeer says no? What if he won't bring me?"

"I took care of that," she says. "I just got off the phone with Robyn. She promised to bring you herself."

"Her word is good," I say. "Mom, you're shaking." I squeeze her hands.

"I can't help it," she says. "You know that not much scares me, Perry. But the unknowns do."

"Unknowns?"

"Like what VanLeer will say. And I'm terrified just thinking about the things I haven't thought of!" She lets out a tiny laugh. She whispers, "Like . . . how after all these years, a long-forgotten swim watch is still out there . . ."

I shake my head no and give Mom a small smile. I let go of her hands, and I reach into my sleeve. I pull the watch out from under the elastic cuff.

Mom blinks when she sees it. "Oh . . . Perry . . ."

I slip the watch under her hand. She curls her fingers around it. "Sorry I didn't tell you. I was trying to keep it safe. But you can keep it safer," I say.

"I love you, Perry Cook."

"I love you back."

chapter seventy-two

ENHANCE!

On Wednesday afternoon I stand at the door to the video room at the library. I have been scheming. Now I have to get my guts up.

"Please," I say, and Brian Morris looks back at me with a blank stare.

"Yeah, please," says Zoey. She's right behind me—my support person for all things difficult.

"I need to make a video," I say. "I have some . . . pictures of old pictures to use. And words." I rattle a piece of notebook paper in my hand. "I need to extract a couple of shots from videos like you did. And I'd like to do that voice-over thing."

"What's the project?" Brian asks.

"My mom's story. Actually, it's my story. Both."

"But what are you going to do with it?"

It's a fair question. Everybody knows the Coming to Butler County project is over with. I might as well tell him

338

the truth. "I'm going to use it to get her out of jail."

Brian's eyes pop open.

"It's true," says Zoey.

"All right!" Brian Morris is so on board he's falling over the furniture to get us set up. "Nothing like the power of video." He says it officially, like he's about to film the Desiree Riggs show.

"Brian, there's one more thing," I say. "It has to be finished today."

"Like, *today*, today? The whole thing?"

"Right. She has a public hearing tomorrow."

"Oooo-kay . . . ," says Brian. "Then we better do this thing."

We put three chairs in front of one computer. Seconds later, my camera is connected. Zoey and I bring up a photo of my room off the Upper East Lounge. At least we know how to do that much. "I want to start here," I say.

Brian is all business. "Okay . . . fuzzy photo . . . here. Let's enhance." He shows me where to click. I do it. The picture gets much sharper. "Do you have a script?"

"He does," says Zoey. She turns to Brian and says, "It's going to be great."

Brian plugs in a mic, draws out the skinny cord, and hands it over. "Click to record when you're ready. Count one-one-thousand, before you speak."

I do like he says. I put my lips close to the tiny mic and say, "Good morning. This is Perry at sunrise."

chapter seventy-three

PAROLE HEARING

The large meeting room is filling up. The parole board is two men and two women. They aren't part of Blue River. They're community people who serve on the board. They take their places at a long table up front. The parole candidate—Mom—will sit across from them. Members of the public will sit in rows of chairs behind Mom. That's where I am. I'm here with Zoey and her mom and Mr. Van-Leer. I have put my name on a list; I am a member of the public, and I wish to speak.

Everyone is watching as the foremen add chairs. I thought it would be just a handful of people. The top of my head is cold and airy. I feel myself tilting in space, which is the way I felt the day Thomas VanLeer came to take me away from Blue River. I threw up that day. I tell myself that can't happen here.

I'm trying not to pull at my crisp collar. Zoey's mom

bought me a button-down shirt and a tie for today. This morning in the hallway of the VanLeer house, she straightened my tie, then VanLeer's. There wasn't much talking.

I'm watching for Mom to come in the side door. The library laptop is under my chair. Zoey Samuels is beside me with the little projector. We're both crossing fingers that we will remember how everything works. Zoey's mom is right beside her, and Mr. VanLeer is next to me. He's pinching a set of papers in his hands. Every once in a while he cranes his neck to see the arrivals. Then he straightens his arms forward. I hear his elbows crack each time.

Mom finally comes in. She is dressed up for this day. No blue chambray. Her hair is in a Miss Gina twist, and her lips are extra pink. Big Ed is at her side. She stops to hug me. She greets Zoey and her mom. She skips Mr. VanLeer at the end of our row. I don't blame her. Who knows what he's going to say, VanLeer with his fist full of papers.

He leans across me and tells everyone within earshot, "I know these hearings are open to the public, but I didn't expect a circus." He smiles as if we are all in this together.

Big Ed says, "Circus, huh? Step right up to get your peanuts."

Mom whispers to me, "How are you doing? Are you all right?"

"I am. Are you?"

"I'm trying to be." She smiles. Her hands are in a nervous knot. She breaks them apart to give me one more hug. Then she goes to her chair, and I can only see her back. I hear Big Ed whispering, reminding her to breathe.

Fo-Joe makes an announcement. "Slight delay. We have an unexpected bottleneck today, folks."

I look up and see it on the security feed. He's right. It's busy. I squint. Someone looks familiar—someone fancy. But who do we know that's fancy?

"We'll get started as soon as we get everyone in," Fo-Joe says.

"Perry," Zoey whispers, and she points toward the door. I look back and see Mrs. Buckmueller and Mr. Olsen coming in together with two other librarians. It makes me wonder who is left to man the circulation desk. Behind them, I see Miss Maya with two teacher friends and Miss Jenrik from the cafeteria. Then Warden Daugherty!

"She's here!" I nudge Zoey. "The warden is here." I want to go greet her, but Fo-Joe is pressing everyone—even the warden—to please find a chair.

"And look!" Zoey says. Her eyes are wide. "It's Desiree Riggs from the TV!"

That's who is fancy! "Oh my gosh!"

Mr. VanLeer has seen her too. He drops his head and mutters, "Oh . . . that woman."

Some of the rezzes have permission to attend, and some who probably don't have permission have lined up in the hall to watch and listen through the glass. Miss Sashonna dips, wiggles, and melts when Desiree walks by. She looks in at us and gestures wildly. She points at Desiree. Then she covers up her finger and melts some more.

Then all is quiet. The chairwoman of the parole board speaks. She tells why we are here. She asks Mom some questions about her time at Blue River. But they already know what's up. They've seen a report and of course they know about Thomas VanLeer's great discovery—me.

"All right then," the chairwoman says. "Let us begin."

Thomas VanLeer is the first on the list. He rises off his chair and clears his throat to speak.

chapter seventy-four

THOMAS VANLEER SPEAKS

"I'm Thomas VanLeer." He smiles broadly all around the room. "I am Butler County's district attorney. As your DA, my relationship with the prison is to review every parole candidate's case before he or she is released. My concern is the public—my community. Today, I'm concerned about a child, one who I feel has been incarcerated right alongside his convicted mother."

"Humph!" I hear Warden Daugherty say it right behind me. She never says things like humph.

VanLeer ignores her. "I'll come back to that," he says. He paces with his papers and makes quick little turns to look around the room. "I'm in favor of prison reform through our courts," he says. "Particularly, I'd like to see reduced time for nonviolent offenders. I believe in second chances. Not every

DA will tell you that." He wags a finger in the air. "I first approached Jessica Cook's case from a standpoint of hoping to recommend that her long sentence be commuted. I arrived to Butler County too late to see it trimmed by much, and yes, the wheels of justice can turn slowly. Still, I was on it."

I wish he'd look at me right now, but it doesn't happen.

"But then . . ." He leans forward then sweeps back up again. "I made the chance discovery that Ms. Cook has been allowed to raise her son—from his infancy—right here at Blue River." He twists up his face.

Mom sits very still. Big Ed pats her hand.

"Sure, prison nurseries are legal in Nebraska, for babies up to two years old. I'm in favor," he says. He shows a nod to the whole room. "But Blue River doesn't have a nursery program. *And* this child was kept here well beyond his baby-hood. It's unheard of! Who gets to do that?" He says it loudly. He sweeps his hand toward Mom and supplies the answer. "Jessica Cook did."

Big Ed lets out a low growl. I'm sweating under my neck-tie, worrying that VanLeer knows just how to say things.

"Think!" says VanLeer. "No other inmate serving beside her has had that same right. She was granted an *extraordinary privilege*." He pushes out the words. "So the question has to be asked, has she truly served out her sentence—as ordered by the State of Nebraska?"

"You're the only one asking," Warden Daugherty says quietly.

VanLeer shoots a look at her. "And what about the greater question? What about a child being raised inside a prison? Who would choose that for a child? Has another crime been committed? At the very least, there has been a mockery of the corrections system."

"If that's so, it's all on me!" The warden speaks louder now.

"Please curb your outbursts," the chairwoman says. She looks directly at the warden.

VanLeer shakes his head. "We are a community. Are we going to pretend that it was all right with us that a young person be confined to a corrections facility—a place made up of cell blocks, kitchenettes, and long dreary hallways?"

But it wasn't like that! I'm dying to say it. Won't somebody say it?

"He went to school, thank goodness. But that's only six hours a day. Blue River doesn't have a playroom," he tells them. "What were his activities? Where was his fun?" VanLeer looks at the papers in his hand. "Did he stock shelves in the commissary? Play prep cook for the masses? Imagine a two-year-old hanging around the prison laundry room—"

"Oh, Perry—he loved that!" Big Ed interrupts with a chuckle. "He'd sit up on the old DynaWash and ride the spin cycle like he was on a pony. Jiggety-jig!" He bobbles his head.

I almost snort. Someone at the back of the room does snort—right out loud. Other people snicker. The warden smiles and nods like she's having a good memory. Mom hides behind her hand.

The chairwoman of the parole board taps her pen. "May we please hold off on the storytelling? All of you." She eyes Big Ed and the warden. She puts her finger on her lips.

VanLeer clears his throat for attention. "My greatest concern is the company he kept. This boy lived with criminals every day." I hold my breath and wonder if he dares to tell them that I took his award—that I'm a thief. "He grew up in a prison! Does that sound right to you? It sounds like a crime to me. And for eleven long years, the parole candidate"—he tips his head toward Mom—"was complicit."

"*Complicit?*" The warden's voice sizzles. "If you think caring for him and raising him makes her complicit, then all right. She is! Perry is goodness and light. You should know." She takes aim at VanLeer. "He's been under your roof for over eight weeks while you dragged your heels on his mother's case!"

"Quiet please!" The chairwoman's face is pinking up.

VanLeer is stopped cold. He's looking at me. I look back. A slow, sick second churns by. He seems to fight for his next swallow, and it finally goes down hard behind his Adam's apple. He looks like he did when I told him where to find his award, when I told him his word was no good. He closes his eyes tightly then opens them again. "This was all highly unusual. I admit that I barely knew how to approach it." He

347

stammers, and his papers rattle in his hand. "It comes down to this: If I can't truly feel that a sentence has been served properly, I have no choice but to pressure this parole board *not* to grant release." He drops his hands. The papers snap against his side. "Such is the case of Jessica Cook."

He doesn't return to his chair. He backs up to a wall that is closer to him. He leans there. He's gone yellow or green or some other bad color. It's not a great day for Thomas Van-Leer.

chapter seventy-five

PERRY COOK SPEAKS

The parole board chairwoman calls my name. "Perry T.
Cook," she says, "it's your turn to speak."

My head feels light and weird. My legs feel like rubber.
Everyone is watching me. I'm going to do this. I came here
to get my mom out. I rise.

"I'm Perry Cook," I tell the parole board. "I was born at
Blue River. This has always been my home." I tell them about
writing the Blue River Stories for my Coming to Butler
County project. "Some of the residents here feel like family
to me.

"For the project, I asked a lot of questions. I heard a lot
of different reasons why people commit crimes . . . or con-
fess to crimes. Sometimes I wonder if they should have been
incarcerated at all. Anyone can make a mistake." I take a
rough swallow. I need to get the next part right.

"I know my mom's story now. It's about a young driver,

349

a hailstorm, an infamously dangerous intersection, and a big mistake. Also, a confession . . . and a death." I say the last words quietly. "That's a list of true things. And after all those things happened, my mom was alone and scared and had nobody to fight for her."

I look at each one of the parole board members. Then I say, "But now she has me." The whole room sighs. I think they might be on our side. "The trouble is, I'm also the thing that's holding up her release now. So I want you to see that I am okay. If you can let me have a few minutes and a corner of the table, I'll show you."

I am surprised how quickly they clear space for me. Zoey knows our plan. She hands me the laptop and hurries back for the little projector. We get everything opened up. Then we panic.

Both machines are silent. We retry the connection. "Is it the battery?" I whisper.

"I-I don't know," says Zoey. Her lip quivers.

Around us, the adults are starting to stir because we need help. Mr. Olsen starts to stand up at the back of the room. But then we hear another voice.

"Excuse me! Coming through. Excuse me." Here comes Brian Morris! I didn't even know he was here. He moves right to the front to help us. He draws a cord out of the projector. He presses a power button, fiddles with the cables. He flicks a switch, and we're in business—with a bright beam of light shining right on squinting Thomas VanLeer. Everyone waits while Brian goes up and guides pale-green VanLeer several steps to the right of where he's been standing. "We need a little more wall," Brian explains. "Is that okay with you? Yeah?" He scoots him just a hitch farther. Then he comes back and adjusts the projector so the video will display larger. We focus and hit Play.

"Good morning," my voice on the video says. Up comes the enhanced photo of my old room. "This is Perry at sunrise. Here's my sunny room off the Upper East Lounge," Video Perry says, "and it was built for me by our best friend on the inside. His name is Edwin Sommers. I call him Big Ed . . ."

We watch me grow up. There's a picture of my first birthday, sock puppets in the laundry room, then six people in blue chambray shirts crowd into the tiny salon to watch Miss Gina cut my hair. I have a new backpack for the first day of school. I lead Mr. Halsey and Mr. Rojas around the crusty Blue River track. I realize something for the first time: I don't look at the camera much. I look at the people around me.

When the video ends I have more to say. "You might think the setting looks wrong. Like maybe Blue River looks like a dull or unwelcoming place for a kid to grow up in. But for me, it always felt like a home." Then I get stuck. Everything depends on today. What if the video isn't enough? What if they don't release Mom? I look at her.

She cups praying hands over her mouth and nose. She

blinks watery eyes. Beside her, Big Ed nods, smiles, and encourages me along.

"Please don't hand my mom a down letter today. She has served a long time for her confession. That's the truest thing I know to say. She wants to make us a home on the outside now. Don't deny her parole just because I grew up at Blue River. I'm okay. I've always been okay."

chapter seventy-six

WARDEN DAUGHERTY SPEAKS

"You've heard me speaking out of turn today," the warden admits. "I apologize for my outbursts, though I meant each thing I said with all my heart. All of District Attorney VanLeer's concerns are *on me!*" She points her finger to herself.

"Blue River is a minimum-security correctional facility, and to me, minimum security has always meant maximum potential. Our residents have made mistakes. But they come here to rise up again, and make good choices.

"But that does not in any way mean that Jessica Cook got to choose to have her son live here with her. No, that was *my* choice. I was Perry's foster care provider, and I was Ms. Cook's warden. Your decision today cannot be about that arrangement. You can only ask, has Ms. Cook served her sentence? You have documentation that indeed she has. She has worked hard here. She took full advantage of programming. She earned a degree, and she has worked an essential position as a social worker here. In case you missed it, she raised an honorable son—a boy who, by his merry presence, elevated the hearts and souls of our population day after day. Innocence raises us all up." The warden points her finger skyward. "We are the better for it," she says.

"Perry was not locked in. I made sure of that. He had rules, but most households do. The walls may not have been pretty colors. But you just saw that he's had the love of many people in his young life." She points to the meeting room wall where the video played. "Some on the inside, some on the outside. A broad circle has looked out for his well-being. Most of all, he had his mother, Jessica Cook. Perry has always been her highest priority."

The warden looks at Thomas VanLeer. "I say, heaven help the community that won't fearlessly welcome her, and heaven help a world that thinks it needs to be protected from the likes of Jessica Cook. She's exemplary."

chapter seventy-seven

THE PAROLE
BOARD SPEAKS

I have heard the residents of Blue River say that parole hearings are yes or no moments. Approved or denied on the spot. But today, the parole board leaves the room to talk in private. We all fidget and wonder. While we wait, I watch Mom's back and shoulders rise and fall with deep, hopeful breaths. Can they possibly know how much their decision will mean to us?

Come. Back. In. I think it to myself. Then, as if I have wished it up, the two men and two women reenter. The chairwoman speaks.

"When we sit down to these hearings we seek to feel satisfied that the candidate has completed sentencing. We listen for concerns from the public. What we often find is that we are moved in some way. This is an odd day and an unusual hearing. But that's fitting because this is an unusual case, and Mr. VanLeer, we will credit you with bringing it to our attention."

There is silence while my heart falls and while Mom stares at her hands. Mr. VanLeer absorbs the moment. His chest rises. He gives a satisfied nod.

"As a board, we read cases in advance of these hearings. We form a strong impression at that time. The purpose of the hearing is to listen for any point that might move us from that impression. I'm talking about a concern as might be stated by the victim of a crime, or a feeling of danger to the public. *Moved* is an interesting word, especially today. We *are* moved by so much of what we have heard here." She looks at me, but she doesn't gush. She looks respectful, and she holds that gaze on me several long seconds. Then she straightens up tall in her chair and turns to face VanLeer again. "You, Mr. VanLeer, inform us today, but you do not move us—not from our basis. You'll be remembered for having picked this scab, perhaps." The chairwoman breathes in. "We are unanimous in our decision . . ."

I close my eyes. I don't think a single soul in the room is breathing now. My knee bounces, and I can't make it stop.

The spokeswoman says, "Ms. Cook, we are sorry . . ."

Now my eyes fly open. My jiggling knee freezes.

". . . sorry for the many weeks of delay. This board wishes you and your son the very best. Your parole is granted."

The cheering is loud. Many voices make it. I jump up

and race forward. I leap into Mom's arms. There is no room for a big swing-around, so we spin tightly together. For several full turns the world is just the two of us. Mom's face is buried close to my ear. She says, "You were awesome, Perry! Awesome!"

chapter seventy-eight

SOMETHING
TO CELEBRATE

There is crying and celebrating. Our Blue River family filters in from behind the glass. Friends from the outside mix with friends from the inside. Fo-Joe tries to stay stern with the crowd. But the rules are suspended—just for a while.

Miss Sashonna circles up Miss Gina and Mrs. DiCoco in her long arms. They pull in Zoey and her mom, and they all collapse into one big extended-contact hug. Mr. Rojas dances the salsa, and Miss Maya shimmies and swings her braids.

Mrs. Buckmueller comes up crying, "Lordy! Extraordinary!" She wraps me in a giant squish. I see Big Ed with both arms around Mom. They cry together while he pats her back. Then Zoey's mom is reaching for me. I hug her and thank her three times over. She has been my support person for many difficult things. In the din I hear Brian Morris telling anyone who will listen, "It's the power of video. I'm telling you . . ."

Warden Daugherty has been standing back and watching the celebration. She has a peaceful smile on her face. I take a step toward her. But Desiree Riggs comes up to shake my hand. Miss Sashonna fake-faints, and Desiree speaks. "I like a good story," she says. Her voice is buttercream. "I like the end of this one the best." Desiree pushes close to Mom. "Ms. Cook," she says, "if ever you'd like to tell me your story as a guest on my sh—"

"No, no, no. Respectfully, no. Thank you very much. I'm going home to live a quiet life . . ."

Mom fans her face with her hand. That reminds me I can loosen my tie now. It tightens instead, and Big Ed comes to my rescue. While he is freeing me, I notice Thomas Van-Leer standing alone against the far wall. He looks less green now that it's all over. It takes me a second to see it, but he gives me a firm thumbs-up. I mean to nod to him, but I'm not sure I do. I'm turning back toward Mom and our friends.

"I can't believe it," Mom says. "I don't even know where we're going to sleep tonight, Perry!" She pipes out a laugh.

"Oh. Right," I say. It's an amazing thought.

"You can stay with me!" Miss Maya says. "The fold-out couch for you, Jessica, and cushions on the floor for Perry." Mom and Miss Maya lean together and begin to make arrangements.

But the warden is still off to one side, still smiling. She bends her head and begins to tap numbers into her phone.

"Gosh, Perry," says Zoey. "No more camp mat in the closet. You're leaving," she says. She blinks, but she also smiles.

"Jessica!" The warden steps forward. She holds a finger in the air and her phone close to her chest. "A slumber party at Maya's sounds lovely, but there is another option." She points to her phone. "I have a certain landlord on hold—the owner of a first-floor apartment on Button Lane. She will gladly meet you there. You can sign a lease within the hour if you wish."

"Button Lane! Really?" Mom clasps her hands together. "Ha! I had forgotten to dream that dream," she says. "Well, Perry, what do you think?"

"Let's go!" I say. "Let's go . . . home!"

"Yeah, yeah, Jessica!" Miss Sashonna is shrieking. She jumps up and down and pulls tiny Miss Gina around with her. "Jessica's got herself a crib!" They laugh and cry and flick tears away.

Miss Maya touches Mom's shoulder. "This is wonderful, Jessica. I'd drive you there myself, but let us call you a taxi instead. You and Perry should go to your new home on your own. This is such a special day."

"Yes, but then please let us help you," says Zoey's mom. "We'll bring Perry's things by this afternoon. What else will you need?"

"I suppose we need a little bit of everything." Mom sputters a laugh.

"We have that," says Zoey.

"Yes we do." Zoey's mom winks at me. "And a day off from school tomorrow to help."

"That's right. Veterans Day!" says Zoey. "And Tom is off too. So after the parade we'll bring the car to Button Lane . . ." Zoey Samuels is on a mission. Her mom begins to steer her toward Mr. VanLeer. "See you later, Perry! See you soon!"

Mom tilts her head back and crows. "I can't believe this. I have no worries!" She tucks me under her arm and squeezes me. "Perry," she says, "I'm going to go pack!"

chapter seventy-nine

GATED OUT

It happens the same day of the hearing. If the parole board is satisfied, the parole candidate becomes a new release. So it goes with Mom.

She is packed up in twenty minutes. All her belongings fit in five shopping bags. Fo-Joe helps us carry them into the quiet common. The other rezzes have gone back to their jobs after this unusual morning at Blue River—except Big Ed. He's her support person to the finish.

"I love you so much!" she tells him. "*We* love you so much. We'll see you soon. Truly. It won't be long."

"Heard about that." He smiles a broad smile and winks. That tips me off. There's a new stink in the clink.

"What's going on?" I say, because all things have changed and I'm Perry Cook who asks questions from now on.

"Something good, my Morning Son." Big Ed waves, and

I choke. I know we will visit. But it's hard to leave him here. Mom knows it.

She says, "Come on, Perry. I'll give you the news on the outside."

We hang her bags on our shoulders. She makes one full turn around the common. She tells Fo-Joe, "Let's gate me out." We go through the big glass doors.

On the outside, the warden waits beside our taxi. She turns to Fo-Joe and says, "So it's all in place?"

"What's in place?" I ask.

"We're coming back!" Mom says with a laugh. "That's the news."

"What!"

Fo-Joe explains. "We don't have another social worker to replace your mom. And we don't particularly want one. She's the newest Blue River hire. Same job. Way better paycheck," he says. "It will be a whole different Blue River experience."

"Mom! This is the best! So you have a good job, and we'll really be back to see Big Ed and the others?"

"A lot." Mom beams. "It's a good plan for us—for right now."

Fo-Joe gives her a grin and calls her "colleague." Then he says, "But no moving the furniture into circles. That drives me nuts—"

Mom says, "Yeah, yeah. Try and stop me."

The warden laughs at what they are saying. She tilts

back her head and the sound comes out high and free. I've never heard her like this before.

"Warden Daugherty, what about you?" I ask.

"Well, I'm all done," she says. "Retired. Time for Blue River to move on without me. I'm at peace with it. The place is in good hands. Say hello to Warden Joe Banks," she says. She pats him on the shoulder.

"I knew it!" I give Fo-Joe a solid high five.

"Speaking of that, I better get back inside," he says. "Jessica, get yourself settled then I'll see you next week, okay?" Mom gives him a nod. We watch the big glass doors close behind him.

Mom and I stand on the outside with our Warden Daugherty. Mom lowers her bags to the ground. She puts her arms full around the warden and hugs her hard. The warden hugs her back.

"How funny to think that I'm the one who's moving on from Blue River," says the warden. She squeezes Mom's shoulders in her hands and looks into her eyes. "You'll be coming back to your job—at least for a while. I'm so proud."

"Thank you for raising me up." Mom can barely whisper the words. "And for always doing your best by Perry."

"Knowing you and Perry is one of my greatest pleasures, Jessica Cook. You are like family. I'll still be in town, and I hope you and Perry will think about having Thanksgiving with Maya and me."

"Oh yes! Thanksgiving!" I say.

"But right now," says the warden, "you two have some-place else to be."

We leave her in the big front circle of the Blue River Co-ed Correctional Facility. We climb into our taxi and head for home.

chapter eighty

JESSICA

Jessica Cook did not mind that she couldn't fall asleep the first night in the new place.

You don't worry about this, she thought to herself. You savor it.

It is so good to lie on this living room floor on two borrowed camp mats and touch hands with your son across the brown wooden floorboards. Turns out, you just want to listen to him breathe.

You want to remember the feel of the two house keys landing in your palm—one for you, and one for your boy. Tonight you have the heat set where you want it. There was an unearthly-good stew for supper, eaten out of hand-me-down mugs, all delivered by Robyn Samuels, who promises to be back tomorrow with some essentials. The rest can come later.

You don't worry about not sleeping. In fact, if you do

sleep you could miss the moment that morning sun will rise into the long windows of these small rooms. Stay awake and know that you'll cook your gorgeous kid a perfect egg—a fried tweet on whole wheat—when he opens his eyes in this new place.

chapter eighty-one

BUTTON LANE

Out in back of the house on Button Lane, Zoey Samuels and I sit on a tippy plank that lies across a pair of cinderblocks. The sun is bright but the chill is Novemberish, like it should be. We pull up our hoods and tuck our hands into our pockets. We are taking a break on moving-in day.

We have carried boxfuls and armloads. Zoey's mom brought us linens and lamps to use, and the last load of my laundry fresh from their dryer. She also brought Thomas VanLeer.

He doesn't come inside, not even up to the stoop. He stays out there on the street and hands things down from the SUV.

Zoey's mom is the champion furniture arranger. Mom, the Blue River U-Hauler, runs a close second. It's not that many pieces. But they keep changing their minds about where things should go. They laugh together, and the sound fills the apartment.

"How's your new room?" Zoey asks me. She jiggles our plank. "Did you sleep last night?"

"Well, Mom and I moved the camp mats into the living room. Just to be together," I say. I don't tell her that we held hands all night, even though Zoey Samuels would never laugh at me for it. "I'm not sure we wanted to sleep. We've waited so long for Mom to be on the outside. Now we don't want to miss a minute." I blink into the sun, knowing we'll have to give that up eventually.

"It's a new place," Zoey says. "You'll get used to it."

"I'm glad we're staying in Butler County," I say.

"Oh yeah!" Zoey says.

"For now," I add. I feel in my bones that Mom will want to go away from here someday. "Hey, Zoey, can I ask you something?" She gives me a curious look. "What are you doing about your Coming to Butler County project? And don't say, oh *that*."

"I've written part of it," she says. She pushes her hands deeper into her pockets. "The part about you."

"Me?"

"Yeah. I wrote about how I was miserable when I got here. You know. Mad-Zoe." She laughs. "But then you came over to talk to me. You told me that story—the one about all the snow and why Surprise is called Surprise," Zoey says. "I wrote all of that. Then I got stuck." She twists her heel into the ground. "Because of you."

"Why me?" I say, and I squint at her.

"The minute we got that assignment you knew what you wanted to write about. *And* you had the most interesting stories from your Blue River family."

"Hmm. I guess."

"But my family is small. We came here because of Tom." Zoey heaves a sigh. "There's no way to tell my story and leave him out." She stops to think. "But he went and messed everything up for you, Perry—and I think he's sorry now. Anyway, it's been hard because . . . well . . . I guess I *do* love Tom." We both laugh because it sounds funny. "I get mad at him for flubbing up. But he tries. And trying is better than *not* trying, right?"

I think about it. "That's kind of hard for me to answer."

"He made a big mistake with you," she says. "But his job—there are a lot of hard parts to it." Zoey scrunches her nose up. "I don't think district attorneys are very popular."

"Hmm." I shrug and give her a small smile.

"My super secret is . . . I'm proud of Tom because he works hard. Seriously hard."

"Then that's your story," I tell her. "Write it just like you told it to me. And Zoey? I need to tell you something . . . and don't be mad." She gives me that curious look again. "Surprise, Nebraska, didn't really get its name because of all the snow."

"No . . . because of the stuff you find underneath it, right? Everything you lost over the winter?" She is sure she has it right.

I shake my head. "That's just a story Big Ed tells."

"What? Perry!" She opens her mouth wide. "You lied? I believed you!" Then she laughs and bumps against my shoulder. I try to hide a grin. "Then how did Surprise really get its name? The whole truth, Perry Cook." Zoey Samuels sits up straight and stares me down.

"A really long time ago a guy came and built a gristmill on the Big Blue River. When he discovered how much water-power there was at the river's headwaters, he was *surprised*. So he decided to name his mill . . ."

"*Surprise?*" says Zoey. Her eyebrows arch up.

"Yep."

"Aw!" Her shoulders drop. She thinks for a second. "I like Big Ed's story better."

"Me too," I say.

"Thanks, Perry."

"Thanks for what?"

"You told me the story that would be better for me on that day. Friends should do that for friends."

Suddenly, it hits me—like a wind across a cornfield. *Mom is out.* I need to be with her. I get to my feet. The plank bounces. Zoey looks up. "I'm going back inside. They might be ready for more help."

"You think so," Zoey sings, "but they're probably still arranging . . . and changing." She lifts her face into the sun and closes her eyes.

"Take five . . . or ten," I say. "I saw some cocoa mix in the groceries that Miss Maya dropped off yesterday. I'll make us some."

"Oooh, now that sounds good," says Zoey.

I love this. Zoey Samuels is at my house.

chapter eighty-two

FEED A DOG

From the side yard I see Mom step out the door and onto the stoop. She squats to lift another box. She's been doing this all morning.

Meanwhile, VanLeer is still out on the street, loafing beside the SUV.

In the night I asked Mom if she minded that he'd be coming with Zoey and her mom today. She squeezed my hand and said, "No. What do I care about old trouble, Perry? It will be my first full day of freedom. Nobody can touch that."

Now suddenly VanLeer is on the move. He strides up to the front stoop—to where Mom stands. I hear an apology falling out of his mouth. "I'm sorry," he tells her. "I—I feel that I screwed up. Badly. I failed to consider the whole picture. But it's come clearer to me now. I didn't help—not in the right way."

There is silence. Mom stares. Then she agrees with him. "You're right. You didn't help."

"I th-thought I was doing the right thing, honestly. I thought Perry needed a home . . ." VanLeer is doing that thing where he talks and talks. He has to fill the quiet spaces. "I was trying to provide—"

"Uttt!" Mom puts both hands out to stop him. "We're not going to do this," she says. "Not on the spot like you're hoping. Forgiveness has two sides, and it takes time." I see her take a breath. "In the few hours that I have been free . . . I've remembered something about living on the outside. It's about *you*. Do you want to hear it?"

"Y-yes?" VanLeer looks interested.

"Even if we disagree with our neighbors, it doesn't mean we won't feed their dog while they're on vacation," Mom says.

"Right." VanLeer's eyes are blinking like he might not get it. I'm not sure I do either.

"I don't like what you did to us." Mom says it plain. "You put a chokehold on my life, and *so much worse*, you put severe stress on my kid. I think it was sick and self-serving." She gazes out at the yard, to the street, and up into the bare November trees. "That's hard to forgive," she says. "But you are my neighbor. So I would still feed your dog for you. Understand?"

"Y-yes! I do."

"Okay then." Mom turns to go indoors, but then she

spins back to face Thomas VanLeer again. "You can still help," she says.

"Anything."

"Two things." She shows him two fingers—it's like she's making the peace sign, or a *V* for victory. "First, if you are really interested in commuting overly long sentences for nonviolent offenders, go look into the case of Edwin Sommers. He's the guy Perry calls Big Ed," she says.

VanLeer nods like a bobblehead. "You said two things?" he reminds her.

"Yeah." Mom points at the round top of a table propped against the side of the house. "That has to come inside," she tells him. "Maybe Perry will help you." She lifts her chin and calls my name. "Per-ry!"

I sprint in from the side yard and take one end of the tabletop in my hands. VanLeer takes the other. (He'll be the one walking backward.) "On my count," I say. "One, two, three!"

And we lift.

chapter eighty-three

OUTSIDE AND INSIDE

The school bus rolls to a stop in front of the Blue River Co-ed Correctional Facility in teeny-tiny Surprise, Nebraska. A boy hops down the steps and up to the door. He's none other than Perry T. Cook. He opens his hand over the square call button. The intercom clicks to life.

"Who's there?" says a voice.

Perry faces the security camera and crosses his huge blue eyes. He tilts his head back, supplying the camera with a shot up his nostrils while he calls, "Who *NOSE*?"

The voice says, "Ew . . ." and Perry laughs while the foreman buzzes him in.

He always looks up the stairs first when he enters the Blue River Common. These days, the door to his old bedroom off the Upper East Lounge stands open most of the time. He makes a run, takes the stairs two at a time, and only grips the red railing in three places on his way to the top. He pokes his head inside the door. There is a circle of chairs where his bed used to be and a desk in place of the cupboard that used to hold his clothes.

His mother turns around, arms open, for a hug and a sloppy sort of swing-around in the office chair—Perry riding one armrest, the chair bumping and tipping. They both laugh when his sneakers thump into the desk drawers. "Go see what Eggy-Mon has for a snack," she says. She kisses his dark head before she lets him go.

In the caf Big Ed and a small crew are rolling down the tables for supper.

"Perry, my man! How are things on the outside today?" Big Ed wants to know.

"Great" comes the answer. Perry always brings a story.

The two talk for just a minute. But Big Ed has work to do—the foreman reminds him of that. The boy opens his pack and starts his homework while his mother finishes for the day. Blue River took in six new female residents this month. Four others are preparing for release. Jessica Cook has been busy firmly planting the beautiful notion of hope inside each and every one of them.

She puts her desk in order then punches the clock. She waves good-bye to Warden Joe Banks.

Meanwhile, the residents come in from the woodshop and the greenhouse to gather in the common before the supper bell. Somebody will always spot the one and only boy on campus at this hour and say, "Mouse in the house! Hey, it's

Perry Cook! All rise!" They do, because it feels good to get a handshake or high five at the end of the workday. That's the way they do things at Blue River.

On Tuesdays and Fridays the Bucking Blue Bookmobile will take Perry and Jessica home on its way back through Rising City. Other nights they are greeted with kindness—a friend from town pulling to the shoulder and calling them into a warm car or the cozy cab of a pickup truck or a family SUV. Someone always comes.

But these two feel no worry walking along the road, where the wide, flat fields open out on both sides. If they had to walk the whole seven miles, they would. Time belongs to them at the end of the day. They're heading home, to the house on Button Lane, where the duck-egg blue chairs sit in a circle around a hand-me-down table.

Soon the first snow will come and float a perfect blanket down on all the rooftops all around teeny-tiny Surprise, Nebraska.

AUTHOR'S NOTE

For me, story always begins with a character in a situation. I gather lots of facts. Then I begin to ask the question, *what if?*

Let me set a few things straight.

There really is a teeny-tiny town called Surprise on the Big Blue River in eastern Nebraska.

It is true that some correctional facilities, including one in York, Nebraska, have nurseries for infants born to incarcerated mothers. Parenting programs are offered to nonviolent offenders. Children may come for extended day and overnight visits in special housing on the grounds. Co-ed correctional facilities are unusual, but they do exist.

For this story I asked, *what if* a boy was born in a prison nursery? *What if* he spent his babyhood there, and then stayed on? What would be his sense of home? Who would be his family?

The Blue River Co-ed Correctional Facility is fictional.

So are the residents and their Blue River stories. However, they are inspired by the stories of real inmates.

One of the most heartbreaking things about being incarcerated is the struggle to stay connected to family while serving out a sentence. At the same time, family love is a powerful defense against recidivism.

About one in twenty-eight school-aged children in the United States has a parent in prison. Many feel fear, sadness, shame, and guilt. Many live too far away from assigned correctional facilities to make frequent visits.

Perry T. Cook, his mom, and all the characters you meet here are real only on these pages. That doesn't mean they won't find a place in your heart; I hope they do.

Leslie Connor

ACKNOWLEDGMENTS

family |ˈfam(ə)lē|
a person or people related to one and so to be treated with a
special loyalty or intimacy: *I could not turn him away, for he
was family.*

With thanks to all my families: one that raised me, one that
I raised, one that sits around the writing table with me, one
that walks with me in the woods, one that publishes me with
great care.

More from award-winning author
LESLIE CONNOR

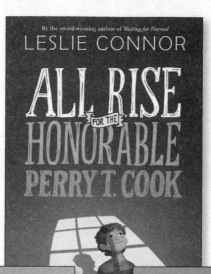